André Caroff's
MADAME ATOMOS

The Mistake of
Madame Atomos

André Caroff's
MADAME ATOMOS

The Mistake of Madame Atomos

Translated by
Michael Shreve

A Black Coat Press Book

Acknowledgements: Thanks to Françoise Carpouzis & Catherine Losserand.

L'Erreur de Madame Atomos and *Madame Atomos Prolonge la Vie* Copyright © 1966, 1967 by The Estate of André Caroff. English adaptation Copyright © 2012 by Michael Shreve. Introduction, *The End of the Brotherhood of the Sword* Copyright © 2009 by Jean-Marc Lofficier and The Estate of André Caroff.
The Way of the Crane Copyright © 2009 by Matthew Baugh and The Estate of André Caroff.
Cover illustration Copyright © 2012 by Jean-Michel Ponzio.

Visit our website at www.blackcoatpress.com

Table of Contents

Introduction

This volume collects the seventh and eighth installments of the saga of Madame Atomos, a series of 17 novels published between 1964 and 1970 in the *Angoisse* horror imprint of French publisher Fleuve Noir. Our introduction to Volume 1 contains a biography of its author, André Carpouzis, a.k.a. André Caroff (1924-2009). More information about Fleuve Noir and its popular brands of science fiction and horror can be found in the introductions to the other volumes translated from their imprints and published by Black Coat Press: Richard Bessière's *The Gardens of the Apocalypse*, Gérard Klein's *The More in Time's Eye* and Kurt Steiner's *Ortog*.

The saga of Madame Atomos (her real name is Kanoto Yoshimuta) is about a brilliant but twisted middle-aged female Japanese scientist who is out for revenge against the United States for the bombings of Hiroshima and Nagasaki—where she was born, and where her family died in the nuclear holocaust.

Madame Atomos seeks to repay the United States by unleashing deadly new threats, such as radioactive zombies, giant spiders, a madness-inducing ray, flaming tornadoes, etc. The heroes opposing her are Smith Beffort of the FBI, Dr. Alan Soblen, and Yosho Akamatsu of the Japanese Secret Police.

Volume 2 introduced the character of Mie Azusa, a.k.a. Miss Atomos, a younger version of Madame Atomos, groomed to continue the fight in the event of her death.

In Volume 3, after Mie fell in love with Smith Beffort, she joined the fight against the deadly Madame Atomos who, in the meantime, had returned from the dead.

Now read on...

Jean-Marc Lofficier

ANDRE CAROFF

L'ERREUR de Mᵐᵉ ATOMOS

ANGOISSE

Editions
"FLEUVE NOIR"

THE MISTAKE OF MADAME ATOMOS

Chapter I

For more than four months there was dead calm. Madame Atomos seemed to have disappeared at the same time as Smith Beffort and Mie Azusa. Some thought that the sinister Japanese woman had given up the idea of reducing the United States to ashes. That was, of course, the opinion of the public at large. But the specialists, James Edward Evans, Yosho Akamatsu, Doctor Alan Soblen and many others knew that there was a better chance that it was just the calm before the storm.

On this particular day, Soblen burst into the office of James Edward Evans and slammed the telegram down on his desk, smiling as he said, "It's official—it's a boy!"

J.E.E. let out a sigh and grumbled, "And none too soon. I was wondering whether Mie was going to manage to give birth before Madame Atomos got back on their trail. Damn, it's a big day, doctor!" He wiped the smile off his face and added drearily, "Even if Beffort's son is French."

"Don't talk nonsense. Smith is American and Mie, also, since they got married. So, little Robert is too. And don't forget that he was born in the American hospital in Neuilly."[1]

J.E.E. nodded unenthusiastically. For him, an Americans couple should be making babies in the United States. "This Robert," he asked reluctantly, "what color is he?" Soblen was speechless. J.E.E. lit a cigar. "What? You looked surprised, but you shouldn't be. Mie is Japanese…"

"And you're afraid that the boy will be yellow!"

"As the future godfather I am fully entitled to worry about it."

Soblen crossed his arms. All of a sudden he was in a bad mood. "Who said you would be the godfather?"

"No one. It just seems natural."

"Not at all, not at all," Soblen said emphatically. "I've known Mie and Smith for much longer than you…"

J.E.E. raised a conciliatory hand. "Let's wait for Smith to come back. No need for us to argue over it, doctor. Especially since no one has asked us anything yet and there could very well be a third scoundrel in the mix. When is Smith and his little family planning to leave France?"

Soblen sat down, wiped his glasses and admitted glumly, "I don't know. Since he's been there, he's become a very mysterious character. We never were able to get his address and the funds we supplied always went through the bank."

"And his famous Green Dragon Force?"

Soblen nodded. "No news. You know that Smith was especially keen on Madame Atomos not finding out

---

[1] See *The End of the Brotherhood of the Sword* in this volume.

that he was in France. And for this he practically burned all his bridges with us."

"Okay, but he achieved his goal," J.E.E. objected. "If the world hasn't heard anything about Madame Atomos for four months, we have him to thank for it. Personally my hat's off to him. And then in spite of everything, we know that Mie gave birth in the Paris area, right?"

Soblen grinned and put a finger on the telegram. "All Smith said was, *Robert Smith Beffort, born today at the American hospital in Neuilly.* And you can be sure that if he risked telling us where he was, it's because he was counting on moving fast."

"So he just may be coming back to the United States?"

Soblen shrugged his shoulders and grabbed his hat. "There's no way to know. We can think whatever we want. Anyway, his wariness is justified. At this moment, Madame Atomos must be moving heaven and earth trying to find him and his wife. Frankly, I wouldn't want to be in their shoes." He held out his hand and added, "Now I have a little work to do. If you get any news, you can call me in the lab."

J.E.E. shook his hand.

"I'll be sure to, doctor, don't worry."

Soblen left the office, went down two floors and then left the Federal Building. After crossing the street to the paid parking lot, he sat behind the wheel of his car. When he went to start the ignition, his fingers felt a thin roll of paper lodged against the handle. He unrolled it and read:

Watch out, doc. Don't look suspicious because you're probably being watched by one or more members of the Atomos Organization. I've been in the U.S. for 15 days. Mie and our son are with me. The telegram you received just now was only meant to throw Madame Atomos off our scent. Now, without telling anyone, get to Kennedy airport. Your plane heading for St. Louis, Missouri, takes off in 20 minutes. The ticket and reservation are in the glove box. In St. Louis take a taxi and go to the Midwest Stock Exchange (319 N. 4th Street). When you get there, one of my men will take care of you. See you soon, doc. The Green Dragon Force awaits you!

Soblen crumpled the paper into a ball and swallowed it discretely. He started the engine, in the same movement checking to see if the ticket and reservation were really in the glove box, and then set off. St. Louis is less than 900 miles from New York. With a jet he would be there in exactly 2 hours and 15 minutes.

The plane landed on time at the Lambert-St.-Louis municipal airport, located 13 miles north-west of the city. Soblen went down the steps with hands in his pockets and crossed the hall to go and find a taxi. 50 minutes later he stepped out onto the sidewalk in front of the Midwest Stock Exchange and waited.

Around him the street was crowded. Too crowded for him to spot a possible lookout. Besides, Smith Beffort had said that one of his men would take care of him, which kept him from taking any action himself. Ten minutes went by and then a small, thin man, carrying a batch of the German newspaper *Deutsche Wochenschrif* under his arm, brushed by him and whispered, "Enter the building and leave through the other door."

Soblen let a few seconds tick off before entering the Stock Exchange. He found himself in a hectic environment among groups shouting in front of boards on which the latest stock values were written. Soblen slipped along the long central wall looking for the exit that the fake newspaper seller had mentioned. He found it without too much difficulty at the end of the south corridor. It was a narrow door, probably used very rarely. Soblen tried the handle and the door opened easily. The doctor entered a corridor and immediately met a man whose face was held together by old scars.

"Keep going, doctor," the stranger huffed as he closed the door and turned the key.

Soblen nodded, strode down the corridor that led into a street behind the Stock Exchange.

"Dr. Soblen, over here!" The call came from a gray Mercury whose door was wide open. Soblen climbed into the car, closed the door and sank down in the front seat. The Mercury shot off, made a sharp turn at the corner and started flying down a quiet street that must have led out of the city toward the west. Soblen glanced at the driver and noted right away that he looked suspicious.

"Were you followed, doctor?" the man asked out of the corner of his mouth.

"I don't think so… but even if someone was tailing me, I have the feeling that he must be far off now. Where are we going?"

The man did not give a straight answer. "My name's Sammy," he drawled, "and I've got to ask you a few questions."

Soblen noticed then that he was driving with one hand. The other had disappeared under his coat where there was a telling bulge. "Go right ahead."

"First of all, can you tell me the number of your hotel room at the Hilton in Palm Beach?"

"302," Soblen answered straight off.

"Second, tell me exactly what the business card said."

"The business card? Can you be more precise?"

Sammy slanted a glance at him; his jaws clenched. The weapon he was hiding under his coat was suddenly pointing at Soblen's belly. "The business card," he repeated coldly.

Soblen wrinkled his brow and said, "To my knowledge there's only one business card that Beffort could think important. If I'm not mistaken, it's text was this: *Mie Azusa, Public Relations Manager, Southern United States*."

Sammy relaxed a little. "Third, doctor, how many witnesses were there in the shop of Toubinsky Junior after the young messenger left and before the stretcher arrived?"

Soblen's mouth dropped open and his face became flushed. The question require a precise answer about events that took place more than a year ago[2]. "Say," he protested, "don't you think that's going a little too far?"

Sammy sat like stone. "Answer doctor. If you are in full possession of your senses, you should remember."

Soblen suddenly realized that the test was really necessary. Smith Beffort was being overly careful, demanding precise answers about particular events in which only he and Soblen had participated. After a four-month absence Beffort wanted to be sure that Soblen had not been enrolled in the Atomos Organization.

Soblen tried hard to remember. "I think there were seven witnesses. Four women and three men. The young messenger was Jack Uron or Uri, I can't remember exactly."

---

[2] See *The Sinister Madame Atomos* in *The Terror of Madame Atomos*.

16

"Jack Urey," Sammy corrected, smiling. "Doctor, Mr. Beffort was right when he said you had a damn good memory!"

Soblen heaved a sigh of relief. "Now can you tell me anything?"

Sammy grimaced, "It wouldn't do any good. Look at this instead."

With a quick movement he pulled out his weapon and handed it to Soblen who took it and was surprised at how light it was. Apparently it was a firearm, but its shape held a few significant differences. Its clip was replaced by a transparent reservoir in which a thick, oily liquid splashed around. The trigger was just a red button on the grooved surface. The thin barrel looked like a welding torch that ended in a kind of sprinkler head with thousands of microscopic holes. The whole thing was about eight inches long and probably weighed around one pound.

Soblen was intrigued. "What is this?"

"A paralyzing pistol, doctor," Sammy informed him calmly. "It freezes in place for 60 minutes every human who's less than 1,000 feet away."

Soblen smiled. "So, Smith did it! We finally have a weapon that can rival the diabolical inventions of Madame Atomos."

It was a gift of fate, but Soblen did not forget that the weapon came from the sinister Japanese woman's arsenal and that Beffort and Mie had barely escaped her after the partial fire in the Governor Clinton Hotel in New York. Four months earlier, being chased by the Atomos Organization, the couple had, in fact, been able to board a Pan Am flight to Paris at the last minute. Since then, Madame Atomos seemed to have given up her merciless vengeance against the United States in order to devote her time to recapturing Mie Azusa, ex-Miss Atomos, whom she had been hunting for months. But this would not last forever. Sooner or later Madame Atomos would resume her attacks because in the end it was the best way to make Smith Beffort come out of hiding.

"We're here," Sammy said. For a while the car had been cruising in the countryside.

"Where are we?" Soblen asked.

"Somewhere west of Saint Louis, doctor. As things stand right now, it's better if you didn't know the exact location of our base."

The Mercury turned sharply onto a narrow path in the forest. Sammy crossed a clearing at full speed and headed straight for a thick bush. A crash was inevitable.

"Watch out!" Soblen shouted.

The Mercury slipped harmlessly through the bush and into a faintly lighted tunnel.

"It wasn't a real bush," Sammy explained coldly.

Soblen relaxed, a little embarrassed by his emotional outburst. He understood that Beffort had completely changed his traditional methods to more or less adopt those of Madame Atomos. The false bush, the tunnel, the paralyzing pistol, all these creepy men in the Green Dragon Force... The Mercury came to a sudden halt in the middle of the deserted tunnel.

Soblen looked around and asked, "What's going on?"

"Nothing, doctor. We're just going through the entrance exam. Right now a camera in the ground is filming certain marks engraved on the chassis of the car. If the codes aren't right, a paralyzing rifle will open fire and we'll be put out of action."

Soblen pursed his lips. Obviously, Smith Beffort had adopted more and more of Madame Atomos' methods! All of a sudden the Mercury shook, turned 45 degrees and shot out into a shaft in the concrete wall. After going down 50 feet or so, it was pushed onto a metal cart and carried like a common package onto a platform under a blinding light from a battery of projectors.

"Get out, doctor," Sammy told him.

Soblen protected his eyes as he stepped out and found himself on a moving walkway that carried him away at 25 miles per hour. Soblen clung onto the handrail and grumbled. Heading down another tunnel he watched the walls fly by until he was thrown into a square room. He stumbled forward and was whisked up by J.E.E. and Smith Beffort.

"Hey, doc," the latter said cheerfully, "good to see you again!"

Soblen stepped away grumpily and pointed a finger at a smiling J.E.E. "So, you were in on all this!" he shouted indignantly.

"Don't be upset, doc," Beffort intervened. "J.E.E. was safe from any Atomos operation whereas you and Akamatsu were prime targets. I couldn't take the risk of letting you in on it. And you can imagine that I couldn't build this base all alone!"

"Still," Soblen muttered, "you could have used me for your research on the paralyzing ray."

Beffort took him by the arm and said solemnly, "Without knowing it, your role was much more important, doc. Thanks to you, being constantly under surveillance by members of the Atomos Organization, we know about one of the hideouts of our mortal enemy. Come on, I'll explain it to you."

Chapter II

Not at all happy, Soblen sat in a comfortable arm-chair that Beffort pointed out while J.E.E. took a place on the other side of the desk. The room was in the center of the base, which was set up fifty feet underground level. There was total silence there.

Beffort pulled down a wall map representing the St. Louis area, picked up a ruler and pointed it at a point between St. Peters and the right bank of the Mississippi. "Here, doc, is where we are. It's practically in the middle of the United States. Therefore, our geographical position is perfect—it allows the Green Dragon Force to get as fast as possible to anywhere in the country."

"Okay," Soblen said, "tell me a little about this Force."

Beffort and J.E.E. exchanged a knowing glance and Beffort sat down. "Doc, I'm going to surprise you."¶"About the paralyzing ray, I know all about it, so you'll have to surprise me with something else."

"I think I will. You see, doc, to fight against the criminal organization of Madame Atomos, I had to create an organization that was like it. It's no longer possible to keep risking the lives of policemen and soldiers in a lopsided fight that hits them hard."

"Yeah, and the FBI agents?"

"There aren't enough," J.E.E. interjected, "and they're already busy with the different crimes that they've been trained for. The life of the nation can't come to a standstill, even if Madame Atomos murders a million Americans!"

"So," Soblen was intrigued now, "where did you fish up the members of the Green Dragon Force?"

"In prison," Beffort said. "Every one of the men here were serving a sentence of at least 20 years in prison. But most of them had got the death sentence."

Soblen's jaw dropped. "Well, I'll be!"

"Keep your cool, doc. Just tell yourself that to crack the whip you have to be holding the handle. My 300 men have nothing more to learn about using weapons, driving cars, burglary, hold-ups or anything else you can imagine."¶"Outlaws! They're going to…"

"Not now," Beffort cut him off coldly. "Society is going to use their knowledge to fight the greatest battle of history. This battle might last for years and will be chock full of hard fighting. My men will risk their lives and whoever finishes their contract will be granted a full pardon and reintegrated into the society that had banished them forever."

"But come on, Smith, they're gangsters!"¶"Of course," Beffort admitted calmly. "And that's exactly why we chose them. We needed killers, commandoes of peace, and now we have them. Your driver, Sammy, was sentenced to 120 years. You could say he was practically dead. Now he knows that he has a chance to pull through and if Madame Atomos of any other member of her Organization runs into him, they're goners for sure!"

"Who knows about this?" Soblen asked.

"A dozen people," J.E.E. answered, "among whom are the highest authorities of the country. Of course, there was never any question about informing the general public through the press. This is and will remain an undertaking stamped top secret! You see, doctor, we trust you."

"Thanks," Soblen stiffened up. "I'll try to live up to it. That said, Smith, what's the lead you discovered thanks to me?"

Beffort smiled to himself at the unspoken battle pitting Soblen against J.E.E. The latter was the head of the FBI. His participation in the formation of the Green Dragon Force was necessary, but it was a fact that Soblen was refusing to admit after he himself had been kept in the dark. "Eight days ago, doc, you attended a conference being held in Houston at the center for space training, the headquarters of NASA, the National Aeronautics and Space Administration, right?"

"Right," Soblen confirmed.

"It was your first major trip in four months and we figured that Madame Atomos would follow you. With this in mind, Eddy Witter and Charles Hyde were charge of your protection. During your trip they noticed that you were being followed by a suspicious couple, so they took some photos and sent them here. After examining them in our archives, we found that the man was Bob Sanders and the woman Madge Geary."

"The girl from the Curtis Hotel in Phoenix[3]?"

"Exactly, doc. Well, the Atomos Organization was interested in you and it was up to us to take advantage of it. After you returned to New York, Sanders and Madge stopped watching you and two other members of the Organization took over. Naturally, Witter and Hyde continued following the Sanders-Madge couple who went directly to Wilmington, North Carolina, which is one of the states that Madame Atomos has not attacked yet. They rented a room in a hotel downtown. The next day at 10 a.m., just after the period of neutralization[4], they

---

[3] See *The Return of Madame Atomos.*

[4] The hour of neutralization (from 9 to 10 a.m.) freed each member of the Atomos Organization from the grip of the Great Brain. Remember that it was thanks to this dead time

suddenly split up. Sanders got away from Hyde, but Witter, who was literally on the heels of Madge Geary, was able to follow her to a small house located on the seaside about 12 miles outside the city. Since then, the girl's been invisible. From our office in Wilmington, we know that the house belongs to a certain Arthur Flower, widower, no children, officially on a pleasure trip somewhere in Europe."

"Hmm," Soblen said, "I'm afraid his trip is going to last forever."

Beffort nodded. "You're probably right. The house looks uninhabited, but our men have noticed some strange comings and goings between the house and the shore during the night. If you knew that the house was only 50 yards from the sea, you'd think like us that Madame Atomos is certainly using it for a port of entry."

"Does that mean that Atomos City isn't far?"

Beffort lit a cigarette and pulled down another map that showed the east coast of the U.S. from Miami to Norfolk. "Off the coast of Wilmington there's a three and a half mile trench. If you remember the attack against Florida…"

"You mean the trench could be the main underwater base of the City, don't you?"

"Everything is leading us to believe that, doc. If we take a few steps back, we see that Atomos City crossed the United States from west to east after suffering serious damage on the Coconino Plateau in Arizona. Now, it was precisely in this area that our radars lost track of the City, which was unable to fly at its usual speed and

that the surgeons in Atlanta operated on Mie Azusa, Yuri Belof and Jean Marchand.

was visible all the way up to a secret base where it could perform the necessary repairs."

Soblen was interested. He took off his glasses and unconsciously wiped the lenses. Beffort's reasoning was strong, based on real facts, absolutely unquestionable. On the Coconino Plateau, Atomos City had indeed flirted with destruction. Attacked by air at a time when its electromagnetic dome was not protecting it, it survived only by fleeing frantically.

But Soblen also remembered that the huge machine seemed seriously damaged. "Great," he said. "Let's say that the City is taking refuge in this trench and that it's still there. What do you plan on doing?"

Beffort leaned toward him, his brow furrowed in concentration, and answered, "This is all very recent, doc, don't forget that. Your trip was only eight days ago and we found out about Arthur Flower's house only 48 hours ago! We got together the Green Dragon Force to try to find a solution. That's why you're here now. No need to tell you that Yosho Akamatsu will be here soon."

A smile smoothed out Soblen's face. "When is he arriving?"

Beffort looked at his watch. "My telegram should have reached him last night in Tokyo. I don't think he'll be long."

At that very moment, Akamatsu was getting off the plane in the Lambert-St. Louis Municipal Airport where Soblen had landed just three hours earlier. When he left Tokyo, he had destroyed Smith Beffort's telegram, being sure to remember the instructions telling him to take a taxi to 411 North 7th Street, the address of the Swiss

Consulate, and wait there on the sidewalk to be contacted about the next step.

Carrying a small suitcase, Akamatsu crossed the hall in his smooth, cat-like walk and headed for the cab stand. He got into the first taxi in line. On the road, the special agent from the *Tokkoka*[5] did not bother to look behind him, which was unusual, but he had no reason to be suspicious. For four months in Japan he could not imagine himself being followed by a member of the Atomos Organization.

When he arrived at his destination, he paid the cab, got out of the car and started pacing back and forth in front of the consulate. Three minutes later a big black Chevrolet pulled up to him. "Mister Akamatsu, would you like to get in?"

Without hesitating Yosho climbed into the back seat of the vehicle next to two men already there and the Chevrolet took off straightaway. As he was putting his suitcase between his feet, he felt a hard blow to his head and collapsed without breathing a word.

In front of the consulate a newspaper seller, who had seen the incident from a distance, ran to the nearest telephone booth.

Yosho Akamatsu regained consciousness much later and he realized immediately that he had been drugged. A bitter taste on his palette; his tongue stuck to the roof of his mouth; it was extremely hard for him to come out of the fog. After a minute the pain in the nape of his neck reminded him quickly of his waiting in front of the Swiss Consulate, the arrival of the Chevrolet and the movement he had made to put down his suitcase.

---

[5] Japan's secret police.

He groaned, opened his eyes onto total darkness and stood up with a crick in his back. They had not even taken the trouble to tie him up, so they must have been sure that he could not escape.

Akamatsu searched his pockets but they had all been emptied. He moved in the darkness, hands held out, and met a rough surface. It was just a wall. An old stone wall whose cement was cracking in places but which would hold up against attack. At least against an attack of fingernails… Farther on there was a door, which was a change—a cold, flat surface. Steel.

Akamatsu finished his little inspection tour, sniffed the air and listened hard. He heard a background noise, a constant, low rumble broken by dull crashes, which he recognized immediately: the sea. As for the air, it was fresh. So, there had to be a ventilation hole somewhere in the utter darkness and he had to find it, no matter how small it was.

He probed the walls again, concentrating on the wall opposite the door, until he felt a light breeze. He jumped, grabbed a rusty iron bar and pulled himself up. Even with his nose against the grill he could see nothing. Beyond the bars the darkness stretched out unto infinity. An infinity that very well could have been just another wall. He let go and sat on the hard clay ground. For the moment he could do nothing constructive. His prison had a few weaknesses but whoever had kidnapped him knew that he could do nothing about it for a long while.

After who knows how long, a key turned silently in the lock and Akamatsu jumped up, glued to the wall, at the very second that a light bulb went on in the high ceiling and a voice said, "Don't tire yourself out, Mr. Akamatsu. If you want to eat, go and sit in the middle of the cellar."

Yosho obeyed, noting that he was in a cellar and that they were watching him in spite of the darkness, probably by means of a wide-angle, infrared lens.

"Thank you," the voiced continued. "Now we can bring your meal. No need to attack your server. Even if you manage to get by him, you will be stopped on the other side of the door by rays that will not be pleasant to your body."

For a minute Akamatsu tried to figure out where the strange voice was coming from. It was the voice of a man, rather metallic, speaking in fluent English. He looked up and right away saw the small speaker, out of reach.

The door turned heavily on its hinges and a man entered the cellar. He put a plate on the ground and stood back up. Akamatsu recognized him easily: Bob Sanders, the third man from the Marchand/Belof team, both of whom the surgeons in Atlanta had operated on four months earlier. For now he was under the control of Madame Atomos, but he would come back to himself tomorrow morning between 9 and 10 a.m.

Akamatsu sat without reacting. It was vital that no observer see that he knew Sanders. The latter looked at the Japanese agent with a cold, empty eye and said, "When you are done, let us know by knocking on the door. Do you need anything else?"

Akamatsu smiled. "I would love to get out of here and back to St. Louis."

His useless request was only made to see the reaction. Soblen, who had already been in Madame Atomos' prisons, had said that there was a delay in the response coming from the Great Brain in Atomos City. In fact, Sanders was only an intermediary. His eyes captured the image of Akamatsu, his ears heard sounds, and everything was collected by the motor-brain in his skull and immediately transmitted to the Great Brain, which responded through Sanders' vocal chords. Therefore, the delay between the question and answer might give an approximate distance between the City and the cellar.

Akamatsu counted 12 seconds before Sanders said, "We will speak about that again when the time comes, Mr. Akamatsu. We know that Smith Beffort and his wife are hiding around St. Louis. Beffort should know by now that you have been kidnapped and he will not stop until he finds you. When we have eliminated Beffort, we will transport you to the City to undergo the operation that you know about."

Through the mouth of Sanders, it was Madame Atomos who was speaking. Akamatsu could have sworn it. "Why are you waiting for the operation?" he asked.

Again the answer took some time to come. 12 seconds. "Our operating room was destroyed on the Coconino Plateau. It has been unusable ever since, but will be ready in a week. You will fight by my side, Mr. Akamatsu, and believe me, I am happy for it. Bon appétit and see you soon."

Sanders turned around, walked through the doorway and carefully closed the armored door behind him. Akamatsu shivered. His chances were one in a million to get out of this one!

Chapter III

The information network of the Green Dragon Force proved remarkably efficient in the hours after Yo-sho Akamatsu's kidnapping. Lost in St. Louis, the black Chevrolet that the newspaper seller had seen was found a half-hour later in one of the parking lots of the Wood Flying Club. From there Beffort's men learned that a private plane based out of Huntington, Kentucky, had taken off 20 minutes before for Chattanooga, Tennessee. The plane was transporting a patient, two male nurses and a doctor.

In Chattanooga one of Beffort's connections found out that the plane had made a stopover at Lovell Field and another connection had spotted it in Asheville, North Carolina. After this, there was a long silence.

Finally at the end of the afternoon, Witter, who along with Hyde was watching the suspicious building in Wilmington, called to say that an ambulance had just entered the property under cover of twilight. Through his binoculars Witter had seen a man in street clothes and two nurses carrying a stretcher into the house. Afterward, the ambulance headed back downtown. Beffort needed no other details; he already knew that Akamatsu was in the dreadful hands of Madame Atomos. Protected by the Green Dragon Force, he, Soblen and J.E.E. took an FBI plane and landed in Wilmington a little after 10 p.m.

Witter had been informed and was waiting for them on the curb in front of their observation post—an abandoned boathouse where Hyde was keeping watch from the second floor.

"What's new?" Beffort asked right off the bat.

"Nothing," the G-man answered. "If we hadn't seen the ambulance come in the gates, we'd swear that the dump was still empty. Come on in so you can see it."

Once inside the boathouse Witter continued, "It's still a little early, but in an hour or two the place is going to liven up."

"What does that mean?" J.E.E. asked.

"They're coming from there," Witter pointed to the sea. "For the most part in a small outboard with no lights on. A casual observer would obviously never imagine that he was sitting in front of a bunch of smugglers, except that they're not unloading merchandise, they're loading it."

Soblen raised an eyebrow. "On such a small boat?"

"Yes, doctor. It seems absurd, doesn't it?"

Beffort objected, "But I don't understand. If goods are being stored on the property, they have to be coming in some way or another. And since you've been sitting here, you haven't seen any delivery truck?"

"Not a one."

"What kind of goods are they?"

"Small crates mostly. The men from the boat each carry three or four, sometimes fewer, and take off for the sea."

Beffort sat on a worm-eaten bench and suggested, "Let's go over this again. We know that the house is one of the refuges of the Atomos Organization, our friend Akamatsu is being held prisoner and some goods are being stored there. This is completely different from the usual methods of Madame Atomos, right?" Everybody agreed. Beffort concluded, "So, if it isn't a trap, we have to say that circumstances are forcing Madame Atomos to stall."

"Wait a second," Soblen cut in. "I think I get it! During one of our last conversations we examined the situation and decided that if Madame Atomos hadn't shown herself for four months, it was no doubt because of serious damage to Atomos City. Let's say now that the City is sitting deep in the sea off the coast with no way to leave of its own accord until the damage is repaired. What does it do? Firstly, get the necessary pieces. Secondly, get food and water for the servants of the Organization living in the City. All this right under the nose of the Coast Guard and without being spotted by our radar or being noticed by the people or the fishing boats. In my opinion this is not an easy job. Especially as far as acquiring the separate pieces. The equipment in the City is extremely complex, like one of our rockets that takes off from Cape Kennedy, and its pieces aren't being sold in the hardware store. Therefore, to get them all together, Madame Atomos has to be very cautious and since she can't buy anything complete, she must have to scrape them together one by one from different places. That would explain the small crates loaded onto the boat and the number of trips between the City and this property. What do you think?"

J.E.E. wrinkled his nose. "For Madame Atomos it's hard to believe! Even if the City is immobilized, there's a whole fleet of flying saucers on board! One of them could fly to Japan in the blink of an eye and get all the necessary pieces!"

Beffort chuckled. "If the computers in the City are out of service, no saucer can take to the air. I think Soblen's reasoning is faultless! Damn, doc, do you really think that Madame Atomos is at our mercy?"

Soblen whistled softly. "Don't go overboard, Smith. This woman has more than one ace up her sleeve and

31

we'd be wise to approach her on tiptoes." He, too, sat down and added, "Unless she's made some fatal mistake? Since she keeps escaping us, maybe she thinks she's invincible…"

"There you go!" Witter suddenly interjected. "Just as I thought. Something's going wrong with the Organization. I felt it while following Sanders and Madge Geary. Tell me, Smith, could you have imagined this just six months ago? At that time every member of the Atomos group vanished into thin air whenever we got close to them."

"It's a trap," J.E.E. said. "You have full powers, Smith, but watch out! Don't forget that the immediate objective of Madame Atomos is limited to capturing you, your son and your wife! To reach her goal she's capable of anything. Look at what she's accomplished already: without the slightest effort she got you to leave Europe and come into this boathouse. She certainly knows exactly where you are right now. Her plan is simple. You're Akamatsu's friend. She kidnapped him to force you to step in." His words were like ice. He, too, had reasoned logically.

Beffort stared at him gloomily and said, "Trap or no trap, it's not the time to pussyfoot around. The Green Dragon Force exists and it has a powerful weapon. I've decided to strike!"

"When?" J.E.E. asked tensely.

"Tomorrow morning at the beginning of the neutralization hour. Exactly at 9:01. In the meantime I need to know where Witter's boat is coming from. Alert the Navy, Eddy—We need a speedboat as soon as possible."

The speedboat was fast, with a Seagull silent motor, and it sped across the water like a skipping stone. All

lights out, black in the blackness, its approach was unde-
tectable except for the soft swish of water under its
sharp-edged hull and the splash of waves that it sometimes caused by planing too sharply.

For ten minutes it kept back from the small boat
that headed for open water after loading a dozen crates
on the beach. Armed with binoculars Beffort, J.E.E. and
Soblen watched it tossing about two miles in front of
them, bearing southeast.

"That's where the trench is," Beffort murmured.
"We should reach it in less than five minutes."

J.E.E. did not respond. He felt uneasy and did not
try to hide it. On the high sea, the speedboat was incredibly vulnerable to the tremendous forces of Madame
Atomos. One shot from a disintegrating ray and the five
men would have lived...

"The boat's turning in circles!" Beffort shouted.

The pilot instantly cut the motor and looked in front
of him, eyes dilated by fear. He knew exactly what it
meant and now seriously regretted having come.

Through his binoculars Beffort saw a whirlpool
form around the small boat. A strange machine rose
slowly out of the water, but the distance and the night
prevented him from identifying it. It looked like a huge
box or a dumpster...

"We saw the same thing in the Gulf of California,"
Soblen muttered. Curiously, he, the short-sighted one,
could see better than Beffort or J.E.E. when the visibility
was at its worst.

"What is it?" J.E.E. asked.

Soblen did not need to answer. The dumpster
opened its jaws, swallowed the small boat, closed up
tightly and disappeared under the dark waves. Beffort

dropped his binoculars and went to the captain whose forehead was dripping. "Where are we, captain?"

The officer shook his head. He had a hard time un-gluing his eyes from the point where the boat had disap-peared, but he was finally able to look at a nautical chart lit dimly by a tiny lamp. "Closer than you think," he said. "It's not much deeper than 600 feet... the trench is still five miles due east. Is Atomos City there?"

"It is," Beffort said coldly, "but over 600 feet down. The jointed arm we just saw is going to take the boat inside the City. Indeed we've already seen this off the coast of Punta Penasco in Mexico, but there the City was only around 100 feet below the surface. Think about it: over 600 feet, that's too much!"

The stationary speedboat seemed even more vulner-able. The officer leaned over the chart again. He had a lot of trouble concentrating, thinking that he was sitting on powder keg whose fuse was lit and burning down fast. He could not do anything about it; his fear in-creased tenfold.

"So?" Beffort was impatient.

The officer glanced at the pilot and read panic in his eyes. He stiffened up, wondering if maybe it was a pic-ture of himself. "You're right," he answered a little more firmly. "I was off by 20 degrees.

"How deep is it?"

"65 feet maximum. We're near The Steeples. It's still sand and reefs here..."

"Not bad," Beffort noted in appreciation. "Here the City isn't at too much risk! The big ships are passing by farther out to sea and the fishing boats shouldn't venture out here too often. Okay, let's go back."

The pilot started the motor and was relieved to turn the speedboat around, heading for the coast, which was invisible in the night. The officer looked through his binoculars and for a minute watched the place where the dumpster had sunk into the sea. He had excellent eyesight but still wondered if he wasn't imagining the four or five periscopes... No, they were there! "Mr. Beffort?"

Smith picked up his binoculars needing no further information, but he saw nothing in particular.

"At water level," the officer pointed out, "in the middle of our wake."

Then Beffort made out the rounded tips of a few periscopes, very far apart from one another, forming a half-circle around the point where the boat had disappeared. "Turn it off!" he ordered right away. "Madame Atomos is watching us!"

The pilot obeyed begrudgingly. Turning off the motor he felt like he was slipping the noose around his neck.

"Hide your binoculars," Beffort said excitedly. "We have to look like we're here fishing!"

The officer reacted, "My boat doesn't look like a fishing boat!"

"We have no choice," Beffort grumbled. "Besides, in the darkness we can pretend... Did you see the periscopes for a long time?"

The officer balked. He was not sure. He was sure of only one thing: if Madame Atomos suspected the truth, she would destroy the speedboat quicker than he could spit.

"Answer!" Beffort was getting angry. "It's important! Were the periscopes already up when we got there?"

"Of course... or I think so. I was paying attention to the boat, but..."

"That's okay," Beffort cut him off. "Tell your pilot to turn around, captain." The officer looked at him in astonishment. "It's the only way to stay alive," Beffort explained, inflexible. "We're fishermen. We're not worried about anything. Except for the reefs. Go on!"

The captain gave orders in a flat voice. The motor started again and the speedboat made a slow, wide turn, pointing its bow to the open sea again and moving forward. Wisely, Dr. Soblen and J.E.E. turned their backs to the periscopes, striking a pose that could lead one to believe that they were, in fact, casting lines. Crouching behind the cabin, Beffort inspected the sea. The periscopes were still there, barely visible between the foam-fringed waves and they were dangerously trained on the boat.

The officer slipped in next to Beffort. "We're navigating with our lights off," he reminded him in a distant voice.

Beffort stiffened up. He had forgotten that detail and understood too late that the speedboat could not be more suspicious. Turning on the lights now would risk alerting Madame Atomos for good. Since the speedboat entered the area, it had made two stops, a u-turn and was getting closer every second to the danger zone.

"Nothing we can do about it," Beffort mumbled. "We've got to keep going like this."

The pilot at his station looked like a statue. Beffort breathed a sigh of relief when he saw that he was cool-headed enough to take off his cap. He looked toward the periscopes again and saw that there was only one (the farthest away) still sticking up. It was a good sign. In the back, Soblen and J.E.E. continued examining the wake of the boat, but a justified anxiety made them look a little mineral—two petrified blocks leaning over the

36

waves… In the distance the periscope pivoted and followed the boat now in profile.

"We should be over the City," the officer whispered.

Beffort did not answer. He kept watching the pilot, who was turning pale, and worried that he would lose control. If he panicked, he might suddenly open the throttle and the boat would fly off much faster than any fishing boat could. Then Madame Atomos would know immediately… He crawled alongside the cabin until he reached the pilot and said softly, "Go a little faster, but just a little, okay?"

The sailor shuddered, gave it a little gas and his cheeks got back some color. The speedboat crossed the reef zone and continued toward open water. Beffort picked up his binoculars and scanned the empty sea—the last periscope had also sunk beneath the waves.

Chapter IV

At eight in the morning six submarines and three torpedo boats left their anchorage and headed for The Steeples area off the coast of North Carolina. Operation Full Stop had commenced.

At the same time a squadron of B-52 bombers took off from Fort Bragg, destination Wilmington, and a hundred men belonging to the Green Dragon Force arrived separately on Wrightsville beach in New Hanover County. This small town was the closest to the house that Witter was still watching and where Smith Beffort had set up his HQ from the old boathouse to the ships at sea.

At 8:30 the deployed fleet was no more than six miles from The Steeples and the bombers were ready to take off from Wilmington. Of course, no special activity revealed that a large-scale military operation was about to unfold. Around the boathouse there was nothing but calm. Still, J.E.E. stayed in radio contact with the Air Force general in Salem and with Admiral Greens, while Beffort was directing his troops by walkie-talkie. The attack on the Atomos refuge and the liberation of Akamatsu were supposed to happen at the same time as the bombs and torpedoes hit the City. A one or two minute delay between the two actions could jeopardize everything and perhaps provide Madame Atomos the means (though Beffort could not see how) to escape once again from punishment. This worried him.

Soblen saw his anxiety and said, "The hour of neutralization starts at 9 a.m. sharp, Smith. Why do you want to attack a minute afterward?"

Beffort looked at him, full of stress. "You think it's too late, doc?"

"Of course! I'm scared that Madame Atomos will take that minute to protect the City with an electromagnetic field that will nullify our efforts!"

"If she's going to do it," Beffort answered, "she won't wait so long. On the other hand, I'm hoping the minute will be used by whoever knows that the surgeons in Atlanta can save them. See, doc, it would be a miracle if a man like Sanders chose this very day to take his chances by escaping on board a flying saucer, but I have to believe in it. There are too many innocent people in the City to condemn them like this in cold blood."

Soblen looked grumpy. "We've already discussed all this. You know perfectly well that we have no choice. We have to strike at Madame Atomos, even if her death spells that of her servants. Why are you hesitating all of a sudden, Smith?"

Beffort shrugged his shoulders and put his hand on the paralyzing pistol hanging from his belt. "I hoped that this weapon would keep us from pulling out all the stops, doc. And I also think that we're going to fail…"

This unexpected confession made Soblen jump. "Damn!" he swore. "Now is not the time for such pessimism! The navy and air force are on the verge of war and your men are just waiting for your signal to invade Madame Atomos' refuge and here you are…"

"I know," Beffort cut him off abruptly. "But like you just said, we have no choice. We have the chance and we have to take it. The City has been spotted, pinpointed and surrounded. No one would understand if we didn't act, would they?"

Soblen spread his arms. He did not understand. "You have full powers, Smith and you alone decided to go into action in spite of J.E.E.'s advice to the contrary when he thought—and still thinks—it's a trap."

"Akamatsu," is all Beffort said.

"Okay, okay, I was hoping you would say that. So, realize that we can't hesitate and you have no other decision… In your place Yosho would do the same thing." The doctor was silent, looked toward the house and said distractedly, "I wonder what he's thinking right now."

One of Akamatsu's main qualities was his tenacity. Since the light bulb was still on in the ceiling of his cellar, he was determined to find the eye through which they were watching him. It took him until the middle of the night. A tiny hole that probably went deep into the armor-plated door with a wide-angle lens. It was really the last place he thought of looking.

He spit into some dirt and made mud to plaster over the hole. It was the best he could do and it would force his guard to open the door if he wanted to see what was happening in the cell. After that, Akamatsu went at one of the bars of the cellar window—a hopeless enterprise. The prong of his belt buckle barely bit into the cement around the bar; it slid off the surface and started bending after a few minutes. Akamatsu gave up and straightaway started digging into the hard dirt ground beneath the window. After four or five inches he hit a slab of concrete and had to abandon that, too.

In no way discouraged, he next tried the wall. His belt buckle crumbled the cement around one of the big stones, scraped against a solid surface and would go no farther. That was no surprise. The wall must have been a good 20 inches thick at least.

Akamatsu took a breather. Now he knew that it was no good attacking the floor, walls and window. So, there was only the door and the ceiling left. Unfortunately the latter was out of reach, just like the light bulb and speaker. As far as the armored door…

Now Akamatsu sat down. He had finally admitted his defeat. Madame Atomos had taken all necessary precautions with him and there was no way out, except for help from the outside.

Without his watch he had lost all track of time. He got up and kicked the armored door with the heel of his shoe. On the other side, nothing moved. Akamatsu continued in vain. The house seemed deserted, which was rather unusual. Madame Atomos was not the kind to leave her prisoners without surveillance, even if she was sure that they could not escape. Now, since the middle of the night, the lens had been useless and no one was curious enough to check up on what he was doing.

That is exactly what the Japanese special agent was thinking of while Dr. Soblen was talking about him.

Eddy Witter raised the alarm. He did it without even thinking, just with a simple statement, "The sun should have risen an hour ago…"

No one took notice of his remark right away. However, it was already 8:40 and it was still nighttime over Wrightsville Beach and the immediate vicinity. A few seconds passed before Dr. Soblen was also bewildered. "Don't you find this strange, Smith?"

"What's that, doc?" Beffort asked, who was busy with his walkie-talkie.

"It's as dark as midnight."

"It's overcast is all."

Soblen nodded and looked at the sky through the hangar's window. No star could be seen; the area looked like it was buried under a dome of darkness. To the east not a glimmer of light was visible. "Still," Soblen mumbled, "an hour late…"

All of a sudden Beffort snapped out of it, jumped up and went to the window. "Incredible!" he shouted. "Doc, can you ask J.E.E. to get in touch with the navy? I want to know if the weather is the same on the sea."

Soblen stumbled down the steep stairs, found J.E.E. sitting on a bench with earphones on and gave him Beffort's request. The FBI chief passed on the message to Admiral Greens and got an immediate answer: the weather was dark off the coast but not bad. On the contrary, a black cloud was covering the zone of operation and apparently spreading overland from Kirkland to Carolina Beach. Naturally Admiral Greens attributed this condition to a meteorological phenomenon.

Soblen climbed back up to the second floor and gave Smith Beffort the news. He went pale. "Weather phenomenon? Come on, doc!"

On the ground floor, Beffort took J.E.E.'s seat and contacted Wilmington. The town was also drowning in the dark of night and the air force general in Salem was wondering how his bombers were going to be able to hit their target. Then Beffort called Jacksonville. There the sun was shining as well as in Southport, Makatolca, Freeman, Currie and Burgaw.

Beffort signed out and put down the earphones. "No doubt about it," he raged, "Madame Atomos is about to slip between our fingers!"

"How's that?" J.E.E. asked.

"Since the affair in Palm Beach[6] we've known that she can control the elements," Beffort informed him. "This artificial night obviously has to thwart our plans.

---

[6] See *Miss Atomos*.

The bombers are going to drop their bombs by guess-work and the navy's going to sail cautiously before opening fire on The Steeples. If the City moves a mile away, you know that our action will be absolutely fruit-less."

"And here's the fog!" Soblen announced from the doorway of the hangar. Beffort went to stand next to him. The fog was, indeed, coming in from the sea, a heavy bank that took only a few minutes to become un-believably thick.

Witter came down carrying his night binoculars. "We can't watch the house anymore," he said disgusted-ly. "I can't see more than 30 feet!"

Beffort looked at his watch. Before the hour of neu-tralization, Madame Atomos was rendering her enemies defenseless in the blink of an eye.

"The navy and air force are asking whether you want to continue the operation," J.E.E. said after getting back to his post. "They're calling the weather conditions appalling. What do you think, Smith?"

Beffort clenched his teeth. He had only a minute to make a decision.

After dumping out the fog and night, Atomos City slid slowly underwater. It was already several miles from The Steeples and was heading for the deep trench where it counted on being safe. In her command post watching the computers Madame Atomos was worried about the trajectory that the electronic brain had calcu-lated to drive the City between the reefs.

Madame Atomos was worried because she had nev-er been so vulnerable. The City could only move very slowly and could use only a fraction of its usual wea-pons—it was reduced to hiding under the sea instead of taking the offensive. The situation had lasted a month already and was coming to an end, but it would still take a week of patient waiting. She had gone through a lot of trouble to get the necessary parts and now they had to put them together and try them out, so the marvelous electromagnetic shield would not be up and running for seven days.

The Americans would have to fail at their attempts to destroy her if she wanted to get farther from the shore, but this would also mean cutting off all sources of supplies. For this, Smith Beffort scored points. Madame Atomos was in desperate straits. She had even been forced to abandon Akamatsu in the house in Wrightsville Beach, as well as all the supplies that had not yet been brought on board.

Nevertheless, in case of a disaster Madame Atomos had one final escape route: a supersonic, guided missile-plane that would take her to her ultra-secret base in the Pacific in less than 15 minutes. But she knew that she would use it only as a last resort because if she lost her City, she would, at the same time, lose all her means of action against the United States and even though this might be possible, it was unthinkable at the moment. Madame Atomos still had terrifying weapons at hand, which she could use even if she were more than three and half miles deep in the ocean. And she was counting on using them.

At 9:01 Smith Beffort unleashed operation Full Stop. The B-52s took off from Wilmington in a fog that could be cut with a knife. They gained altitude and were very quickly flying over the zone that was still sunk in darkness. At the same time, the submarines and torpedo boats arrived in range of The Steeples. Whereas it made no difference for the subs, the ships on the surface had a lot of trouble staying on course. In spite of this, Beffort ordered them to fire at 9:05. A rain of missiles struck point zero and all around the reefs, destroying some of them, but it was impossible to judge the results for the time being.

At the same time, the Green Dragon Force flooded into Arthur Flower's house and met no resistance. All the doors were open except the one leading to the cellar, which they had to blow up to free Akamatsu and subsequently find a huge stock of supplies.

At 9:15 everything stopped. The bombers went back to their base and the ships turned around, but the Green Dragon Force stayed where they were. On board a speedboat, Beffort, Soblen, Akamatsu and J.E.E. drove out to The Steeples. The small craft searched the water in every direction for 30 minutes but could not find the smallest piece of wreckage or even a drop of oil.

"It looks," Soblen said, "like our bubble's been burst." Under the circumstances that was black humor.

"I knew it," Beffort said. "From the moment that Madame Atomos found out that we were going to attack, she made all the necessary arrangements to escape us. And yet the fact that she didn't counter-attack proves that she's weak right now."

"I agree with you," Akamatsu seconded. "Otherwise she would have taken me on board the City like she had planned."

Beffort turned to him. "Did she talk to you?" ¶ "Only through her servant. Now that we have some time, I can tell you that I was being watched over by Bob Sanders during my short imprisonment."

Beffort only then realized that his friend did not know what had happened since Madame Atomos' jailors had captured him when his plane landed in the United States. Therefore, he immediately explained how he had managed to build the famous paralyzing ray and then revealed the existence of the Green Dragon Force.

Akamatsu did not looked surprised but said with regret, "In fact, you were forced to change your plans because I was stupid enough to let myself get captured by our enemy. I'm really sorry about that, Smith." He winced and then in a rather cold voice asked, "Are your wife and son okay?"

"Yes, thanks," Beffort answered distractedly.

Akamatsu took his arm and looked him straight in the eyes. "It's not just a polite question, Smith. It's obvious that Madame Atomos has acted pretty much to get you here along with most of your men. In your shoes, I would make sure right away that my family is safe and sound."

Beffort shrugged, "No use. Mie and my son are in hiding."

"Still, make sure," Akamatsu insisted.

"He's right," J.E.E. agreed. "From the start I've been telling you it's some kind of trap!"

Beffort nodded. He only had to make a simple telephone call.

Chapter V

Beffort called the cabin in Columbia, Missouri, a little after 9 o'clock and was connected with his wife right away. Everything was fine. Robert was sleeping. The four men from the Green Dragon Force were at their posts and nothing out of the ordinary had happened since Mie and her son had moved in.

With this load off his mind he hung up and reassured his friends, bringing the conversation back to Madame Atomos. "The City can't be far," he said with conviction. "I'm absolutely sure that she's taken refuge in the ocean trench three and a half miles under the surface. How can we get to her under such conditions?"

J.E.E. lit a cigarette and piped in, "To reach her is nothing. But we first have to make sure that she's really there. Then it'll be child's play to send a few tons of explosives to her. The trouble is that locating her won't be an easy task. If the City isn't moving, there's no way to detect it with sonar…"

"Ultra-sound depth sounder," Soblen proposed.

"Easy enough to try…"¶"It won't work," Soblen interjected after thinking about it. "If the City is stuck on the bottom, the reading of the sounder by magnetostriction won't tell it apart from the relief of the sea bed."

"Therefore?" Beffort asked.

"We have to go and look," Soblen decided.

There was a moment of silence. Everyone understood that if a submarine detected the City, Madame Atomos' devices would, at the exact same time, detect it.

"That would be suicide," Akamatsu mumbled.

"Exactly," Beffort said. "We can't take such a risk. We have to find another way, doc, using machines."

47

As Soblen raised his eyebrows and motioned toward the window, which the fog was covering in thick layers, he said, "Take your time—we have plenty of it. This darkness and fog proves that Madame Atomos is still in the neighborhood."

At 10 a.m. a helicopter from the naval aviation dropped a dozen ultra-sound depth sounders over the trench and flew back to the coast. The devices were going to sink while emitting a ray at a 20-degree angle. The ultra-sound ray was supposed to reflect off Atomos City or go through it if it was not too dense and give back echo-reliefs of the seabed that was very well known in this area. Thus, any anomaly would show up on the reading, which would be instantly sent back to the navy headquarters in Fort Fisher where Beffort and his friends had gone and thereby the location of the City would be known with absolute precision.

Twenty minutes after launching the devices the operator announced that the reading was not normal. He thought that a huge school of fish had swum between the sounder and the bottom of the sea and it was so dense that it was holding up the echo relief for the moment.

A minute passed and then something started whistling. It came from all sides, gradually getting louder.

"What's that?" Beffort shouted.

The operator shook his head. "I don't know. It sounds like it's coming from the port."

Beffort and Akamatsu went outside. The sound was deafening, but the source remained a mystery. An officer ran by and Beffort grabbed his arm. "Do you know what's happening?"

"What is that?"¶Beffort had to yell to make himself heard, but he could not hear the answer. The noise was unbearable now, drowning out all other sounds and making conversation impossible. Akamatsu took a notebook and ballpoint pen out of his pocket. He wrote something down and showed it to Beffort:

"Madame Atomos, to keep us from spotting the City." Beffort nodded. It could not be anything else.

Soblen took a piece of chalk and went to the blackboard that Beffort had brought into the office. He wrote:

"The dictionary says that the decibel is one tenth of a bel, a unit used to measure the intensity of sound. Symbol: dB. The average voice measures 55 decibels, the sound of thunder is 77. The sound that we are hearing right now is close to 100 dBs. We can't hear anything else except this sound, which is steadily increasing every 15 minutes. It's obvious that Madame Atomos has found a way to keep us from spotting her City and that she has defeated our sounders by emitting other ultrasounds. She is preventing us from acting effectively by drowning us in decibels.

Soblen had got to the bottom of the blackboard. He turned around to get the approval of Beffort, J.E.E., Akamatsu and the high-ranking officers from Fort Fisher who were present at his talk.

An hour later the situation developed in a surprising fashion. Solely because of the strange whistling, all activity in the area was paralyzed. Conversation was impossible, so businessmen could not dictate their letters, make telephone calls or listen to the radio or television. In the shops they had to use signs to make themselves understood. To take a taxi it was necessary to write the address down on a piece of paper, etc.

In short, everyone was deaf and dumb. Besides this, the shrill whistling grated against the nerves and had already caused a number of breakdowns among people whose sensitivity was exacerbated by fatigue or by the constant bustle of modern life. Then the situation emptied the schools, workshops, post offices and all places where they had to talk in order to work. There followed a noticeable shift in the daily routine that upset people even more.

It was useless to plug your ears or close the doors and windows; the whistling infiltrated everywhere to bore into the eardrums like a powerful electric drill. Everyone was deaf to sound, totally deaf. Drivers on the road could not hear the motors and had to change gears by feel, honking mute horns out of habit and ending up feeling like they were driving in outer space. And yet nothing was broken—it was just that nobody could deal with all the silent objects. Every action is accompanied by sounds that are followed by a series of movements. In the absence of familiar noises, mistakes were made and everyone became even more irritated.

But all this was nothing. The doctors predicted that half the population was at risk of going crazy if the whistling continued for more than 36 hours. In fact, it was to be expected that no one could sleep during such a racket. Babies were already choking in their beds and the night shifts were losing their precious time of rest. After 36 hours, the lack of sleep could be fatal...

Dr. Soblen erased what he had just written on the board and gave the floor to whoever wanted it. Beffort took the chalk and wrote: *If Madame Atomos acted at the precise moment that we were dropping the sounders over the trench, it's obviously because the City is there. Taking this as nearly certain, all we have to do is strike hard and fast. I ask this of the navy officers present here: how can we hit, without fail, a target sitting three and a half miles down on the bottom of the sea?*

He made sure that everyone had read his message, erased the board and left his place to the highest ranking officer, who was a ship's captain. He took the chalk firmly in hand and wrote without hesitation: *Give us the green light, Mr. Beffort, and let us chose the means.*

Beffort broke the chalk, took one piece and started a dialogue:

I don't doubt your effectiveness, captain, but Madame Atomos is a dangerous adversary. It's more than likely that she won't let you get close to her and it's useless to risk the lives of your men in a hopeless endeavor. How do you plan to proceed?

The officer wrote, *First of all, we have to cut the City off from every possibility of retreat. Mr. Beffort, you don't remember me, but I was in San Francisco Bay when Madame Atomos blew up the Maine[7].* He stopped writing, erased the board and resumed. *At that time the Maine was surrounded by an impassable electronic net and it would not have blown up if Madame Atomos hadn't sabotaged it from the inside. At Fort Fisher we happen to have the same kind of net. It's so big and strong that our most powerful ships can't break through without being seriously damaged. So, I propose that we fill the net with cement blocks weighing around 1,000 pounds each and drop it down there. If everything works right, the City will be imprisoned under the steel mesh and stuck on the bottom under several tons of ballast.*

Beffort shook his head, wiped off the text and wrote, *Your net will be sliced or disintegrated by the City in a split second. Instead of dropping a net down there, we should drop underwater mines that are set to explode at the bottom. And we should send Madame*

---

[7] See *Madame Atomos Strikes at the Head* in *Miss Atomos*.

Atomos so many that she can't destroy all of them before they reach her. A rain of explosives, captain, that's the answer!

Soblen came up and simply wrote, *Net + mines. The latter first.*

The officer nodded and by habit picked up the telephone. Realizing that nobody could hear it ringing, he hung up. The whistling had, in fact, become even louder, probably reaching 300 decibels. In the night and the fog that was still covering everything, the strange whistling sounded demonic and terrifying.

The ships' captain and the other officers left the building and disappeared in the fog. Beffort, Soblen, J.E.E. and Akamatsu followed. Not being able to communicate with the navy, air force or the Green Dragon Force, they were forced to count solely on the sailors at Fort Fisher.

Loading the huge steel net, the cement blocks and the mines took practically all morning. At 2 p.m., the big, 25,000-ton cargo ship the Eagle finally left the dock, cruising at 16 knots, with an unusual crew of 150 men. Informed in writing, the admiral had agreed and done what was needed so that no other ship would cross its path during the operation. Moreover, the sky was covered by the air force, which stood ready to intervene in case the City tried to escape by leaving the water.

On the pier Beffort watched the cargo ship enter the night and fog. The whistling drowned out the sound of the machines, making it terribly complicated for orders to be given from the bridge to the different posts. Beffort easily imagined how difficult it was going to be for the ship to accomplish its mission.

In a few seconds the cargo ship was swallowed by the fog. Beffort returned to the control room where he found J.E.E., Soblen and Akamatsu. An operator was in written contact with the Eagle and there was also the captain. In the next room they were watching the Eagle's progress on the radar. The atmosphere was tense, charged with electricity. Everyone was prepared for the worst.

At 2:15 the Eagle signaled that everything was fine on board and it was following its plotted course. 15 minutes later it sent the same message and added that it was passing by The Steeples. Another quarter of an hour went by and then the ship sent a third message: the fog was unbelievably thick, like it could turn solid at any second, and the temperature had dropped several degrees.

At 3:15 the Eagle announced that it was above the trench and it would start the drop. There were three minutes of silence and then the fifth message arrived, astounding: *We are stuck in ice! Spontaneous formation of a vast ice floe that keeps us from moving. Impossible to drop the net and mines! Awaiting instructions.*

Since the captain hesitated, Beffort dictated the response himself: *Clear off the Eagle immediately! It'll mean your life! Confirm reception.*

The operator communicated the order and waited for an answer. A few minutes went by without a sign from the Eagle. The captain called them five times in a row but got no response. He turned to Beffort and looked at him questioningly. The events were beyond him; he was facing a situation that he was not prepared for; he was visibly asking for advice.

Beffort did not know which way to turn. If Madame Atomos had sunk the Eagle, it was impossible to go and verify. The formidable woman had succeeded in striking terror in her enemies. Night, fog, noise, ice floes!

Moreover, Atomos City was becoming totally invulnerable. If Madame Atomos could change water into ice at will, it could be expected that the ice floe would reach deep into the sea.

Dr. Soblen took a pencil and piece of paper. *Nothing to do for now. Madame Atomos is trying to gain time, probably to repair the city, and won't let anything get close. But when she decides to leave the trench, we'll have to be ready.* He turned the paper over and continued in his clear writing. *Can your paralyzing weapons pierce the armor of the City?*

Beffort wrote, *I really don't know. We never tried that.*

We have to try. Right now it's the only really effective thing we can do.

Beffort grabbed another piece of paper. *For that I'd have to gather my men. Some of them are carrying more powerful paralyzing rifles with a greater range. So, right now we have to get back to Wrightsville Beach. Does anyone have a better idea than our friend Soblen?*

Akamatsu, J.E.E. and the captain all shook their heads. Beffort wrote for the captain, *You should inform the admiral about the disappearance of the Eagle and tell him that all operations have been suspended until further notice. The next action will depend on how effective our arms are against armor.*

The officer showed that he understood and watched the four men climb into a military vehicle that the navy had put at Beffort's disposal. He was thinking that going back to Wrightsville Beach in the middle of this fog and night would be a real feat.

Chapter VI

From Fort Fisher to Wrightsville Beach, passing through Winter Park, is about 20 miles. Normally the trip takes 30 minutes, even counting on bad traffic, but this day nothing was bound to be normal. With the headlights on Beffort, who was driving, could not see more than 30 feet through the fog and was lucky just to hug the shoulder of the road. A long line of cars and trucks stretched out in the other direction, not moving because of an accident at the entrance to Fort Fisher. The whistling, of course, drown out all sounds, including the sirens of the fire trucks and police, who were trying hard to clear the road but could not get through. Things were slowly getting worse. It started with chaos among people on the edge, but who knows where it would end.

A little before Kure Beach, on Highway 421, Beffort was stopped by a van. It had crashed hard into another vehicle coming in the opposite direction, trying to pass on the left in order to gain some time, and the road was completely blocked. The two drivers were swearing at each other at the top of their lungs for nothing since the diabolical whistling covered their voices they looked grotesque trying to scream over the din.

Beffort and his passengers got out of the car. It was absolutely necessary to clear the road and reach Wrightsville Beach before evening. It was already 5:30. Time was passing quickly and every minute that passed played into Madame Atomos' hand.

While Beffort, Akamatsu and J.E.E. went to see if there was a way to clear the road, Soblen set off across the fields. He was feeling his way over the ground to see if there was a possible detour. In the night and fog it was not easy. The little doctor bumped against a tree trunk, scrambled through thorny bushes, but finally ended up on a road after hooking around. Then he went back to examine the ditch that ran between the road and the fields: it was a natural formation, but it could still prevent a car from reaching the other side. He found the same tree trunk again and the same bushes and all of a sudden splashed through a puddle that he did not remember. He stood still, not sure what direction to take. Because of the whistling he could not use his hearing and the headlights from the vehicles on the 421 could not be seen. The fog surrounded him on every side and when he stretched out his hand, he could barely see it.

Soblen took off his fogged up glasses and set off again blindly. He counted 100 steps and figured that he should have reached the road long ago if he had gone in the right direction, so he turned around. Another 100 steps and he figured that he was back where he had started. He continued straight ahead without running into anything.

Ten minutes later he was still walking and he knew for sure that he was lost. He hoped that Beffort and the others were not too worried about his disappearance and that they would keep moving to Wrightsville Beach. Personally, he was embarrassed, nothing more.

He climbed up and down a few slopes, walk a while longer on slimy ground and then almost ran into a wall. To the touch it felt like a building made of boards. He guessed that he had come to a barn and the farm was probably not far off. He felt along the boards until he found a door, but it was closed tightly with big padlock. He moved on, dragging his feet so that he could feel the ground better. After a few yards he stopped next to a high chain link fence, planted solidly in the ground. He tried to walk around it, but after a short while he was once again feeling the boards of the shack.

For a few long minutes he tried to escape from the trap that was fencing him in, but he could not forge through the thick bushes to follow the fence all the way and thus lost contact with it, wandering in the darkness and each time bumping up against the shack. He got tired of the endless game and gave up trying to find the entrance through which he had come in, apparently by pure chance. Leaning against the fence, he knew it would be impossible for him to climb, so, since he did not want to walk around in circles all night long, he decided to break into the shack.

His luminous watch showed 6 p.m. It had been one half hour since he had left the road. It was nerve-racking. Soblen hated to waste time and if he absolutely had to, he would rather it be somewhere comfortable. The comfort of the shack could only be relative, but it would still be better than the icy fog that was chilling him to the bone.

Soblen armed himself with a rock and went at one of the eyebolts that the padlock was hooked to. He struck blindly but could not hear his blows because of the whistling, which was as loud as ever. He had no idea if his efforts were paying off. For a good 15 minutes he fought with the padlock without getting any results and then it came to him that the shack must have a window.

He felt like an idiot as he walked around the small building, feeling along the boards from every angle, but finding no opening whatsoever. Which was weird. As weird as the fence. Why bother putting up a fence, waste all that material just to protect a simple barn in the middle of the countryside? And wouldn't it be unnecessary after putting on the padlock? And if the shack were protecting something valuable, it would probably have been better to give it a good solid door with a strong lock instead of a padlock that any decent tool could snap off.

Reflecting on this, Soblen returned to the door. He picked up the big rock and went at the padlock again. In the darkness he often missed his target, so he was very surprised when he suddenly found the padlock sitting in his hand. He dropped it, pushed the door open and by reflex searched for a light switch. He found one right away and flipped it. The light flooded the room and Soblen stood there agape.

The shack measured around 12 by 15 feet and had no ceiling! It was completely filled with a powerful transmitter whose loud speaker, like a huge funnel, was pointed at the sky. Soblen shook himself, kicked the door closed and approached the machine.

It was obviously working thanks to a series of transistors arranged in circles within circles above five giant batteries. In one corner an antenna made a constant sweep around a half-circle zone centered on the door. Intrigued, Soblen put on his glasses and leaned over. He had the feeling that the whistling was louder, but he would not swear to it. Besides, he had not yet established the connection between the machine and the noise that had been dominating the region for almost 12 hours. Then, through the wires, he saw a disk turning inside a Plexiglas dome and this find put him on the right track.

He had chanced upon one of Madame Atomos' transmission posts! As usual the sinister Japanese woman had anticipated the events and set up a series of installations all along the East Coast that ran by themselves and could keep her safe. But it was done in a hurry. The fence, the shack and the padlock proved it. Nevertheless, the result was the same: since morning, the region had been paralyzed.

Soblen unhooked the battery terminals one by one and with a great deal of trouble he finally pried off the last one, straightened up and looked at the disk. It started slowing down and at the same time the whistling diminished. When the disk stopped turning, the sound transmitted by the loud speaker got softer and softer until it finally died out with a strange screech from the phonograph whose springs had wound down.

Soblen was suddenly standing in silence. But the silence was relative because in the distance the whistling was still raging. At least now he could hear himself breath and he heard the sound of his footsteps, the rustle of his clothes...

Soblen imagined that a good part of the coast must have also been experiencing the same, sudden calm. "Damn!" he shouted, just to enjoy hearing his own voice, "that feels good!"

Like at a signal a car horn suddenly honked outside. Soblen jumped to the door and heard the sound of a motor and then a voice yelled, "Doc, where are you?" It was Beffort.

Soblen shouted, "Over here, Smith. On the other side of the fence!"

Headlights cut through the fog and Beffort's voice asked, "What are you doing in there, doc? Do you want to get electrocuted?"

Soblen walked toward the lights and felt the first drops of rain. He rounded the bushes, went between two poles and slipped out of the half-open, chain-link gate. In the dark it was a real miracle that he had entered the enclosure through such a narrow passage.

"Come on, doc," Beffort said, "and tell us why you're risking your life."

Soblen turned around and saw the sign in the head-lights: *No Entry! Risk of Death! High Voltage!*

Soblen laughed. Madame Atomos had anticipated everything except that one of her servants had left the gate of her so-called transformer open!

At 8 p.m. the situation was remarkably improved between Southport and Kirkland. 30 of the transmitters had been put out of service by the army and police so that the whistling was completely turned off all along the coast. Of course, there were still some posts to be found farther inland, but now that they knew the cause of the ill, it was simply a matter of bringing the cure. That was Soblen's job.

Then the rain started falling and did not stop. It swept away Madame Atomos' artificial fog and, for once, nature waged war against the terrible Japanese woman.

Nevertheless, the sea was still protecting the City. A few patrols had sailed within a mile of the trench, but the ice floe kept them from going any farther and the sailors were not authorized to venture onto the ice. The navy was being cautious since the disappearance of the Eagle and Beffort was not sure that it would follow his orders. Besides, he preferred to get back into battle in his own way—he wanted to change the front that Madame Atomos was used to, to leave her in the dark about the enemies she had to battle. In a word, Beffort wanted guerilla warfare.

"Great," J.E.E. objected, "but that helps our enemy. She wants to gain time and you want to give it to her! She won't be going on the offensive."

It was the moment chosen to try Soblen's suggestion. On Arthur Flower's property, the men of the Green Dragon Force had set up four steel plates that were each one-inch thick. In fact, it was unlikely that the City's armor was as heavy, so Soblen thought it was definitely exaggerated. When everything was ready, two volunteers took cover behind the armor and Beffort opened fire with a paralyzing rifle. The two men were unscathed behind the steel plates. Next they tried three plates, then two, then one without any results. The paralyzing ray did not pass through.

"One inch," Soblen mourned, "it's not so much."

"I don't agree," Beffort shot back. "Some tanks don't have any better protection. Do you think the City could fly if it had to lift a hull like that?"

"Damn!" the little doctor was beside himself. "Why did you start with four plates in that case?"

"Curiosity, doc," Beffort answered coldly. "The weapon is new and it's necessary to find out how effective it is. Now we're going to experiment on thinner plates. Sammy, send in the next one!"

The former inmate stuck his pistol in his belt and helped his three colleagues bring out a half-inch steel plate. While the tests were being carried out, the men of the Green Dragon Force (there were about 100 of them) kept watch around the property.

Beffort started the new test and this time the two volunteers did not leave their shelter. Their partners carried them into the house and laid them on the carpet. They were completely paralyzed for one hour, but after that time they would regain full consciousness.

"There you go," Beffort concluded. "Now we know that the ray can cross through a half-inch steel plate from 100 yards away! Now let's see if we can go farther back." He made another try, but the ray would not pass through beyond 100 yards.

Akamatsu looked sour. "It's not exactly the ultimate weapon, is it?"

Discouraged, Beffort shook his head as he sat down on the front steps. "It's almost midnight and we still haven't found a way to attack the City. All our conventional weapons are useless. I don't see how we're going to do it. Especially since the City is sitting three and a half miles deep in the ocean."

J.E.E. came forward, his face haggard and tired, "Smith, I see only one solution. We have to use an atomic bomb."

Soblen countered vehemently, "In Birmingham General Stuart tried the bomb without warning us. A plane dropped it on one of Madame Atomos' flying saucers and it was bounced back by an electromagnetic ray so that it exploded on Stuart, his headquarters and six armored companies! The result? Thousands of fatalities in our camp![8]" He took a breath and continued, "I beg you not to make this decision because you won't be able to live with the responsibility."

J.E.E. shrugged his shoulders. "You're overdoing it, doctor. The bomb will explode three and a half miles underwater."

"As long as Madame Atomos doesn't throw it back in our faces like a tennis ball! And how do you plan to get through the ice floe?"

"With an icebreaker."

---

[8] See *Miss Atomos vs. the KKK* in *The Return of Madame Atomos*.

"Stop!" Beffort ordered. "This isn't getting us anywhere. We have to look at the problem from another angle."

"What does that mean?" J.E.E. sounded spiteful.

"Madame Atomos is untouchable as long as she's sitting down there, we have to admit it! So, we have to make plans for when she decides to resurface."

He stood up, poked Soblen in the chest and asked, "In the meantime, doc, tell me something: in your opinion, how are Madame Atomos and her 2,000 servants able to breathe down at the bottom of the ocean?"

Soblen grimaced and whistled. "Good grief! I never thought about that, Smith!"

"Think about it, doc," Beffort said coldly, "because I think that if we can mix a little gas with the air that they're breathing, it would do the trick for us."

Chapter VII

The next morning Soblen had his theory and J.E.E. had his. Akamatsu and Beffort likewise had their own notions. But strangely, all of them agreed on one point: underwater for at least four months Atomos City could not be manufacturing the oxygen needed for the lives of its inhabitants. Therefore, the oxygen had to be coming from someplace.

There was where the choice lay. Either the City came up at night to get its supply of fresh air or it was using a ventilation system coming from the outside, i.e. from the surface. The two options were both feasible and stirred the imagination of the whole team. Beffort walked to the window and looked outside. The artificial night was still covering the country, but the incessant rain had kept off the fog.

Beffort went back to the table where his friends were finishing lunch, drinking their coffee, and he said to them, "In 35 minutes the City will start its neutralization period. It's just enough time for me to make a trip out there."

Akamatsu got up. "I'm going with you, Smith."

"Hey," Soblen said, "that wasn't in the plan!"

Akamatsu smiled and spoke softly, "You made all the decisions without me, but you forgot that I am the special envoy of the Japanese police. My country would not be very pleased if its representative remained inactive when it came to fighting against Madame Atomos."

J.E.E. fidgeted in his seat. "I understand, Yosho, but do you really have to risk your life like this? I told all of you that I'm against this expedition. I think it's useless. Only an armed attack can be decisive!" He persisted in his original idea, in spite of everything and everyone, figuring quite fairly that a reconnaissance mission had no justification if it was not accompanied by a brilliant attack on Madame Atomos.

"Before going on the offensive," Beffort said patiently, "the greatest military chiefs need to know the land on which their troops will be fighting. To venture out there under the present conditions would be making the same mistake we made in sending the Eagle over the trench. If my friend Yosho wants to be part of the expedition, no one can stop him without seriously offending the Japanese government. Madame Atomos is one of its nationals and…"

"Okay," J.E.E. cut him off furiously. "Do as you as like since you have carte blanche."

Beffort slipped the strap of a paralyzing rifle over his shoulder and motioned to Akamatsu to do the same. As he was going out the door he said, "We'll stay in touch by walkie-talkie. If anything happens, you'll know about it instantly. I think that should make you feel better, right?"

Soblen grimaced and reproached him, "You're acting as if you were single, Smith. If *anything* happens to you, as you say, we won't even be able to tell your wife since we still don't know where she's living."

Beffort smiled thinly, "Don't worry about that, doc. Mie will be informed by the Green Dragon Force in good time. And between us, bad news travels fast, doesn't it? Are you coming, Yosho?"

Akamatsu followed him into the yard where a car was parked. Sammy was behind the wheel and three men from the Green Dragon Force were sitting in the back. Akamatsu and Beffort climbed into the front and Sammy took off right away.

Five minutes later the car stopped at the beach. The six men got, walked to the shore and climbed into a dinghy, which brought them to the boat that Beffort had chosen for the reconnaissance patrol. A speedboat was lowered into the water; it had a thin bow, two Daytona 500 HP motors and could reach a top speed of around 60 miles per hour. Beffort did not exactly know how his men had acquired the marvel and he did not want to.

"You like it, boss?" Sammy asked.

"It's okay. How long can we use it?"

Sammy balked, grinning. "Uh, if it stays night, I guess you can keep the boat for a few days."

Beffort was sure that the speedboat had been *borrowed* from the nearby marina, but he did not want to know how. "Who knows how to drive this thing?"

Sammy beat his chest. "I'll take care of it, boss."

Beffort slanted a glance at him. "I didn't know you were a sailor..."

"I became one last night."

"That doesn't make me feel better," Beffort grumbled. "I'd rather have someone with experience. This is no time to be playing by ear."

After examining the boat Akamatsu lifted up his head. "I can drive it, Smith."

The Japanese special agent never committed himself lightly. Beffort nodded and took a seat in the front of the speedboat. Sammy and his partners sat in the back while Akamatsu started the engines. The boat shook a little, turned slowly to face open water and then gradually picked up speed.

"Direction, Smith?" Akamatsu asked.

Beffort unfolded a nautical chart while Sammy grabbed a waterproof box with navigating instruments that he was told to acquire. Beffort and Akamatsu worked out the route to follow. This time they would circumnavigate The Steeples, head toward the east and then south and come back west. If Madame Atomos were using any detection devices in spite of her ice floe, they would most likely be pointed toward the coast. Coming from open water was the only real strategic choice.

The boat skimmed over the water at full speed and yet stayed remarkably stable. Its two motors purred and Beffort appreciated it, giving Sammy a thumb's up. "I wonder if you aren't a sailor after all. Who helped you pick out the boat?"

Sammy took a sailing magazine out of his pocket and pointed to an article. "I did some research," he said modestly. "This is a racing boat that's got a dozen wins under its belt. The last one was the Offshore Powerboat Race. It's been up for sale for over a week, but the door of the hangar wasn't closed very well."

Beffort ignored the last phrase. Sammy could open any safe with the simplest of tools. His three partners did not even smile. Beffort had chosen them carefully. One was the famous Ralph Stutton. 61 hold-ups to his credit; six policemen, four bank employees and a night watchman were unfortunate enough to get in his way and were resting six feet underground. Beffort signed him up when he was getting ready to plop down in the electric chair.

The second was Art Baxter. He had committed a lot of robberies and did ten years in a state penitentiary in Georgia. Three days after being freed, he and his team attacked the Harris Trust & Savings in Chicago. They were caught by the police, but during the shootout he killed a dozen officers. Beffort had literally pulled him out of the gas chamber.

The last was Lucky Simms, who had been a war hero in the Pacific. On his return to civil life he rebelled against readjustment. His gang scoured six states and put out of combat five upholders of law and order. Lucky was arrested alone. He refused to *give up* his accomplices, took full responsibility and saw his death sentence communed to life imprisonment. Beffort was convinced that he was not as guilty as he claimed and had a certain respect for him.

It was certainly a pretty disreputable bunch, but one that would definitely cause a lot of problems for the Atomos Organization.

"We've just passed The Steeples," Akamatsu announced flatly. "What time is it, Smith?"

"8:50. We should slow down, Yosho."

Akamatsu reduced the speed and peered into the night. The day before it was impossible to see more than 30 feet ahead because of the fog. Now the visibility was pretty good and the moon was breaking through the dark dome fabricated by Madame Atomos. Akamatsu saw a long, white streak on the sea and called out to Beffort. The G-man came over to him and looked at the water through his night binoculars.

"That's the famous ice floe, Yosho," he murmured. "Apparently Madame Atomos is still using the same defense mechanism. Veer off to the left; we're getting close."

Akamatsu turned the boat to head northeast, which would take them away from their target. At 8:59 Beffort figured that the boat could get closer without too much risk. Akamatsu gave it some gas, leaving the large loop he had started ten minutes earlier, and drove straight for the west.

A few seconds passed before the ice floe came suddenly into view before them. Akamatsu cut the engines and let the boat drift forward, bumping gently against the thick layer of ice. There was no swell to speak of, so the boat was completely still.

Beffort raised his arm. Straightaway Sammy, Ralph, Art and Lucky jumped silently onto the ice floe. They were incredibly calm carrying their paralyzing rifles. Beffort sent a message to Dr. Soblen with the walkie-talkie, saying that everything was fine and the target had been reached.

"It's 9:02," Soblen answered nervously. "Don't forget that you only have 53 minutes with a safety margin."

"Don't worry, doc," Beffort whispered, "and stay on the line. Contact every five minutes. Okay?"

"Okay. I have to tell you that J.E.E. has chartered a chopper!"

"Don't let him play the lone cowboy," Beffort growled. "What does he want with a helicopter?"

"For once," Soblen retorted dryly, "I totally agree with you."

"Tell me, doc," Beffort was getting annoyed, "you're making us lose time."

"Rescue mission. In case you get hit hard, we'll pick you up off the ice. It's a Cobra. Three 13.2 machine guns and a rapid-fire cannon. I feel a little better with it, Smith. Over and out."

Beffort signed out and turned toward Akamatsu. "Yosho, I'm going to ask you stay on board." The Japanese was startled. Beffort quickly added, "Your role is essential and you're the only one who can pull it off. When we're on the ice, we might get lost. If we walk straight ahead, it's obvious that we'll reach the edge of the ice floe, but not necessarily where you'll be waiting for us. At 9:55, I'll flash this light three times. It's up to you to come and get us before the end of the neutralization hour."

Akamatsu wrinkled his brow. It was a heavy responsibility. Beffort's life and the lives of the four men from the Green Dragon Force were in his hands. "You're hard on me, Smith."

"Proof that I trust you, my friend. I'll admit that without you I'd be going out on the ice with a lot more worry on my mind. See you soon, Yosho."

He jumped onto the ice floe, joined the group of men waiting for him and headed east. Each of them knew that henceforth it was necessary to be absolutely silent or at least to talk only in case of extreme necessity and only in a whisper. Beffort had trained the Green Dragon Force in some traps that they would have to face: ultrasensitive microphones, panning cameras, etc. In their refuge in St. Louis, the ex-lifers and death row inmates had experienced an accelerated but complete training. Beffort was as confident in them as he was in himself.

In anticipation of this moment, Beffort and his men were equipped with boots with nonslip soles, night binoculars and strong flashlights. Their clothes were dark and their faces painted black. Between the night and the ice it was either black or white—Beffort was not sure he had made the right choice.

The commando team moved slowly along line 60-foot line, carefully examining the terrain. For the moment, the flashlights stayed holstered. If some object were protruding from the ice, it would be easy to spot on the immaculate whiteness. Beffort had warned his men to watch for any spindly thing sticking out, like an antenna.

After slowly covering about half a mile, Ralph Stutton, who was on the right wing, flashed his light at Beffort, which meant that he had just found something. Beffort took no time joining him. The former killer showed him a strange apparatus that was barely poking up from the frozen bed. It was rounded, like half a balloon, and was pierced with four big, screened holes. At first sight Beffort could not say what it was. Anyway, it was certainly no microphone or camera.

He motioned to the four men to keep their distance, lie down and arm themselves. Then Beffort crawled up to the mysterious object, feeling a terrible cold slowly penetrate his body. When he was ten feet away he knew that the object was used to make ice by lowering the temperature; it became so cold that he had to retreat.

He huddled his men together and whispered to them why he had come back. There must have been a number of these devices scattered over the ice floe. There was no need to worry too much, but it would still be better to avoid them. Objective: possible air ducts.

The commandos lined up again and began their slow advance over the hard ice. The silence was extraordinary and the night darker. They were approaching ground zero, that is, directly over where the City was immerged, and Beffort felt a tremendous anxiety rising up in him. Never in the past had Madame Atomos let him get so close.

Then Beffort thought better—after all, the City was still three and a half miles underwater! The fact that it was measured vertically did not change the distance. Between his group and the City there was a thick layer of indestructible ice and miles of water. In reality, Madame Atomos was in no danger for the moment.

All of a sudden, on the other end of the line, Lucky Simms made the prearranged signal. He flashed his light at Beffort who ran to the mound over which Lucky had stopped and saw a metal device, painted white, that was faintly humming. Lucky took his boss' arm and then tore off a small piece of a cigarette paper, placing it on the ice. The paper started whirling around, moved back and forth and suddenly slid over the ice and was swallowed by the device.

Beffort smiled. Lucky had just proven that Madame Atomos was pumping in fresh air from the surface of the ice floe!

Chapter VIII

Over the next 20 minutes Beffort and his men found six devices of the same type. Some were sucking air in, others blowing out. Of course, there were probably other devices to keep the air fresh in the City, but there was no way to locate them at the moment. And time was of the essence.

Beffort gave the signal to retreat and the group headed west. In 50 minutes, including stops, the commando team had crossed the floe. At 9:55 Beffort was at the edge of the ice. He turned on his flashlight, swept it twice over the surroundings and then pointed the light at the sky. The toughs of the Green Dragon Force stood around him waiting calmly. Akamatsu had surely seen the signal and should have been rushing to its source. A minute passed but no sound of an engine could be heard. Then Beffort's walkie-talkie began blinking frantically. The G-man knew that Soblen was panicking.

He pressed the button, put the microphone close to his mouth and whispered, "Don't get in a sweat, doc, we're waiting for the boat."

"It's 9:56, Smith," Soblen also whispered.

"Stay calm. Akamatsu will be here."

"I'll stay on the line," Soblen said in a hollow voice. "What exactly is your position?"

"We're at the west end of the floe," Beffort murmured as he peered into the night.

Soblen did not answer. Beffort took the opportunity to listen carefully, but he could still not hear the engines of the speedboat. Lucky Simms looked at his luminous watch, raised an eyebrow and put up three fingers. Beffort nodded in silence. In three minutes the hour of neutralization would end. Madame Atomos could use her servants again and restart a mess of detection devices, which would go over the entire surface of the ice floe with a fine-toothed comb and the commando team would not have the slightest chance to escape.

"Smith," Soblen's voice came over the walkie-talkie, "less than two minutes and 40 seconds! I'm in radio contact with the helicopter flying over the beach. It can get to you in no time. You want me to send it out?"

Beffort hesitated. The situation was becoming critical and his men were starting to look a little nervous. Still, calling the helicopter could compromise everything. So far it really seemed that Madame Atomos had not detected the little group. This was the result of the precautions taken by Beffort and his men who had walked on the ice with infinite care and tried to avoid any hidden microphones like the plague. The operation had succeeded in its two first phases: approach and inspect the terrain. For it to succeed completely, they would have to get away without a hitch. Otherwise, Madame Atomos, at the slightest alert, would drastically change her means of defense. The City would only have to move one mile and everything would start from scratch.

"Smith!" Soblen said. "Less than two minutes!"

Beffort clenched his jaw and looked at the ray of light showing their position. Akamatsu must be able to see the signal. So, what was happening?

All of a sudden, Art Baxter raised his hands and pointed to his ears.

"Smith," Soblen insisted, "if you don't answer, I…"

"Shut up, doc!" Beffort barked.

Soblen kept quiet and Beffort heard a furious roar break through the night. Two seconds later the speedboat literally jumped out of the darkness, headed for the group, and swerved around at the last second. It stayed briefly on course and then its motors pushed it in reverse until it hit the ice. The men were already on board. Beffort got on last and was grabbed by Sammy as the boat shot off. He collapsed onto the bench at the exact moment that Soblen shouted, "Smith! The helicopter is heading for you."

"You can call it back," Beffort laughed, with a huge load off his chest, "We're on the boat!"

The walkie-talkie no doubt amplified Soblen's sigh of relief, but Beffort was sure that the little doctor had almost had a nervous breakdown during the last few minutes.

Beffort lit a cigarette, shook out the match and continued, "Now we know the exact position of Atomos City and we're sure that it's not three and a half miles deep. Its ventilation tubes and its air coolers can't be more than 40 or 50 feet long, so the City is sitting directly under the ice floe."

J.E.E. twisted his face into a smile of contentment and concluded triumphantly, "Ergo: we have to attack!"

Beffort agreed. "Yes," he admitted, "and we have to strike hard and fast. This time the bombers will fly at 10,000 feet so Madame Atomos won't be alerted. Doc, call General Salem right now. We need a group of B-52s before 11 o'clock."

"The target?"

"The helicopter will direct the fire and modify it if need be. Go on, doc, it's the perfect opportunity!"

The Cobra was a good distance from the target, but Beffort could make out the ice floe perfectly through his binoculars. The helicopter banked away and slowly headed back to the shore. Beffort's watch showed 11:03 when the pilot shouted, "That's it! They've taken off!"

Beffort slipped on his headphones and immediately heard the distant voice that rattled off a series of codes. "Group leader to Cobra. Position 20... Position 19... Altitude 6,000 feet... Are you receiving me?"

"A-OK," the pilot answered, "And you"

"Roger. Position 14... Position 13..."

A second passed and the positions of the group and their altitude kept changing as they got closer to their target. Thus, at zero hour, the helicopter could direct the stream of bombs if it felt it necessary, change the firing line or confirm the number of hits. Strangely, in this modern warfare, they reverted to the old system of an observer perched on top of his bell tower!

"Position three... two... one... zero!"

A white rocket shot out of the sky like a meteor and crashed into the ice floe which exploded into countless sparks.

"Point zero, okay!" the Cobra pilot yelled.

The group leader was calm, his voice a monotone, when he started reporting his second approach. "Zero elevated... plus eight... altitude 9,000 feet... position plus six..."

The Cobra took a wide turn, descended to sea level and sped off at almost 200 miles an hour toward the eastern edge of the ice floe. Now Madame Atomos could detect the B-52s, but it did not matter. The attack was on and she could not sneak away!

"Position plus two... plus one... zero!"

A few agonizing seconds passed by before the ice floe went up in flames and the din and blast of the explosion shook the Cobra. "Bull's eye!" the pilot screamed.

"Point zero on the nose," the group leader said calmly.

The pulverized ice was still floating in the air when the second wave of B-52s dropped their huge bombs. One line was lost in the sea, but most of the powerful missiles hit the target full on. The Cobra bobbed in the air like a cork and Beffort had to cling onto his binoculars. He saw that the ice floe was shattering and disintegrating into tiny splinters that whistled eerily through the night.

From now on Atomos City was directly under the bombers assaults. It had already lost its ventilators and coolers and the severed tubes, blown to bits, were turning into mere water pipes. Beffort tried to imagine the panic that must have been spreading through the City when the third wave of B-52s let their tons of steel fall on point zero.

The stream of bombs crashed into the sea, which leapt up in a wild gush of foam, and they exploded dully, almost discreetly, under the surface. Dark waves rose up and tumbled back down. And then a splattering drizzle that should have sounded the death knell for Madame Atomos.

The fourth and fifth waves finished the work of destruction that had begun three minutes earlier before they flew off toward Wilmington. The sea was calm and still again, too peaceful to Beffort's liking. Nothing floated on the surface. And the night prevented them from seeing if any streaks of oil were rising up from the unfathomable depths.

Since Beffort was so anxious, the Cobra pilot brought his machine down, hovered at sea level and turned on a high-power beam that brightly lit up the rippling water. The two men took a few seconds to accustom their eyes to the blinding light until they finally noticed the oily substance that shined on the sea. 30 feet away huge bubbles had just burst and large oil patches were spreading out.

"Hurray!" the pilot yelled as he soared back up.

Beffort waited, a knot in his throat, his eyes fixed on point zero. He still could not believe, could not bring himself to admit that Madame Atomos and her unreal City had finally been wiped off the face of the earth. The battle had lasted for years. Madame Atomos had been cornered a number of times, had her brush with death, but her superior intelligence and her perfected inventions had always helped her get out of the worst situations.

And here now, with laughable ease, a group of B-52s had sent her to the depths for good!

"Shall we go back?" the pilot asked cheerfully.

"No," Beffort's voice was dark. "Go back down."

Surprised, the pilot turned his machine around and went back to skirt the sea where the oil was floating. Beffort leaned out, scrutinized the black water being lit by the beam and suddenly straitened up. Below him, the oily bubbles were moving!

"God damn!" the pilot swore. "What's going on?"

Beffort did not answer. Atomos City was hit, that was sure. Maybe it was dying, but Madame Atomos was bound to do everything in her power to save it from an irreparable disaster. And Beffort knew that the power of his mortal enemy was immense.

Suddenly the oily bubbling stopped and after a minute a few air bubbles burst on the surface. And that was all.

"It's over," the pilot said.

Beffort shook his head. "It's not that simple. Atomos City is a veritable underwater town. The sea should be scattered with its wreckage for miles around. Plus, the 2,000 people who were part of the Atomos Organization can't have just disappeared like that, in a flash, without trying to get to the surface…"

The pilot's face went pale, staring at him. Until then he had not thought for a second about all the people, all the lives that the B-52s had tried to crush under their bombs. Now that the action was over, he could think about it calmly and the feeling he had was not of victory.

"And then," Beffort was speaking to himself, "Madame Atomos should have a means of escape. If she didn't use it, it's because she still has some hope of saving her ship. A few gallons of oil on the sea don't prove anything."

At that moment the aircraft radio crackled and the tense voice of J.E.E. vibrated the speaker. "Well, Smith? We're waiting for news…"

Beffort admitted to himself that he had completely forgotten that hundreds of people were sitting on pins and needles by the radios. He grabbed the microphone and said softly, "The City has disappeared and the sea is covered with oil."

"You don't seem very convinced," J.E.E. remarked. "Is something wrong?"

"It disappeared too fast and too quietly," the G-man confessed his innermost thoughts to hundreds of listeners. "Madame Atomos can't die like that!"

A low murmur came through the speaker. J.E.E. must have been surrounded by a crowd of military men, journalists and the merely curious. The crowd expressed its disapproval; it wanted to believe that the City was destroyed forever.

"Weigh your words carefully, Smith," J.E.E. advised. "You're live with the media. The entire population of the United States is listening to you." He paused dramatically and said rather melodramatically, "Smith Beffort, can you tell us whether you believe that Madame Atomos and her diabolical ship have been destroyed?"

He was putting on a little act, which made Beffort scowl and cut off contact. The cabin was silent; there was nothing but the beam of light shining on the oily sea.

"Damn!" the pilot sounded worried. "You just hang up in their face like that?"

Beffort smiled. "Don't worry about it, old boy. Turn off your little lamp and slip over north-north-east... All lights out. Maximum altitude."

"You know what you're doing, right?"

"I hope so. Step on it, will you!"

The pilot turned off the beam and the sidelights and slowly gave it some gas. The Cobra slid quickly to the left and rose up as its whirling rotors howled. The pilot obeyed reluctantly and showed it.

Beffort hid his smile and asked, "What time is it?"

"11:30."

"In the morning, right?"

The man threw him a surprised look and answered suspiciously, "Of course."

Beffort stared at him and spoke casually, "So, if Atomos City has been destroyed, aren't you surprised that it's still night?"

The pilot jumped. "Damn!"

Beffort's voice became more biting. "The bombs literally pulverized the ice floe and no machine could have escaped the hammering. Therefore, the City is still making it nighttime. It's down, for sure, but not out! Because of the darkness I think it will try to surface. Get us higher, friend, and fast. Any second now the area is going to become unsafe."

The Cobra shot up into the sky like a missile, suddenly emerging into sunlight. The transition was breathtaking, incredible. The sky was blue as far as the eye could see, but underneath and for miles around darkness hid the landscape.

"Fuel?" Beffort asked calmly.

The pilot got a hold of himself and glanced at the instrument panel. "About an hour's worth."

"Great. Go back down."¶"But you just said that the area…"

"Not at 1,500 feet," Beffort cut him off, "and then we can watch the sea. You know, Madame Atomos can't do anything without light."

Jaws clenched, the pilot brought the Cobra down.

Chapter IX

Far from there, in the immediate suburbs of Columbia, Missouri, Mie Azusa-Beffort was sitting by the radio listening to the unfolding battle that her husband was fighting against Madame Atomos. The cabin had been chosen very carefully by Smith. It was perched on the top of a hill in a pine forest. Except for the clumps of trees, the sides of the hill were bare of any vegetation and could easily be watched by the four toughs of the Green Dragon Force who were in charge of protecting Mie and her baby against any possible attack by the Atomos Organization. But their work did not stop there. They were also responsible for the supplies, the cooking, the cleaning, etc.

In the living room Mie had her ear glued to the radio. J.E.E. had just been replaced by a commentator from KSTL, located in St. Louis, who was getting information directly from Wrightsville Beach. The man did his job, dramatized Beffort's abrupt silence, tried to persuade his listeners that Atomos City had been destroyed and the sinister Japanese woman was not preparing a bloody counterattack against the USA. Mie turned pale in her armchair while listening to him.

At the French doors Owen Bernitz could not hold back. "The bastard! He's going to scare the hell out of everyone."

Owen did not mince his words. He was a big guy with the face of a boxer, continually chewing on his cigar, which was usually unlit. A murderer three times over, sentenced to death, he was drinking a glass of rum when Beffort got him out of a tight spot. Since then Owen found life downright beautiful and was mighty grateful to Beffort and his family. He was rough, but when it came to little Robert—whom he called Bob—he was extremely gentle, whether it was pulling up his covers or burping him after his bottle.

Mie trusted him wholeheartedly. She looked up and said, "What he's saying doesn't bother me, Owen. My husband didn't answer J.E.E. just now."

Owen Bernitz shrugged his heavy shoulders and the paralyzing rifle slung over one of them bobbed. He spoke in a throaty voice, "You don't have to for the boss. He's got mama what's-her-name in the bag. Probably didn't answer 'cause the other guy's ribbing him... Is the kid still snoozing?"

Mie was used to this kind of language. "I think I heard him, but it's better to let him rest."

"It's almost time for his scotch, but you're right. My old lady always said you should never wake a snoring kid. Say, instead of getting all spooked in front of the tuner, why don't you go out and get a little sun?"

Mie waved him off and leaned toward the radio. Owen gave up trying to change her mind and went back out onto the terrace where he could watch the dirt road leading up to the cabin.

Behind the building John Torpey was guarding the south side. Big Foster Tyre was keeping one eye on the west side and on the north was little Brady Castleman, who once in a while glanced down at the old quarry while he was fixing lunch—this was the calmest side, since it was almost impossible to get to the cabin from this way.

Owen Bernitz sat in the shade and rested his rifle between his knees. After a minute he rolled his cigar over his lips, spit in the dust out of the corner of his mouth and crossed his feet over the rifle butt. His little pigs' eyes looked blank, but they were deceivingly aware. In prison he had learned to watch without seeming to see. He heard the background noise of the radio and a branch cracking in the wind and the metallic sounds of the cooling Cadillac engine.

All of a sudden a new sound, an unfamiliar noise, mingled with the concert. Owen tried to identify it and locate the source, but he could not. He stood up slowly. It seemed to be coming from the bottom of the slope where an embankment hid part of the cornfield that extended to the train tracks. Owen listened intently and caught a fleeting glimpse of a glare behind the embankment. Exactly the kind of glare that a ray of sun makes when it flashes off the barrel of a rifle or a car windshield.

Owen crouched in the shade of the railing, put two fingers in his mouth and gave a loud whistle. The radio turned off immediately, a door slammed and the faint sound of a bell meant that someone had just picked up the phone.

30 seconds went by and then Mie's calm voice could be heard in the living room. "That's it, Owen, the phone's been cut."

"You sure?" he rasped without turning around.

"Absolutely. I can't hear a dial tone."

Owen grabbed his paralyzing rifle and readied it. "Okay, Mrs. Beffort, go and get Bob."

Over the past few days, there had been several false alarms, but this time Owen knew that it was real. They were spying on the cabin from the cornfield. They had cut the phone lines…

Like a snake, little Brady Castleman slid next to Owen. He laid a paralyzing rifle onto the cement as well as the blackened barrel of a flame-thrower with a hose hooked up to a 200-gallon tank of octogel in the cellar. Owen thanked him with a puff from his cigar and pointed to the embankment. Brady winked, took off his apron and crawled away. In less than a minute John Torpey and Foster Tyre had got the same equipment.

Owen did not budge. His penetrating gaze scanned the landscape beyond the embankment inch by inch. The cornfield rippled in a weird way, but it always did that when the wind blew in from the south. Owen heard wailing and smiled frugally. Bob had just woken up and was crying at the top of his 15-day-old lungs for his bottle; he would not shut up until the nipple was in his mouth.

All of a sudden the unexpected happened. A police car appeared, driving down the road that led up to the cabin. It was still far away, far beyond the cornfield, but Owen would have recognized this type of vehicle just by the smell. For the moment he did not smell anything, but he recognized the colors and, above all, saw the two-toned lights flashing on the roof. Then he could hear the rumble of the engine. Soon Owen could count the number of passengers. There were six, all in uniforms, three in the front and three in the back.

"What's the meaning of this, Owen?"

The big man turned his head and saw Mie through the half-open French doors. She was pale, holding an almost empty bottle in her trembling hand. In his room Bob started bawling again—short pauses followed by furious howls.

Owen frowned. "Go back inside, Mrs. Beffort, and feed the little one."

"But..."

"No buts. Get going! Maybe I became a killer because I had to wait too long for my bottle!"

Mie tried to smile, but only grimaced. Her eyes were glued to the police car, betraying a terrible anxiety. She tried to soften up Owen. "If something happened to Smith…"

"It's not the cops who would tell us," Owen snickered. "Go on back inside, Mrs. Beffort! It's a trap. Cops are bastards, but they don't cut telephone lines!"

Mie withdrew and Owen started mumbling to himself. He estimated how far he still was from the car and slowly raised the barrel of his paralyzing rifle. At 300 yards he pressed the trigger button. Nothing happened. No flash, no bang, but the police car swerved suddenly to the left, flew across a ditch and crashed into a bank, engine stalled. The policemen were in their seats, stiff as wooden stakes, eerily formal. Owen laughed and said that 60 minutes of rest would do them some good. If they really were cops, they would wake up in an hour and have no clue about what happened.

Big Foster Tyre popped out of nowhere, unprotected. "Are you crazy, Owen? Those cops in uni…"

A bright flash shot out of the cornfield, hit Foster and enveloped him. There was a puff of smoke, then Foster disappeared, like he was erased, and there was only a little pile of ashes, which the wind was already blowing away, to show where he had been a second ago.

Owen swore under his breath and huddled a little closer to the railing. *That damn Foster! But he knew what he was dealing with. Beffort kept harping on all the methods for almost two weeks! Disintegrator rifle! Range, 500 yards! Instant death! That damn Foster…*

Behind Owen something rustled and then Brady appeared. All he said was, "Foster?"

"Offed," Owen grumbled.

Brady whistled. "How?"

"Disintegrated. Warn Torpey. There's some guys from the A.O.[9] hiding in the corn."

Brady's prying eyes scrutinized the field, finally falling upon the police car. "Cops?"

"Phoneys. They came to have a little fun with us. Drop your dishes and pick up a peashooter. Don't forget to get the word to Torpey. The horn's cut and the A.O. guys aren't here to deliver groceries."

As Brady was starting back, Owen said without even looking at him, "Watch out, chef, that disintegrator rifle is a real bitch."

Brady lay a little flatter and crawled into the living room like ectoplasm. Owen had not blinked. In the shadow of the railing he knew that they would not spot him very easily if nothing forced him to show himself. He was already being terribly careful before Foster's death, but now he was nothing but a ball of nerves with all senses alert. He remembered Beffort's speeches, word for word, and etched into his memory the position of every bush, every shrub, every bump in the ground.

He suspected that the A.O. guys would not attack head-on from the embankment. A moment earlier they had made a little noise, just enough to attract some attention and then liquidated Foster because the opportunity was too sweet. But their job was more along the lines of diversion—that was clear.

The grand offensive would come from somewhere else. Something sneaky, unexpected, underground... The last word petrified Owen a little more. Beffort had beaten it into them how much Madame Atomos loved to dig tunnels to surprise her victims. With this in mind, the embankment was a perfect starting point! They could

---

[9] Atomos Organization.

bite into the hill there without being seen from the cabin. Furthermore, the corn would hide the work and take all the rubble so that nothing would be visible from the road.

Owen moved a few inches and stuck his ear to the cement floor of the terrace where the support pylon was sunk into the ground. He knew that concrete could be a great conductor of sound, so he was hoping that nobody moved in the house. He listened for a long time and then heard a muffled thumping. His eyes opened wide, but he realized that he was only hearing the sound of his own heartbeat. He breathed deeply, lay down and listened again with his ear barely touching the cement. The thumping continued, at a constant rhythm. Like clockwork!

Owen scowled and then whistled. Two seconds later little Brady crawled over. "Take my place here," Owen told him, "I have to see about something in the cellar. And stay behind the railing, whatever happens. Got it?" Brady nodded, snaked over and slipped into the shade. He was smart, fast and not easy to fool. Owen backed away slowly, all the way through the living room until he felt the wall against his heels. He stood up and found Mie staring at him. The young woman was sitting there, stiff, with a blank expression on her face. She had dragged her son's cradle into the living room and was sitting next to it, gripping the blackened tube of a flamethrower—the same flamethrower that Foster was supposed to use in case of trouble.

"Where are we at, Owen?"

"Things are fine, fine… the kid's dozing?"

"He just fell asleep. What happened to Foster?"

Owen waved nonchalantly and smiled. "He made a mistake. I'm going down to the cellar."

Mie grabbed his sleeve as he went by. "What's happening in the cellar? Come on, Owen, you can tell me everything, I know the stakes."

She spoke in a hushed tone so as not to wake her son, but her voice was still very firm. Owen crouched down next to her. Suddenly he felt like, in some way, she was as hard as he was and she could take any shock whatsoever.

"I have the feeling that the A.O. is trying to get to us from underneath," he whispered. "From the embankment, with good tools of the Atomos kind, it would be a piece of cake, wouldn't it?"

Mie nodded. When she was Miss Atomos, she traveled underground more often than she did in the open air. All she could say was, "Be careful, Owen."

"Okay, okay, it'll be alright." He stood up, winked at her, and went down the hallway.

From a room in the corner, John Torpey was watching both the south and the west. He was chewing gum and, like always, relaxed. "Hello, Owen. Looks like Foster got shriveled up?"

"Yeah. Keep an eye out, I'm going down to the cellar."

Torpey understood right away. He, too, remembered Beffort's lessons. "The A.O. is being moles, eh?"

"Not sure yet. I'll tell you when I come back up."

"Where's Brady?"

"East side."

"That means there's no one on the north. I don't like this much, Owen. They can dig from the road there, too. And there are trees."

Owen shook his head. He had always thought that they needed more people to guard the cabin. Now that Foster was gone, the situation could go downhill fast.

But Brady would go back to his post in no time. It was only a matter of minutes. He told this to Torpey, opened the door to the cellar and went down after turning on the lights.

The cellar was completely empty. Only the flexible hoses connecting the flamethrowers to the octogel tank were sticking out of the hard dirt floor. On Beffort's orders, the cellar windows had been cemented over, but they had to leave two ventilation holes to let the fumes out.

Owen lay down and put his ear to the ground. He immediately heard the same rhythmic thumping that had raised his suspicions on the terrace, but it was closer. Moreover, he could hear a constant rolling sound like a mountain stream. The machine being used by the A.O. was remarkably silent, but it still could not keep the rocks and dirt from tumbling away.

Owen listened a minute longer until he was sure that the sound was coming from the east. So, his first impression was right: the A.O. was digging a tunnel from behind the embankment. This made Owen feel better. As long as the A.O. was counting on this to invade the cabin, it would not attack. Its goal was obviously to take Mie and her son alive. Cornered off the east coast, unable to escape, Madame Atomos was in dire need of these two hostages to guarantee her safety.

Owen smiled scornfully and ran upstairs. If his plan worked, all this crazy digging of the A.O. would be for nothing.

Chapter X

It was 12:30. In the badly damaged City the air was getting thicker every minute. Soon it would become unbreathable and the inhabitants would drop like flies. But this did not bother Madame Atomos too much.

For the moment, the wicked woman had only one goal, only one thing on her mind: on the control screen of the Great Brain, she was watching the underground progress of her commando team. And as she tried to estimate how long it would be until her grand victory, she bit her nails impatiently. Once again she would have Mie and her son in her power and she would be able to dictate her own conditions to Smith Beffort!

This alone interested her. The fact that her servants had managed to find the hiding place of Mie at the most critical moment was, in her eyes, a sign of destiny. For, Madame Atomos knew perfectly well that from now on she had no choice. Before the hour of neutralization, the City could have fled to the high seas or taken flight over the United States. It no longer flew like lightning, but it was still fast enough to reach the base in the Pacific. There, on the secret deserted island, they could proceed with the repairs in peace. But now the time had passed. The bombers had hit their target and broken through the hull of the ship in several places. The compartment with the flight computers was flooded and the flying saucers were out of service.

The City had a gaping hole in its dome like a mortal wound. Its disintegrator cannons were not working, its electromagnetic ray emitter was definitely destroyed and the spare parts that she had taken great pains to gather were in a flooded room. In short, the City was unable to move, except on the surface. And only as fast as a cruise ship and without the possibility of defending itself other than with its disintegrator rifles within a 500-yard range. The other solution was to stay underwater while waiting for the capture of Mie and her son. After that, Madame Atomos would warn Beffort and demand safe passage, as well as a ceasefire, for as long as she needed to get back to the Pacific base at low speed.

That was the reasonable solution that Madame Atomos had chosen. But her error was not committed yesterday. It dated back four months to the exact moment when she had temporarily abandoned her vengeance against the USA to go hunting Beffort and Mie. And that because she believed they were running away, while the whole time they were preparing the Green Dragon Force and the paralyzing rays. Now she understood and knew she had been fooled. Nevertheless, she was risking the existence of the City on a coin toss: Mie and her son would fall into her hands and she would be saved or else they would escape and everything would be lost for a long while.

Madame Atomos cleared her mind. She had trouble breathing and was sweating profusely. It was then that she decided to surface…

The Cobra cruised for 30 minutes in the darkness without seeing the City, but slowly, the night thinned out and in certain places the dawning sky let in a few rays of sunshine. A chiaroscuro of undergrowth…

The pilot rose up from the water and without looking at Beffort said, "It looks like Madame Atomos needs some light. Do you think she'll come up to the surface?" He often posed questions like this, giving the impression that he thought Beffort was a seer. It was naïve, kind of endearing, but really annoying.

"If she has to, "Beffort said, "she'll surface, but that will admit her defeat at the same time. To show herself is to expose herself to the weapons of the air force and navy. With nothing but what we have on board, we'll be able to inflict heavy losses on her... We have to be patient, pal."

The pilot nodded, but his brow was furrowed nervously. He was not a timid person, but he would rather be able to see the enemy he was fighting against, which was not the case. The Cobra was flying 150 feet above the water, which was stained with long streaks of oil, and which, at sea level, was starting to show a pale light.

Madame Atomos' night was diminishing, melting into its perimeter, and would soon be reduced to a ridiculous little black cloud that would be swept away by the wind. It was a symbol of her power and Beffort watched the coming day with growing joy. In his eyes, the danger was represented by the City, that gigantic laboratory stuffed with dreadful weapons that had made the world tremble.

Even if Madame Atomos survived the disaster, she could not rebuild such a ship too quickly. It would take 20 years to reassemble the necessary elements to satisfy her hatred, 10 years to develop the infernal machines that had killed thousands of Americans... From the beginning the sinister woman was aging. Now she had more experience, but would she have the strength and courage to start over from scratch?

"Look!" the pilot suddenly shouted.

Beffort leaned over to see where he was pointing. A little ways away, a huge dark lump was taking shape under the water. Atomos City was rising! Beffort motioned to the pilot to gain some altitude. He did not think that Madame Atomos would give in without a last ditch effort and he wanted to check the state of the ship before giving the green light to the air force waiting on the airfield in Wilmington.

Through his binoculars, he watched the City rising and he grunted with pleasure when he noticed that the B-52s had ripped open the gray shell in several places. Damaged as it was, it seemed unlikely that the City could still float! But floating it was…

"Get on the radio," Beffort ordered, "and call General Salem direct for me."

The pilot understood that he wanted to keep the journalists out of it. The suspense had already lasted too long. If the City managed to escape again, panic might break out in the country. He called the base and got an immediate response after which he engaged in an almost incomprehensible conversation, in a weird military jargon that would have staggered J.E.E. is he were listening.

Beffort himself did not understand a thing. He looked questioningly at the pilot who signed out, winked and explained, "Falcon is me. The sardine is the City. Bear is General Salem. He will be on the mic in three clicks, that is three minutes. When we're on maneuvers, these code words allow us to talk together without being understood on the ground."

Beffort thanked him and turned around to look at the coast. He did not see anything yet, but was sure that it was only a matter of time. The artificial night was fraying now in big streaks, giving way to the sun. If it continued, the air force could attack on sight.

Below, the city opened its dome to reveal blurry figures running across the grey shell. The pilot reached out and wrapped his fingers around the trigger of the twin machine guns.

"Don't do anything stupid," Beffort warned. "If you drop below 500 yards, they can wipe us out with a disintegrator rifle. Hold your altitude and get out of here."

The Cobra shot up and then soared to the south. The pilot was nervous; he brutalized his equipment.

"Gas?" Beffort asked.

"Fifteen minutes."

The Cobra banked again. Beffort adjusted his binoculars and swore out loud. The figures had disappeared and the dome was shut tight. The City was already diving back into the waves.

"We're screwed," the pilot raged.

"Not for long. In an hour or two it will have to resurface to get air." He was beginning to wonder why Madame Atomos was trying to play for time like this.

Owen Bernitz and John Torpey were sweating bullets. For more than an hour they had been digging a narrow ditch in the bottom of the cellar. Upstairs Brady Castleman and Mie were standing guard, but no sound came from the outside. Earlier Brady had hit the passengers of the police car with another 60 minutes of sleep. On that score, there was nothing to fear.

Owen stopped digging to wipe his forehead with the back of his sleeve. "Listen."

Torpey stopped as well. They could hear the rhythmic thumping of the A.O. machines getting closer. "Less than 40 feet," Torpey estimated.

"It's a race, John. If we don't get to the bottom of the tank before they do, we'll have to drill it where we are…"

Owen's idea was simple: pierce the tank as low as possible so that the fuel could leak into the soil and soak the tunnel that the enemy was digging. When the tank was empty, all they had to do was light a match.

"The octogel's gotta flow fast," Torpey huffed as he dug wildly. "But 200 gallons doesn't pour out in a flash."

Owen tossed out a few shovels of dirt. "If we're lucky enough to hit the drain plugs…"

From the start they had been digging for that, but they were not at all sure they chose the right side of the tank. Of course, Owen was present when they installed it; he had even helped bring down the boilerplates… "You outta remember," Torpey complained.

"I didn't pay attention. At the time it wasn't important and we thought we would never have to use the drain plugs. If the A.O. guys attacked on solid ground, the tank would be emptied from the top, not from the bottom."

Torpey snorted and swung his pickaxe, which bounced back with a metallic ring. Owen swore, dropped his tool and started digging with his bare hands where the pickaxe had just struck. Very quickly his fingers felt the flap of a drain plug. He continued digging and found a second, then a third…

He stood up, smiling, and put his finger to his lips to be quiet. He was happy and worried at the same time. The plugs were there and all they had to do was free them from the dirt, but the A.O. guys were dangerously close. Now they must be going at the foundations of the cabin because the sound of falling rocks was louder, like it was coming from directly under them.

Torpey scowled, then made a sign that meant he doubted Owen's plan would work, pointing instead to the paralyzing rifles. He was obviously thinking that they would be better off greeting the newcomers with a point-blank welcome.

Owen leered at him, braced himself on his spread legs and pried off the first plug with great effort. A creaking noise rang out and then the octogel started flowing, spilling into the narrow trench before being soaked up by the loose soil. Owen knew that it would not last. The earth was going to soak up the fuel and then stop if there was a layer of clay underground. So, the octogel would fill up the trench as high as the tank and they would not be able to get to the other plugs.

Owen waved Torpey over to help him out. The two men joined forces to struggle with the second plug. They had to beat a quick retreat when the fuel came rushing out. Standing on the edge of the trench, Owen watched the level meter and clenched his jaw in frustration. The octogel was flowing in slow motion; it must have been blocked by an impermeable layer because the plugs were designed, in case of an emergency, to empty the tanks in record time.

Under the two men's feet the rhythmic thumping was shaking the earth. In a very short time, the servants of Madame Atomos had stopped digging horizontally and had turned the machine toward the surface. If they came out in the cellar at a point far from the tank, Owen's plan would fall apart and they would have to defend the cabin with their paralyzing rifles. Against the disintegrator guns of the A.O., Owen and Torpey did not feel up to snuff. Of course it would be whoever hit first, but they had to figure that Madame Atomos had her own plan.

All of a sudden the thumping stopped. Owen picked up his weapon and dragged Torpey to the stairs. The two men hid behind a bend in the flight of stairs and waited. Owen held his rifle in one hand; in the other he had a cotton pad soaked in octogel and a box of matches.

A minute went by, then the A.O. drill started grinding away at the ground. The sound of it was different, more muffled, almost inaudible. Its teeth bit into the hard, dry ground, which cracked and crumbled like old wood. Now the machine was certainly in the area drenched in octogel as it tore through the soil like a knife through butter.

Owen kept an eye on the level meter. Its red needle did not move—it was stuck on 950. In the ditch, the fuel had not gone down an inch. The temperature in the cellar was high and the fumes from the octogel were becoming heavier and heavier, almost solid. If Owen lit a match in the volatile atmosphere, the cabin and everyone in it would be disintegrated by the power of the explosion.

Torpey understood this on time and ran across the north wall to get the pickaxe. In a violent outburst and without caring about the noise, he smashed the brick that filled one of the cellar windows, opening a hole big enough to let in some air right away. The sudden ventilation cleared the cellar of its noxious smell and two golden beams flooded the electric light, shining on the dial where the red needle was still motionless.

Torpey dropped the pickaxe and got back into position on the stairs. Underground the machine puffed away, slowly but surely eating away the distance that separated it from the surface. Owen felt like he could stare through the floor. He literally saw the drill and the men operating it… And now they must have been directly under the tank.

Madame Atomos and her Great Brain were never off. With diabolical precision, they guided the drill to their bull's eye. All of a sudden a frightening screech broke through the relative silence: the drill had just touched the bottom of the metal tank.

Hundreds of miles away, the Great Brain recorded the obstacle and its nature. Madame Atomos thought that Beffort had protected the cabin with a metal covering. She had a wild smile on her face when she gave orders to continue.

The drill attacked the metal, carved a six-foot gash and then rammed through it. Instantaneously the fuel poured out and drowned the men and the machine, gushing into the tunnel like a waterfall.

Owen watched the red needle of the meter with wide eyes; it fell at a dizzying rate. At 10 gallons he lit the cotton pad. At zero he tossed it into the trench, which still had a puddle of octogel.

Chapter XI

The tunnel, dug 30 feet under the surface and solidly shored up as it went along, was what is commonly called a great achievement. If it were not so well built, it would have collapsed and exploded, sending tons of dirt into the air. As it was, it became a conduit, a kind of gigantic gas jet that carried the burning octogel toward the cornfield as straight as gun barrel shoots a bullet at its target.

Dragging along the men in its fiery breath, the deadly jet of fire erupted into the open air with infernal violence, charring the two A.O. trucks in the blink of an eye, as well as the other group of servants who were watching the cabin. At the same time, the corn caught fire and the field turned into a huge inferno.

While the members of the A.O. were being grilled, another tragedy was playing out in the cellar. Owen had backed away as soon as he threw the cotton and was almost at the top of the stairs when the blast from the underground explosion blew the cover off the tank. The shockwave moved in more than one direction. The tunnel was not a cannon and the tank cover, which turned into a breech, had no recovery brakes or any possibility of recoil able to tamper the backdraft of flames. So, the cover flew up and smashed into the ceiling as a maelstrom of fire filled the cave, grilling John Torpey before whirling out the north and south windows. Owen was grazed by a tongue of fire, but ran into the hallway, slamming the door behind him and rolling on the floor. The door heated up, cracked and split. Pieces of plaster peeled off the walls. The floorboards bulged and the entire cabin vibrated violently like a cork ready to pop out of a champagne bottle.

Then the 200 gallons of fuel were burned up and the flames lost their energy at each end of the tunnel, finally being absorbed back into the ground and going out in a final burst of black smoke, which bellowed out of the two exploded cellar windows. Down in the field the corn was still burning, but the fire would not burn farther without anything to feed on.

Owen walked away from the door into the living room. Little Bob was sleeping calmly in his cradle. Mie and Brady Castleman, petrified in the doorway, were watching the smoke coming up from the cellar. When they heard Owen's footsteps, they turned around.

"Torpey?" Brady asked.

Owen sliced through the air with his open hand and sat in the armchair. He felt drained by all the tension that his nerves had supported over the last few minutes and understood that a battle with the A.O. had nothing in common with a bank hold-up.

"What are we going to do?" Mie asked.

The big man jumped up, suddenly realizing that it was not over. Madame Atomos had just lost a round, but she was no doubt preparing to win the next. Beffort had told him that the sinister Japanese woman acted fast, so they had to act faster and change the siege war into a moving war. In the garage the Cadillac engine should still be warm.

"We're getting out of here," Owen said.

"Where?"

"The base in St. Louis seems the best place to me. Brady, you pack the bags. Mrs. Beffort, I'm going to help you take the cradle." Brady was already gone, so he could order in a gruff voice, "Don't forget the kid's teddy bear."

On her television screen, Madame Atomos had just witnessed the demise of her last hope. She did not understand what had happened, but she was sure that not a single servant had survived the catastrophe. The blank screen confirmed it.

For the first time since she attacked the United States, Madame Atomos was receiving no information from the outside. All the members of the Organization were on board the City, which was on the brink of death, and from now on she could not count on the resources on board because they were extremely short, ridiculously limited compared to the fantastic power that she had at hand just four months before.

When it was 1,000 feet under the water, the City was certainly invulnerable, but how long could it stay there? Soon it would have to surface to renew the air, open the dome, let out the ventilation tubes... The operation would last only a few minutes, but if Beffort launched the bombers, those minutes might sound the death knell for the Atomos Organization!

Madame Atomos left her post and went into the control room where a dozen screens displayed what was going on in the City. Everyone everywhere was feverishly busy trying to put the huge ship back in order. The means were not lacking, but the urgency of the moment quashed everything. Nevertheless, the repair teams had just managed to seal the main water line. Several pumps were pushing water back out and in a few hours it would be possible to start the repair of the flight computers and flying saucers.

Madame Atomos sat in the room from which she had given her orders of attack against the USA. She looked long and hard at the hive of activity in each of the dozen areas of the City and little by little she began to regain hope. Even reduced, her power was still considerable. If Beffort did not unleash an offensive before nightfall, the repair teams would have valuable time and might fix the indispensable flight computers that automatically guided the saucers, which, when in the air, could fend off the B-52s from any attempted attack. With their lightning speed the saucers could strike at 500 yards with their disintegrator guns and be out of range a second later. Then they would suddenly show up over the Wilmington airport and destroy the super-bombers on the ground...

Madame Atomos dreamed for a minute and came back to reality reluctantly. Beffort would not give her the luxury of repairing the City. He knew her too well for that. To think that he would wait for the next day was the height of fantasy. When she surfaced next time, a deluge of bombs would strike the City and send it to the bottom of the sea without any resistance. Therefore, she could not go back to the surface!

Too many lungs that were useless at the moment were pumping the oxygen in the ship. To save the latter, her logic told her to keep the vital workers and sacrifice the others.

Madame Atomos left the control room, went to the Great Brain and changed the program. By punching in a half-dozen cards, she had just condemned to death more than a thousand of her servants.

It was 4:30 p.m. The Cobra was returning again from filling up and was flying over point zero. On the

Wilmington airfield, a group of B-52s and six fighter squadrons were on alert. The offense was unusually long and wearing down the nerves of everyone who knew that this final attack could free the world of the Atomos threat.

The Americans had been informed by the television, radio and newspapers, so that many of them were following the developments of the Cobra on their little screens. Once again Madame Atomos had paralyzed the United States, mobilized the US Navy and Air Force, captured the attention of millions of listeners and spectators and brought the best journalists and commentators of the country to the east coast. And all this while remaining invisible!

Two years earlier the same thing had happened around Dallas, Texas. At that time the Pooley was gobbling up the countryside, the trees and the inhabitants[10], but they were not taking Madame Atomos seriously yet. The spectators licked their ice cream cones while waiting for the spectacular event and talked calmly among themselves. On the whole they were pretty relaxed.

Today it was different. A terrible anxiety loomed over the United States. People talked in a whisper so as not to show their fear to their children; they chain-smoked; they forgot appointments and other suddenly unimportant little cares; and they did not ask each other what they were going to do tomorrow. Depending on what would happen over the coming hours, there might not be a tomorrow...

The result of all this was that the speakers, journalists and editorialists of the main outlets of information

---

[10] See *Madame Atomos Sows Terror* in *The Terror of Madame Atomos*.

went way too far. To give the people a thrill, they went beyond the truth, claiming that Madame Atomos felt trapped and was going to react with unheard-of violence. They were exaggerating, at times, but strangely enough everyone knew that nothing was too crazy when it came to the sinister Japanese woman. With her the unbelievable became real, fiction stayed in the wings and imagination remained idle. Her reputation was well established. They knew she was invincible and nobody truly believed that Smith Beffort had her at his mercy.

In the Cobra the G-man himself was starting to doubt. According to his calculations, the City should have already resurfaced two or three hours ago. But nothing was happening. The sea looked normal, the sky was blue and the temperature mild.

Beffort had to force himself to believe that the City was still off the coast of Wilmington. The pilot, however, did not bother. It was a sure fire bet for him that Madame Atomos had managed to escape.

"Well, Smith?" J.E.E. was impatient, asking for news every five minutes. Beffort clicked the microphone nervously and said coldly, "Nothing."

"The buoy?"

Beffort leaned out and saw the buoy and its big balloon bobbing on the waves. He owed this idea to Lucky Simms who had fished a number of times in the Canadian great lakes. They did not use radar there to detect schools of fish. A fishing fleet of small boats stayed close to shore while the scout went out on the hunt. When he hooked a nice one, he tied a nylon string around its tail and let it go. The other end of the string was tied to a red balloon that always let them know the position of the guide-fish. Since the latter automatically rejoined its fellows, the fleet only had to fish around the red balloon.

Of course, Beffort improved on the system. The Navy had supplied the material and built it: a raft weighed down by a very powerful magnetic keel, which was attached to almost two and a half miles of cable tied to a weather balloon with luminous paint. A motor on the raft was guided by remote control from the Cobra. When the City appeared, they just had to drive the raft against it and the magnetic keel would stick to the metal hull. At the same time the raft would be cast adrift by an electrical charge, completely detached from the keel, cable and balloon. If the City escaped the bombers assault, if it dove before the attack, it would not be lost in the waters. The balloon would follow it everywhere it went, revealing its position night and day.

Beffort looked away from the buoy and finally answered J.E.E.'s question, "We've tried it out and it works great, like a child's toy. For our part, we're ready to go. We're just waiting for the City."

"Can it logically stay underwater for such a long time?"

"Proof," Beffort grumbled.

"Answer me, Smith," J.E.E. insisted. "Just a minute ago you agreed with Dr. Soblen and me when we said that the City couldn't hold out for more than two or three hours, considering the number of inhabitants. Knowing that it can't make its own oxygen, that it hasn't resurfaced, that it isn't getting any fresh air on the bottom of the sea, can't we reasonably assume that it's gone for good?"

Beffort snickered, "That would take care of everything for you, wouldn't it?"

"The journalists on the street are waiting," J.E.E. apologized.

"Let then charter a boat and come to see for themselves!"

"The admiralty is blocking the ports and it's been declared a zone of operations. You're the only one who can see what's going on. Make a statement, Smith!"

"Go to hell! It's not a football game!"

"The country has the right to know," a voice that Beffort recognized cut in. "You can't leave it ignorant of its future. A grave danger is weighing on it..."

Beffort saw an object coming to the surface, then another. He turned down the volume and said to the pilot, "Something at five o'clock."

The pilot leaned out and blinked. Now twenty objects were scattered over the sea. Beffort dropped the microphone and grabbed his binoculars. What he saw froze him.

"What is that?" the pilot asked.

"Corpses," Beffort groaned.

The pilot brought down the helicopter, brushed over the waves and came to a halt over the macabre scene. The bodies, all dressed in the black A.O. uniform, were bobbing up by the dozens, dancing on the waves like corks.

"Unbelievable!"

Beffort quickly counted the corpses. In a very short while they numbered over a hundred. And the dead were still ascending from the depths.

"Smith," J.E.E. yelled, "answer, answer!"

With a mechanical movement, Beffort turned up the volume, grabbed the mic and stated icily, "You want news, this one's for the journalists: the sea is covered in corpses."

"Excuse me?"

"You heard me. The sea is covered in corpses. They're members of the Atomos Organization. Right now I see around a hundred bodies, but they're still coming up."

"So the City is sunk!" J.E.E. shouted.

"No," Beffort said sharply.

"How's that? Are you off your rocker, Smith?"

"They're floating very nicely, which proves that their lungs are full of air, not water. In my opinion, Madame Atomos is getting rid of the extras, killing whoever isn't necessary for the moment. She must have murdered them a few hours ago, which explains why she's still keeping the City underwater."

"That's atrocious!"

"But very helpful for us," Beffort replied. "The more Madame Atomos kills, the fewer enemies we'll have. Now, look, there must be 200…"

J.E.E. was speechless.

"The sharks are coming," the pilot said.

Beffort nodded and repeated the news to J.E.E, hearing him announce it to other people who were obviously next to him. A loud racket instantly shook the speaker and literally drown out J.E.E.'s voice.

Beffort had a bitter smile on his face. There's nothing like the dead to captivate the living.

Chapter XII

While Madame Atomos was unloading the City of its dead and Mie Azusa-Beffort, her son and their two bodyguards were heading for the base in St. Louis, six men, whom everyone had forgotten, regained consciousness inside the police car.

With their uniforms they could fool anyone, but they belonged body and soul to the Atomos Organization. They were still alive because Owen and Brady were satisfied just paralyzing them before leaving the cottage. Time was too pressing for the two men of the Green Dragon Force to waste precious minutes on destroying their adversaries for good. It was a terrible mistake, but at the moment nobody could have guessed it.

So, the six fake policemen woke up and shuddered, but did not leave the car. Conditioned to passively obey orders from the Great Brain, they could make no decision without being remote-controlled. They stayed in their seats and their eyes stared blankly at the landscape they had seen when Owen's rifle stopped them on the edge of the bad road.

The images were sent back through their motor-brains to the Great Brain. On the control screen, Madame Atomos suddenly saw the cabin and the hill with trees on top of it. At the same time, the identification board started blinking, giving the numbers of the six men. Madame Atomos jumped up and fed the Great Brain with the cards corresponding to the numbers. Immediately the Great Brain launched a series of orders, the ones that Madame Atomos had programmed before noon.

The police car started up and drove to the cabin. The fake policemen climbed out of the car and entered the deserted cabin. They were armed with disintegrator rifles, but they acted just like robots, without fear or any kind of emotion.

Madame Atomos saw that Mie and her son had escaped, but she realized that she could take full advantage of her servants. She changed their orders. The police car drove off from the cabin and got on the road to Columbia. With the siren blaring it got to the city in 15 minutes, continuing on its way until it arrived at the airfield. Once there, nobody tried to stop it. They were wearing official uniforms, sitting in a regulation vehicle and acting with urgency, which implied a special mission. They represented the Law in action... People cleared the way for them to speed onto runway 3 where an airliner was getting ready to take off.

Siren wailing, lights flashing, the car caught up to the airplane and one of the policemen waved the pilot to stop. The latter swore, but instantly slowed down the engines, put on the brakes and stopped the plane on the runway.

"What do they want?" the copilot complained.

"Probably a passenger identification check."

"Regular cops?"

The pilot shrugged his shoulders in boredom as he watched the six policemen head for the steps that the crew had just let down from the belly of the plane. Three minutes later the passengers, huddled together on the runway, watched in amazement as the airplane took off, carrying away their baggage. A little later they learned that the pilot was not responding to radio calls and the plane was flying toward an unknown destination.

1,000 corpses were now food for the sharks.

The sea frothed under the lashing tails, was tainted with blood, rags and human flesh. The sharks gathered by the hundreds, literally swarming over point zero, sometimes fighting each other for a share of the feast.

The Cobra pilot had tried to disperse them with machine gun fire, but the sharks who were shot were immediately devoured by the others and the extra blood only attracted bigger and meaner sharks to the place.

"Disgusting," the pilot winced.

Smith Beffort nodded unconsciously as he examined the sea through his binoculars. He thought that Madame Atomos was going to take advantage of the situation to come to the surface, so he forced back the nausea that he felt at the sight.

"A sorry end," the pilot mumbled.

"If it's any comfort," Beffort said, "remember that most of the servants of the Atomos Organization have been dead for a long time. At the beginning, Madame Atomos recruited her troops from the cemeteries. Later she operated on the living, giving them a motor-brain that guaranteed their mechanical immortality. When one of them was mortally wounded by a bullet, he or she died biologically, but woke up to lead an artificial life under the impulses of the domesticated atoms... Madame Atomos is the general of an army of the dead!"

In saying this, he thought of his friend Sam Forbes, of Maggy Fairbanks, of May and George Maxwell, all dead for months, and he wondered if they were among the corpses that the sharks were fighting over.

Just then the radio crackled and J.E.E. asked, "Still nothing, Smith?" He had already forgotten all the corpses floating in the water. He was demanding more news, even more sensational.

"Nothing," Beffort said, "but if you want my opinion, it won't be long... unless Madame Atomos decides to do some more extermination."

She was not dreaming of it. On her screens she was watching the quick progress of the airplane that was approaching the Wilmington airfield. Things were suddenly turning in her favor, thanks to the six survivors of the cabin combat in Columbia.

In the city the air was thinning, but the work went on at breakneck speed. Two out of eight computers had been fixed. Four flying saucers would be ready to take flight in 12 hours and they could insure the complete protection of the City for months. Nevertheless, a total victory depended on the immediate success of the six false policemen. They were about to attack the B-52s and the fighter jets stationed on the runways in Wilmington.

During the course of this surprise attack, the City would resurface to refresh its air in total security for the second time in the day. Two other ascents would take place later in the night. The surfacing would be without any risk under the cover of the night and would allow the teams to finish the current repairs the next morning.

Madame Atomos was feeling better as the hours passed. She was already thinking of the formidable offensive that she would unleash against the United States. This time she would show no mercy; she would destroy the most powerful armament in the world, cut off its lines of communication, drive it into famine and plunge it into despair...

The sinister woman shook with wild laughter. Then she got a grip on herself, brought her attention back to the screen showing images from the outside. Through the eyes of her servants, she could see the first pass of the airplane over the Wilmington airfield. The plane returned to fly over the hangars: it swung wide of the control tower and banked back to get on the axis of the main runway.

On the ground they tried to get in radio contact with the pilot of this mysterious plane. The airport was off-limits since it had been a zone of operations for the last 24 hours. Only military planes could use it and the civil aviation authorities had been duly notified so that no one should be unaware of the prohibition. Except in cases of emergency, the airplanes were supposed to land in Jacksonville. Now, the plane that was getting ready to land looked in perfect shape. However, it was not responding to the radio calls and this might mean that something was wrong on board. That was one of the reasons that kept General Salem from sending his fighter jets to force it to turn around. And the super-bombers lined up on the runways did not have much to fear since they could defend themselves against any attack.

So, they let the airliner touch down on runway 1. But just in case, they sent out an ambulance and fire truck. The landing was routine and the plane slowly rolled to the central hangar while the ambulance, fire truck and two MP Jeeps converged on it. Then, when everything seemed to be proceeding without a hitch, tragedy suddenly exploded on the Wilmington airfield.

Six men dressed in Missouri police uniforms jumped to the ground and aimed strange weapons at the fast approaching vehicles. Six bright flashes and the cars disappeared in a split second. Nobody had fully understood the astounding sight when the disintegrator rifles opened fire again. Before the stunned eyes of General Salem, 12 bombers and their crews were wiped off the face of the earth, simply, noiselessly, as if it were the easiest thing in the world. Then the six fake policemen turned around and disintegrated a squad of fighter jets and the two hangars behind them, which was holding three airliners.

At this moment, the men who were witnessing the massive carnage finally reacted. A heavy machine gun started firing from a newly built watchtower in the south, covering the area where the fake policemen were attacking. The bullets hit their targets over and over and they could even see the men staggering under the impact, but it was not enough to bring them down. The metal was hitting corpses, hacking dead flesh that the motor-brains and the domesticated atoms kept in working order under any condition.

A 40mm quick-fire gun entered into action. It fired at practically point-blank range (100 yards) from the north angle of the opening formed by the service buildings and workshops. Its angle of fire was almost horizontal, frightfully lethal. One of its first shells decapitated one of the A.O. men. The next round tore off the leg of another and blew out the chest of a third. The survivors flattened themselves to the ground and disintegrated the guns. During the lull that followed, they destroyed another line of bombers.

A second later and all the arms in the camp opened fire. The last three servants of Madame Atomos were quickly surrounded by a living hell, tossed into the air by the explosions and blown apart before they hit the ground.

When they were no longer moving, the weapons stopped firing and a heavy silence fell over the airport. General Salem, still dazed, contemplated the airfield, which was empty of planes around the corpses of the

A.O. men, and the devastated runways, which was now useless. The calls from the radio came to him like in a dream. He stumbled over and clearly heard the statement that J.E.E. had been repeating for five minutes: "The City has just surfaced! Smith Beffort wants an immediate attack by the air force! General Salem, respond!"

Salem pushed the operator out of the way and grabbed the microphone. "Salem here," his voice was almost unrecognizable, "we've been attacked by the Atomos Organization. Out of my squad and my group I only have four B-52s and six fighters left. Plus, the airfield is out of commission..."

Over point zero the Cobra was watching the City, dome and ventilators open up, peacefully getting its fresh air. It had been there for five minutes. From the first second, Beffort had asked J.E.E. to send out the air force, but no plane could be seen in the clear blue sky. The G-man played nervously with the radio controls, finally switching it to broadcast. "Goddamn," he swore furiously, "what's the air force up to?"

J.E.E.'s gloomy voice came back, "Madame Atomos has played us, Smith. While we were waiting for her to show herself, her commando team attacked the base in Wilmington. The bombers and fighters have been destroyed and the runways are all churned up. We can't attack for the moment. It's a disaster!"

"And the A.O. commando team?"

"Crushed under a flood of steel, but it's cold comfort. Some other planes are going to take off from Fort Bragg."

"When will they be here?"

"Not for at least 20 minutes, given the fact that they weren't on a state of alert. It's a real feat, but I'm afraid they'll get there too late."

"They'll be too late," Beffort agreed. "Tell them not to take off."

"But…"

"Don't argue! No one's going to stop the City from diving back down. Considering where we're at, it'd be better to wait for the next time it comes up. Keep the bombers in Fort Bragg on alert, give them more fire-power and make sure they can get here in three minutes after I call. I'm going to stick the balloon on the City. Stay tuned."

"Okay, Smith."

Beffort made a sign to bring the Cobra down. The pilot did what he was asked and hovered at 1,800 feet. Because of the disintegrator rifles, it was the closest he could get.

Beffort took his binoculars and looked for the raft that was keeping the magnetic keel afloat with its two and a half miles of cable and the big weather balloon. He found it 300 yards from the City and estimated that it was far enough that Madame Atomos could not spot it. The balloon could be seen from a distance if you were over the water, but should have remained unseen by the City. The sea was rough, waves reaching up to 20 feet, edged with froth that the wind dispersed on high. At sea level the spray and mist probably limited visibility.

Counting on this, Beffort eased the remote control into action. The raft started moving immediately, head-ing straight for the City. Beffort stopped it, figuring that it should advance right after the dome and ventilators closed. In a few seconds the magnetic keel would find no surface to latch onto.

"It's closing," the pilot warned.

Beffort leaned over and saw that the City was, in fact, preparing to dive. He worked the control feverishly, giving it maximum power. Down below the raft jumped over the waves, dragging along the weather balloon, which sparkled in the sun. At that speed, Beffort could see that he had no reason to worry. The navy seemed to have calculated better than the air force.

The City still had not dove more than an inch when the raft was on it. At the same time, the magnetic keel bonded to the hull of the ship, the raft opened up and the balloon rose into the sky as the cable slowly unwound.

In the second phase of the operation, the raft was cast far away by its remote controlled engine and the cable unwound faster and faster. When the City was below the water, the balloon was still hanging on. The cable was stretched out, changing color every 30 feet, whereby they could estimate how deep the City went to within around 15 feet.

Chapter XIII

When night fell, all the observers knew that the City was moving slowly at 6,500 feet below sea level, but nobody was sure of its real position. In fact, the weather balloon at the end of the two and a half mile cable was not staying steady, that is completely vertical out of the water. The winds were blowing it around in different directions, so that it was sometimes carried toward the coast and sometimes out to sea.

In the thick of the night, the observers knew that, contrary to what they had been told, spotting the City was no easy task. Certainly, the luminous balloon was there, but nobody could determine the precise angle of the cable connecting it to the underwater ship.

"It doesn't matter," Soblen said calmly. "At dawn the bombers and the navy will be ready to attack."

Beffort turned around. "You forget that Madame Atomos is working hard this whole time, doc! The last time she showed up, I could see that the main waterline had been sealed. By tomorrow morning, who knows, maybe she'll have her magnetic shield up and running? Even now you can see she's moving. Slowly, perhaps, but it's a clear improvement over the forced immobility she suffered before. And I'm worried that she'll detect the magnetic keel stuck to her side."

Akamatsu jumped in, "That's very possible, Smith. If all the machines on the City were working, this operation would fail. But in case you decide to go on the offensive, don't forget that I'm your man."

"Easy to say," J.E.E. grumbled.

Beffort shrugged. "There is, at least, one possibility of attack and I'm surprised that nobody's thought of it."

"Yourself?" J.E.E. scoffed.

"Exactly," Beffort agreed sportingly. "I was also obsessed by Lucky's idea, wanting to put it to use at all costs without thinking about changing it. In short, what's good for the Canadian fish is good for Madame Atomos."

"Well said! So?"

"So, we've tried to fight against Madame Atomos with new weapons because she was using them, too. It was a failure, wasn't it?"

"Seems so," J.E.E. admitted reluctantly. "But you're not going to start pelting her with stones because of it..." The business in the Wilmington airport had come down on his head and it was a bitter pill for him to swallow. It made him angry, sarcastic and extremely unpleasant.

Beffort ignored his bad mood and continued, "The magnetic keel stuck to the City without a problem, right?"

"We all saw it... where are you going with this, Smith?"

Beffort raised a finger and asked, "What would happen if that keel were replaced by one or more magnetic mines?"

It was so simple, the results so obvious, that no one could think of anything to say.

Beffort went on, "During the last war, the armor was blown up by such mines. Do you think that the City's plating would fare any better?"

Soblen furrowed his brow and said, "Right, but you're talking about the past, Smith. Right now the City is under water and nothing like that can be repeated."

"I said that there was at least one way of attacking, doc, now I see two! The first, which is far from easy, would be to wait for the City to resurface. We'll know this by watching the balloon, which will rise with it and when it's up at 6,500 feet, a cargo plane could drop enough mines to sink Madame Atomos and her infernal ship. Except..."

"Of course," J.E.E. said, "it's too simple!"

"Except," Beffort continued, "we know that the balloon will not necessarily show the exact position of the City. Therefore, the mines might fall off target and be lost before doing any good..."

"Forget it," Akamatsu intervened. "The other solution?" ¶"Follow the lead..."

"Excuse me?"

"Drop the mines down the cable," Beffort explained. "Like that they'll automatically reach their target!"

A silence followed his statement, which was strange, to say the least. Finally Soblen mumbled, "It's pretty crazy, but not unfeasible."

J.E.E. leapt up and roared, "Impossible! Let's stick to standard procedure! At dawn the bombers will drop their bombs and it'll all be over!"

"At dawn," Beffort repeated, "Madame Atomos will surely have enough means at her disposal to keep the planes from getting close. We have to act tonight, as soon as possible, and even if we fail, at least we can say we tried." He turned his back to J.E.E. and addressed Soblen, "Do you see how we can put my idea into practice, doc?"

Soblen puffed up his cheeks, looked thoughtful and then declared, "It's not too complicated. We only have to attach something to guide the mines down the cable. The hardest thing will certainly be to find the mines, fit them with the attachment, load them onto a suitable ship and carry them out there all before dawn. Moreover, if the ship is on point zero when Madame Atomos decides to come up for air, what will happen?"

Beffort smiled. "The ship, the mines and the crew will be disintegrated, doc. Personally, I think it's worth a shot."

"Me, too," Akamatsu said.

Soblen stood up, wiped his glasses and decided, "In that case, I'm with you."

The ship was the same class as the *Eagle*. It carried 20 mines fitted with insulated straps, a crew of 10 men, Beffort, Soblen, Akamatsu and J.E.E., who did not want to be accused of half-heartedness. "This is what's called putting all your eggs in the same basket," he grumbled. "If we're disintegrated, Madame Atomos can break out the champagne! When Washington learns about this…"

Soblen scowled, "If you hear them talking about it, it will mean that you're still alive, Mr. Evans. If you're still alive, it will be because we succeeded. Therefore, Washington will do nothing but congratulate your heroic conduct."

J.E.E. grimaced and put his cigar back in his pocket, remembering just in time that it was forbidden to smoke. He glanced toward the bow. The *Raleigh* was making good progress in spite of the waves, heading for the luminous point that was drawn out of the darkness by the weather balloon. At two and a half miles away, it was only as big as a pea, so they had to know its approximate location to tell it apart from the stars that studded the sky.

With his binoculars Akamatsu had kept constant watch since the *Raleigh* left the dock. If the balloon started rising, it would mean that the City was resurfacing and the *Raleigh* would stop its engines and inform Fort Bragg where a new group of B-52s was on alert. The rest of the mission would then fall on the pilots of the super-bombers, but Beffort doubted their effectiveness. To detect the City in the middle of the night would take a downright miracle.

At 1 a.m. the *Raleigh* was exactly underneath the weather balloon. The men were petrified. The ship was in the danger zone and would have a lot of trouble getting away if the City suddenly rose up from the bottom of the sea where it was hiding. Everyone stared nervously at the balloon. With the gusts of wind it started blowing due south, suddenly flew north and then the weight of the cable, stretched to the breaking point, swung backward. The shifting positions made it look like it was always moving away so that it would be hard to tell it was actually rising up.

"This is not good," Soblen groaned. "We can sail around in circles for hours before finding where the cable is coming out of the water."

Beffort made a sign of helplessness and shouted over the sound of the waves, "We have no choice, doc. We have to find that damn cable or give up!"

"And if the City suddenly shows up in front of us?"

Beffort tapped the paralyzing rifle that the doctor was carrying. "This is our only chance. Right now I think that Madame Atomos isn't able to defend herself from the combat stations set up on the City. Her men even had to come outside of the shell to unhook the ventilation tubes. They'll have to be eliminated first because they'll be armed with disintegrator rifles. In sum, whoever has the element of surprise will win the round."

Soblen blinked and said, "It's a game with many rounds, Smith. I've lost count of them, but I know that this has to end once and for all. Tonight it looks like Madame Atomos is winning. On the whole, out situation is exactly the same as the *Eagle!*"

Beffort did not answer. Soblen was not a pessimist. He was looking at the situation objectively and concluded rightly that Madame Atomos had the advantage. She could appear at any location around the *Raleigh* and if she were within 500 yards, a single disintegrator rifle in the hands of one of her A.O. servants could wipe out the ship and crew with a single shot. On the other hand, admitting that Beffort and his friends opened fire, the City would lose only a few men before diving again. It was really disproportionate.

All of a sudden the wind shifted and a commotion broke out in the back of the *Raleigh*. Beffort and Soblen turned around and saw a sailor sprinting up to the bridge. Three seconds later the captain left his post and headed for Beffort, screaming the whole way, "The balloon is rising!"

At the same time, Akamatsu came out from behind the baffles and confirmed the bad news. Beffort lifted his binoculars to watch the balloon. It was, in fact, gaining altitude and its ascension was fast, dangerously fast because it obviously meant that Atomos City was rising.

"Stop the engines," Beffort ordered, "and tell your boys to keep their eyes on the sea."

The captain went back to the bridge and gave the orders. The diesel engines went immediately silent and an eerie silence fell over the *Raleigh*. Beffort glanced around. He could see the sailors carefully examining the night. They were searching, above all, for the cable that tied the City to the balloon, but it was hard going. Although relatively clear for sailing, the night was heavy when it came to spotting a steel cable that was only half an inch thick.

Beffort himself did not see what was happening beyond the bridge. Along with its engines, the *Raleigh* had cut its lights, drifting slowly in the darkness. The waves hit the ship sideways, breaking against the hull furiously and then crumbling before being scattered by the wind, which blew the rain onto the already soaked bridge. Thus, the swell increased the pitching and the mines that had been loaded on the beach began to roll around dangerously between the support frameworks. Still, the weather could have been worse. Only the dramatic situation gave an impression of impending doom, making the men even more nervous to the point of turning the tiniest incident into disaster.

A winding tackle broke loose and flapped against a yard. Beffort jumped and gritted his teeth. In the tense atmosphere, the snapping sounded like an explosion.

Soblen took off his glasses by habit to dry them. He sighed, "This is taking too long, Smith. The men are losing their nerve. They might panic when the time comes for them to act."

Beffort nodded, but did not comment. The cards were dealt and nobody could start the game over. He took a moment of silence, then said, "If I'm right, doc, we're going to have to try our luck with the air force."

Suddenly pale, Soblen stared at him. "You say that so calmly."

"It does no good to get wound up, does it? J.E.E. is all for the B-52s. He wants to give them a chance to get revenge for their comrades in Wilmington and he sincerely thinks that they can hit the City. Nevertheless, and perhaps unconsciously, he's also hoping to clear himself with the bigwigs in Washington. I wonder what he'll think when the *Raleigh* is surrounded by the bombs?"

He looked up at the bridge and saw the men getting excited. Leaving Soblen behind, he dashed up to the command post. At the head of the stairs he understood that things had deteriorated between J.E.E. and the captain of the ship. He went closer and listened.

"I'm ordering you to let me use your radio," J.E.E. was saying firmly. "The City can surge up at any minute and we have to warn the air force!"

"It's too risky," the officer replied. "I'll let you alert Fort Bragg if you authorize me to head back to the coast or any other destination that takes my ship out of the firing range."

"That's insubordination if I've ever seen it!" J.E.E. exploded.

"I'll take full responsibility," the officer said calmly. "No one can force me to deliberately expose my ship and my crew to a bombardment."

"You volunteered!"

"For a battle, not for suicide."

Beffort snuck away. He knew that the captain would not give in and agreed with him one hundred percent. Madame Atomos was enough by herself to create the danger of death that everyone was waiting for and afraid of. And there was the tragic accident of the *Eagle*.

"What's happening?" Soblen asked when he saw Beffort return.

"J.E.E. has hit a snag. The captain of the *Raleigh* is refusing to let the air force intervene. I must admit that this takes a big load off my mind."

Soblen agreed and once again aimed his binoculars at the sky.

Beffort asked, "How high is the balloon?"

"Hard to say exactly, but I'd estimate that it must be over two miles."

"More than half a mile in ten minutes," Beffort translated, "which means that in ten more minutes the City will emerge. Damn! If only we'd found the cable."

As if in answer to his wish a long scraping sound ran through the *Raleigh*. It stopped when the ship dropped to the bottom of a swell, but it started up again even louder when the ship rose. Soblen and Beffort turned around and saw that a hoist was sagging strangely under an invisible weight.

They sprinted off, but arrived later than a third class petty officer who screamed out with relief, "The cable! Captain, it's the cable!"

Chapter XIV

The cable was, indeed, coming out of waves a few arm lengths away from the *Raleigh*, stretched at a 20-degree angle and scraping against the ship's forecastle. At the very moment when the petty officer saw it, the cable had just hooked onto a hoist that was acting as a kind of runner for it.

It was stroke of luck. The ship had been drifting for a while and had run into the cable all by itself while the men were scrutinizing the night for nothing.

The captain, Beffort and his friends huddled together at once, fully conscious that every second was vital.

"We have to make a decision right now," Beffort said. "The situation looks better, but we only have nine minutes to hook the mines onto the cable. Is that possible, captain?"

The answer rang out spontaneously, "No!"

Beffort did not blink, but J.E.E. jumped and shouted, "You're really no help at all, captain! You say no to everything. First to contact the air force and now you don't want to try our chances! Why?"

The officer turned to him. The tension showed in his face. "The distance of the balloon proves that the City is surfacing at record speed, Mr. Evans. Right now it's at over half a mile and rising at 300 feet per minute. To get the electric crane up and running on the prow will take four minutes. The same to back up the ship and draw it level with the cable. When these two operations are done, eight minutes will have gone by. The City will only be a few hundred feet from the surface. When the first mine goes down, with the slow speed we calculated, the City will be 100 feet away. I'm saying all this to make you understand that when the mine explodes, the City will only be 50 feet underwater and the *Raleigh* will blow up along with it."

J.E.E. was speechless, but Beffort said, "Your logic is flawless, captain. Any ideas?"

Akamatsu stepped forward. "Let's let Madame Atomos come to the surface and we'll get out of here."

"And the cable?" Soblen asked.

Akamatsu kicked a coil of rope. "Do you have many others like this, captain?"

"Yes," the captain answered in surprise. "The *Raleigh* is a cargo ship. It has a lot of cordage, cables, ropes…"

"Placed end to end how long would the reach?"

"I don't really know… maybe 300 or 400 yards?"

Beffort looked at his watch and intervened, "Less than seven minutes, Yosho. If you have a plan, let's have it!"

Akamatsu snapped up the end of the rope. "We attach this end to the cable. The *Raleigh* sails away from the hot spot. Little by little as we get farther away, the crew can tie together all the ropes on board. In the end we'll be hooked to the cable by our own rope and we can easily find it again when the City dives back down."

The captain, Soblen and J.E.E. agreed unanimously.

"Okay," Beffort accepted, "it sounds like it'll work. It's your call, captain."

The officer walked over to work the Engine Order Telegraph and came back barking orders while the diesels groaned back on. The crew, sensing the danger, ran to the ropes, cords and cables. In no time at all they freed the hoist and fastened a rope to the cable linking the City to the weather balloon.

The *Raleigh* was already heading out to sea, dropping little colored buoys on the way, which would keep the long makeshift rope afloat.

At 350 yards from point zero, the last rope was stretched out. The captain stopped the engines and ordered a buoy to be dropped, which would keep the ship in place as much as possible. And the wait began.

"Under 30 seconds," Soblen whispered. He and Beffort were on the bridge. The G-man was keeping watch with night vision binoculars. Below, at the pump, Akamatsu and six crew members were pointing their paralyzing rifles at point zero, even though they could not see it. At Beffort's call, they would open fire in the hope of neutralizing the A.O. servants if the *Raleigh* were spotted. But Beffort was hoping that this would not be necessary.

The *Raleigh* was low enough in the water to melt into the darkness. Beffort was thinking that Madame Atomos had too many worries on her mind to waste time on the surface. Still, the A.O. men might see the magnetic keel by chance while they were opening and closing the ventilation ducts. That was the chief danger.

The magnetic keel was stuck to the hull of the City haphazardly. No one knew, even roughly, where it was. If it happened to be on the dome or on a ventilation tube, Madame Atomos would know instantly that she had been monitored all night long. If that happened, the terrible woman's reaction would be immediate, violent and deadly. Being 350 yards away, the *Raleigh* was in range of the disintegrating rifles…

"Less than five seconds," Soblen indicated with composure, just like a stopwatch.

On Beffort's mark, the third class petty officer brought the whistle to his lips and blew shrilly, gloomily. From this second on nothing was supposed to move on the ship.

All of a sudden, Beffort saw the sea open up, crash and foam, then the well known form of Atomos City took shape in the double prism of his binoculars. Because of the distance and the night Beffort could not make out the keel. He knew that it would remain a question mark until the end. Only his quick reflexes could save the *Raleigh*. If an A.O. man discovered the secret...

Again Beffort had to guess at the reaction of the man who might find the keel. A totally wild guess. An order given without reason and Madame Atomos would reply instantly to the paralyzing rifles.

"Do you see anything, Smith?"

"The City has just surfaced, doc. The dome is opening... A group of servants is scattering over the ship, opening the ventilation ducts..." He stopped suddenly and held his breath. A shadowy figure was leaning over near the dome and looking at something that Beffort could not see. The figure stayed in the same place for a minute. Beffort imagined his eyes sending one single image back to the Great Brain—of the magnetic keel, for example—and Madame Atomos was going to make the only decision she could.

The G-man dropped the binoculars from his right hand and was about to give the order to fire. But the figure was still not moving. Moreover, around the ventilation ducts, other men were standing frozen. The City was filling up with fresh air, getting rid of the bad, breathing like a human being who had gone without oxygen for a long time, just as regularly and with relief. It was like a huge beast with Madame Atomos as its heart and thousands of arms in the form of its servants. For now it was motionless because wounded. It would very soon become extremely violent if given the chance to lick its wounds. In a way, the *Raleigh* and the men on board represented the last chance for the United States.

Smith Beffort, Soblen and the others were aware how important their behavior would be over the next hour. Never had Madame Atomos been so near her end. But in spite of this, it would take next to nothing to turn her defeat into a dazzling victory. Indeed, everything was riding on this moment.

Soblen, even though he was burning with impatience, dared not open his mouth and the crew members were stiff as boards, eyes wide open onto the thick night where death was waiting to jump out at them.

Kept facing the waves by the floating buoy, the *Raleigh* barely rolled. Sometimes a muffled creaking arose out of its infrastructure when the swell got bigger or the mines scraped against the support framework. There were a bunch of usually unheard sounds, which took on immense importance in the silence. J.E.E. was sure that the noises carried over the sea and the microphones of the City would pick them up. His trembling hands gripped the rifle even harder.

Soblen went up to him and whispered ironically, "You tremble, carcass…[11]"

J.E.E. shrugged. "It's nerves, doctor."

"Would you be afraid of dying?"

"I'm not afraid of dying, but I'm not afraid of living either," J.E.E. shot back aggressively. "Can you say that you're totally relaxed?"

---

[11] You tremble, carcass, but you would tremble even more if you knew where I was taking you." –Turenne, the decorated general, in his old age when he felt danger approach. (Editor's note)

Soblen was honest. "I'm scared to death," he admitted. Then he added a little more casually, "Do you realize that if neither of us makes it, little Bob might not have a godfather?"

His joke calmed James Edward Evans a little. "Speaking of which," he said, "I have the feeling that Smith has already chosen me."

Soblen patted him on the shoulder. "We'll talk about that later, Mr. Evans, we'll talk about it later." And he went away, certain that he had done his good deed for the day, and shuffled silently back to Beffort who was still keeping an eye on the City. "What's happening, Smith?"

"Nothing," Beffort heaved. "It's starting to get annoying. I have the feeling that the City is staying up longer than it used to. How long has it been?"

Soblen looked at his watch. "12 minutes."

Beffort let out his breath. "Another three minutes and it should dive… if everything goes as planned, of course."

He was terribly suspicious. Under other circumstances, he had been able to judge how cunning Madame Atomos was when things were against her and it was probably because of his suspicious attitude, his vigilance at every moment that Beffort was still alive.

The 180 seconds ticked off in slow motion. Finally, Beffort saw the outlines of the A.O. servants moving over the ship. "That's it, doc! Madame Atomos is getting ready to dive!"

"Doggone, things are going our way!"

Through his binoculars Beffort watched all the activity before the dive. The men plugged up the ventilation ducts and went back under the shell, which was slowly closing. Then the City dove and disappeared under the waves.

Immediately Beffort turned his binoculars to the sky. It took a few seconds, but he found the weather balloon. A few more seconds and he verified that it got closer to the sea as the City descended. He looked at Soblen, smiled and said in a vibrant voice, "The cable's still connected to the magnetic keel, doc! This time, I believe we've got Madame Atomos!"

Chapter XV

Soblen grabbed the binoculars that Beffort had just dropped and watched the weather balloon for himself. "You're right," he almost did not believe it. "The balloon is going down... and going down fast!"

Then everyone looked up in the air. The *Raleigh* was still motionless. Before getting the engines running, they had to be certain that the City was really diving. Now, there seemed to be no doubt about it. The balloon was losing altitude very quickly, getting bigger in plain sight.

"Two and a half miles!" Soblen announced. It was only an estimate. The balloon was blowing in the wind, soaring off and then snapping back up straight, but they saw it better and better. "Just over two miles now," Soblen said.

A minute passed, then the little doctor declared it was clear that the City was going no deeper. The balloon stayed the same distance from the sea, stubbornly. They were waiting for more evidence, but Beffort decided that the moment for action had come. The engines of the *Raleigh* propelled the ship toward point zero and the crew pulled in the strangely fashioned rope, hauling on board the colored buoys. Everything went smoothly. Everyone had calmed down, more or less convinced that the sinister woman would not escape her just desserts.

In spite of everything, Beffort and the ship's captain kept watching the sea. They were both afraid of a last minute trick by Madame Atomos. A quick resurfacing or the blinding flash of a disintegrator rifle and the *Raleigh* would join the countless victims of Madame Atomos in the void.

Even with this justified suspicion, the ship arrived at point zero without meeting any obstacles. The point zero, of course, was just symbolic. The City had moved during the night and the three and a half mile trench was now more than ten miles behind them.

At last the makeshift rope met up with the cable and the ship was shut down. After a skillful maneuver, the cable was brushing the bow of the *Raleigh*. They kept it in place using several hooks supported by a capstan and the first mine was pushed toward the rope, lifted by the electric crane and hooked firmly onto the cable.

At this instant, the captain looked at Beffort inquiringly. A little pale now, Beffort nodded. For him, having fought against Madame Atomos for years, this was an historic moment.

In the nervous silence, the mine was brought down to the sea and then the crane dropped it. It sank under the dark waters. Right away, they loaded another mine, which followed the first. And then a third…

"How much time, doc?" Beffort asked.

"20 minutes, Smith."

"That's too long!"

"That's what was anticipated and you agreed."

"I won't be able to wait that long," Beffort grumbled. "The mines have to explode sooner."

Soblen shook his head. "Impossible. The success of the operation relies directly on what time they hit. The mines stay on the cable just like a train on the railroad tracks. Like that, they will definitely reach their target. The first will cut the cable and the others will free fall—if you allow me this expression considering the density of the water—and explode directly on the target."

Beffort knew that Soblen was making sense. He went off to the back of the boat and tried to shake off the anxiety that was crawling inside him. All of a sudden, and for no apparent reason, he was convinced that Madame Atomos could not be destroyed so easily. Indeed, it was more a hunch than an analysis, but Beffort knew that his subconscious rarely betrayed him. Even after the death of Madame Atomos in San Francisco[12], he could not share in the general rejoicing. The course of events largely proved him right.

With his nerves on edge, he came back to the bow and saw that almost all the magnetic mines had been dropped. A quick glance at his watch showed that 15 minutes had gone by. The *Raleigh* was already clearing off, backing away after disengaging the cable—as a precaution, in case a mine stayed hooked to the cable for some unknown reason to explode near the ship.

Soblen, who had become the human stopwatch, announced the time remaining to get away before the first explosion. At two minutes, he counted the seconds. Less than 30 seconds and the *Raleigh* was 200 yards away from where the cable entered the water.

"Five, four, three, two, one, zero," Soblen droned.

Although they were expecting a dull explosion—since the mine would be blowing up at a great depth—or a huge splash of water, nothing happened. Beffort clenched his jaws and shot a questioning look at the captain, who was waiting in the doorway of the sonar room. The officer shook his head, meaning that the machine had not registered anything.

15 more seconds ticked off in silence and then, without a sound, the sea rose up violently above point zero, shooting a long spray of water into the night and raining back down. And then there was the chain reac-

---

[12] See *Madame Atomos Strikes at the Head* in *Miss Atomos*.

tion Soblen had predicted. Other mines hit the target, but for the passengers on the *Raleigh*, there were only sprays of water, a little ridiculous compared to the dreadful upheaval that must have been taking place 6,500 feet below the surface.

However, the sonar recorded the explosions unerringly and no one could doubt the effectiveness of the operation. Soblen touched Beffort's shoulder, pointing to the weather balloon that was climbing fast toward the stars. Down on Atomos City, the cable had snapped in the first explosion and the balloon was dragging it along on its endless journey.

Still petrified, the crew, Beffort and his friends waited a little longer before jumping for joy.

Madame Atomos felt the floor give way under her feet. She fell and rolled into a corner of the room, hearing a loud explosion. At the same time, the television screens went off and the whole City started shaking while the mines tore apart its metallic hull as if it were some flimsy skin.

Madame Atomos knew right away that her marvelous ship was lost. She cried out in rage, crawled to the door of her laboratory in the pitch black and found the command lever for the generator. The lights came back on immediately, but only in the lab, which was henceforth totally separate from the rest of the ship. Armored, waterproof, soundproof—it would be her tomb if the radio-controlled missile refused to take off.

Fighting against the tilted floor, Madame Atomos opened the door of the launch tube, which went through the center of the City and came out a few feet away from the dome. Her heart was beating fast when she turned on the board of the ten control posts. Only four lights flashed on. That would mean that the launch tube was breached and water was already flooding it.

After taking her seat in the missile she closed and locked the latch. She strapped herself in, put on the oxygen mask and adjusted the bottles of oxygen. Now she could not leave the missile whose electromagnetic latch would only open when she reached her secret base in the Pacific.

With a steady hand she initiated the blast off.

A second passed and then a powerful thrust plastered Madame Atomos against her seat. The missile shot off into the tube at a dizzying speed.

The *Raleigh* came back to point zero, chopping through the waves that were lit up by all its spotlights. On the surface, a huge oil spill and all kinds of debris proved that Atomos City had just been sunk. Moreover, the sea was bubbling in several places—the air that the City had stored was now floating to the surface.

"It's over, Smith!" Soblen laughed.

Beffort looked glumly at his watch. "It's only been two minutes, doc. When it comes to Madame Atomos, that's not enough. Her death throes are not over... if they've even begun."

Soblen and J.E.E. challenged him, but Akamatsu solemnly agreed. Like Beffort, he knew the Japanese woman too well to believe wholeheartedly in her death.

"She's not immortal," J.E.E. offered. "You finally have to admit it! Sorry, but I'm sending a cable to Washington! The entire United States should hear the good news..."

Not far from the *Raleigh*, something shot out of the water, hurtling into the sky and leaving a long trail of fire in its wake.

"What was that?" J.E.E. stammered.

Beffort did not respond. He watched the rocket disappear into the west. He was not surprised or disappointed. For a long time he had known that Madame Atomos would find a way to escape simply because she anticipated everything.

"It doesn't," Soblen commented, "take away the fact that Atomos City is lying on the bottom of the ocean. Even if she's alive, it'll be months, maybe years, before she can attack our country again. I think that this is a great victory!"

He was right and he had the final word.

*This short story was originally written for a French an-
thology dedicated to the memory of science fiction writer
Jimmy Guieu (1926-2000) and is included here because
it mentions the birth of Smith and Mie's child in France.
The four main protagonists are the heroes of The Brotherhood of the Sword, a short-lived series Guieu had
begun in the early 1960s, but quickly abandoned in favor
of the far more popular Gilles Novak, a journalist spe-
cializing in the investigation of UFOs and other para-
normal phenomena. In this story, fiction imitates life,
and the aging Brotherhood also passes the baton to its
younger successor...*

Jean-Marc Lofficier:
The End of the Brotherhood of the Sword

Paris, Spring 1967

Spring had come early that year, and the sun's hot
rays flowed freely through the open bay windows and
warmed up the richly-furnished three-bedroom apartment located on the Quai Voltaire, on the banks of the
Seine.

Jeff Mauroy was sitting comfortably in one of the
four leather armchairs of his living-room, a glass of
scotch whisky in hand, facing his three friends, Ray-
mond Duchenal, Gilbert Cartier and Robin Alexander.

Three years prior, the four friends had solved a
couple of baffling mysteries and, after locating one of
the mythical Templars treasures, had christened themselves the "Brotherhood of the Sword."

"We need to have a serious talk," said Jeff, the leader, in a tone that poorly concealed his irritation, "For some time, frankly speaking, we—the Brotherhood, I mean—have been messing around. It's like we've lost our sense of purpose, we've forgotten our mission…"

An uncomfortable silence reigned in the room.

"Honestly, look at you," Jeff continued. "We haven't had undertaken one single case worthy in the last six months!"

"Well, I've been very busy at the office," said Ray Duchenal, the biologist of the team. "I'm responsible for setting up the biology department of a new organization. It's going to be called the *Bureau International de Prévention Scientifique*. It's going to be huge. We hope to start in three or four years. But it's given me the opportunity to think, Jeff. In the future, missions like ours will best be handled by large organizations of that type. Four men like us, even with the best intentions in the world, and the treasure of the Templars at our disposal, are ill-equipped to save the planet…"

"Wait a minute!" said Jeff, offended. "Don't you forget that only last year, we ensured the protection of the Beffort baby at American Hospital in Neuilly, against the forces of Madame Atomos? And how about Indochina…"

"Indochina was more than twelve years ago, Jeff," said Alex Robin, the youngest of the group, who had begun to gain weight because of his wife Clara's excellent cooking skills. And was now the proud father of two adorable children, Olivier and Philippe. "That's all in the past. You're not young anymore. Do you still climb the five flights of stairs to your apartment two steps at a time?"

"Er, no, I take the elevator now," Jeff Mauroy was forced to admit, in the tone of a child caught with his hand in the candy box.

"And when it comes to fighting for the good cause," said Ray Duchenal, "the secret services don't need us anymore. They have Calone, and Gaunce, and Kovacs, and..."

"And the guys of S.N.I.F.," added Alex.

"OK, OK, but it's still thanks to us that France was able to save the anti-gravitation device of Professor Lancry, don't forget that!" said Jeff.

"Ah, yes, about that..." Gilbert Cartier began. He was a physicist attached to the laboratory of nuclear synthesis of Ivry-sur-Seine.

"What about it?" asked Jeff.

"Well, it seems that it only works at the size of the original model. Once you enlarge it, the anti-G force dissipates. We can, at best, fly a flat iron, but nothing else. And for that, we needed all the energy generated by the Marcoule nuclear plant for two hours."

"It can't be!" said Jeff, with an air of despair.

"It has to do with quantum mechanics," Gilbert murmured, shrugging.

A new silence weighed was in the room, disturbed only by the sound of the ice cubes in Jeff Mauroy's glass, whose hand—probably due to a nervous tic?—had begun to tremble slightly. Then, in a resigned tone, Jeff turned toward Alex:

"We still funded the research of Professor Clairembard on the lost continent of Mu. That's worth something," he said.

Alex Robin, the anthropologist of the Brotherhood, appeared slightly embarrassed, just as his friend Gilbert earlier.

"Professor Clairembard's research... Er... Yes... Well..." he muttered, his eyes trying in vain to avoid those of Jeff. "You know I've never been very good at finances, Jeff... And, well, there were some unexpected setbacks... We lost a bathyscaph..."

"How much did we spend?" asked Jeff, growing somber.

"But the Professor is certain that, this time, he's on the right track..."

"How much did we spend?" Jeff repeated.

Alex leaned over and whispered a figure in Jeff's ear. Having stomached the blow, Jeff asked:

"OK. How much do we have left?"

"After the Clairembard expedition?" asked Alex.

"Yes, after the Clairembard expedition!" Jeff replied, angrily.

"Approximately..."

New whispers.

The electronics engineer, former helicopter pilot and judo black belt, who had never been afraid of anything or anyone, blanched, emptied his glass in one swoop, got up and refilled it. Gil and Ray noted that his tremor was now much more pronounced.

"I've come up with the idea of an investment that would be completely in keeping with the spirit of our mission," Ray began, suddenly. "There's this guy who's been recommended to me by Francis Dalvant, the reporter of *L'Eclair* with whom we worked last March. He knows a colleague who's trying to revive an ailing magazine, but no one wants to lend him a penny..."

"That's ridiculous! Do you see us becoming Press barons?" Jeff threw, his face reddened. "Why not invest in night clubs while you're at it?"

"Don't judge so quickly, Jeff," said Ray, keeping his calm. "This would be a magazine that would help usher mankind into the Age of Aquarius, while maintaining a connection to the past. It would deal seriously with everything the official media ignore: the Templars, UFOs... The guy was turned down by Dassault, who told him that Atlanteans would never buy any of his Mirage planes and, therefore, he wasn't interested. Filipacchi asked him if there were female Templars willing to be photographed in scanty clothes. We're his last chance."

"Hum. And what is it called, that magazine?"

"*Panorama de l'Insolite*. Right now, it isn't worth a penny, but this man has ideas on how to relaunch it. He would make a fantastic editor. I took the liberty of inviting him to come here and present his project in person..."

Ray got up, headed for the door, and opened it.

"My friends, let me introduce you to Monsieur Gilles Novak..."

Credit where credit is due: The Bureau International de Prévention Scientifique was the star of a French TV series called Aux frontières du possible *which aired in 1972 and 1974. Calone, Gaunce, Kovacs and the S.N.I.F. are popular spy series of the 60s and 70s created respectively by Alain Page, Serge Laforest, G.-J. Arnaud and Vladimir Volkoff. Professor Clairembard comes from Henri Vernes' Bob Morane series and journalist Francis Dalvant from Paul Béra's Leonox series.*

ANDRE CAROFF

Mme ATOMOS PROLONGE LA VIE

ANGOISSE

Editions "FLEUVE NOIR"

MADAME ATOMOS PROLONGS LIFE

Chapter I

It started very simply on a farm not far from Coventry, which was a little town in the state of Rhode Island in the northeast of the United States[13]. It was in July, 1966. The weather was beautiful and if you believed the forecast, in the next few days it was going to turn into a downright heat wave.

So, the farm in question was located on a hillside surrounded by gentle, pleasant-looking hills. For the time being, it was the only thing pleasant at the Smiths. In spite of the warm temperature, the plentiful crops and the surprising good health of the family, Bob Smith and his wife Jeanne looked worried watching Dr. Humphrey's movements.

Dr. Humphrey was a pediatrician and for more than twenty minutes he had been examining little John, who had just turned 13 months old. He picked him up delicately, put him on the balance and slumped discouragingly.

"I don't understand," the doctor grumbled, "he's in perfect health, but he hasn't gained an ounce or grown an inch in the last two weeks." He wiped his glasses and

---

[13] It is interesting to note that Rhode Island is the smallest state in the Union: 37 miles wide by 48 long.

look dumbfounded at Bob and Jeanne Smith. "Has he been eating well?"

"Very well, doctor."

"Sleeping okay?"

"He never wakes us up."

The doctor sighed and sat down.

"Is it serious, doctor?" Bob Smith asked.

"Well, no," Humphrey assured him nervously. "Your son is in very good health, I guarantee it. I can truly say that I've never seen such a strong baby."

"He's so small!"

"When I say strong," Humphrey clarified, "I mean that his physical state is remarkably well-balanced. His heart, stomach, intestines, all his organs are in perfect condition. He eats well, sleeps well and his bowel movements are regular... In fact, Mr. Smith, this baby has absolutely no need of me or of medicine or vitamins of any kind. We must let nature takes its course, that's all!"

Humphrey stood up, closed his bag and buttoned his coat. "I'll come back in eight days. I'm sure that between now and then the boy will still be fine and he'll have grown and put on weight. Don't worry, he's a fine piece of engineering."

He took Jeanne Smith's arm and asked, "And you?" His question was friendly, that's all. The young woman had a heart condition and the birth had presented a few problems.

Jeanne shrugged her shoulders. "I'm doing fine, doctor."

Her response was spoken coolly, which proved that she really was fine. A sick person who no longer talks about his ills can be considered definitely cured and Dr. Humphrey made no mistake about it. So, he did not question Jeanne Smith further. He got back in his car and drove off to his next appointment.

It was unfortunate, this lack of curiosity on the part of Dr. Humphrey, but that's the way things go.

The next day, a few miles from the Smith farm, a nurse was giving an injection of gamma globulins against whooping cough to little Mason. She was acting on behalf of the attending physician who was called away on an emergency to treat a dying man and thus unable to perform this simplest of procedures.

Later that evening, little Mason was struck with a partial paralysis. The sciatic nerve was pinched and he could not move his leg. It was not serious. Another doctor came to confirm it for the panicking parents. The paralysis would not last long and there would be no after-effects; he would probably be better within the week.

See, for a child, as we all know today, a simple shot in the butt is not very easy nor without risks. The baby is often anxious and fidgeting. All he has to do is tighten up and the shot can cause sciatic paralysis.

The doctor went on his way, but, and this is the amazing thing, little Mason recovered full use of his leg less than an hour after he left.

The doctor who took care of Mason was totally unaware of the miraculous recovery of his young patient. He went off to the other side of the county where old Douglas was dying. The man was almost 80 years old and had just suffered a brutal stroke and, rather cruelly, a cerebral hemorrhage to boot. The doctor, whose name was Wallace, had no false hopes about his chances of survival. Douglas was already worn down by old age and would not put up much of a fight when death came to take him away.

He arrived at Douglas' place as night was falling and went straight to his patient's bedside. The old man's color was strangely healthy, pinker than it had been over the last few weeks. Moreover, he looked extremely lucid and, astoundingly, the cerebral hemorrhage, which normally brought on a partial or total paralysis, seemed to have had no effect at all on him.

Wallace leaned over, gave him a quick examination and stood back up, clearly surprised. "Well," he whispered to Mrs. Douglas who was standing behind him, "I have the feeling that he'll be just fine."

The old woman dried a tear, found the strength to smile and murmured, "Thank heaven, doctor! I thought he was a goner and just now he spoke to me..."

She was a former nurse and had taken care of her husband for a long time, so she had known instantly when he was struck ill. Naturally Wallace thought that she was mistaken, overreacting, and that she had phoned him for what was, finally, just a simple dizzy spell. After giving a prescription that he knew would be of little use, he went back home.

The next morning, old Douglas was on his feet, fresh as a daisy and the picture of health, but his wife did not think it necessary to tell Wallace the news.

It is weird, but it has been proven for centuries that good news rarely travels to the general public through the press and other mouthpieces of information. In truth, nobody really cares about people in good health, happy as larks and leading quiet lives.

However, that is exactly what was happening in the tiny state of Rhode Island. No one died, no one got sick, no one got colds or suffered from rheumatism. On the other hand, the children did not grow or gain weight; they stayed the same as they were a few weeks before. As for the adults, it was no different, but no one noticed it because it was less easy to see.

Thus, six months went by before a vague rumor reached the ears of Smith Beffort. It was the end of January, 1967 and heavy clouds were looming over New York. Beffort was reading the *Herald Tribune* while Mie Azusa-Beffort was playing with their son in the next room.

For more than six months, Madame Atomos had not shown herself and some people were absolutely convinced that she had not survived the destruction of Atomos City and the death of all her servants. Certainly, the terrible woman had managed to escape on board a supersonic rocket, but those who had the privilege of witnessing the remarkable event were pretty much sure that the machine had crashed in the Pacific Ocean. Beffort just waited[14].

In the past he had believed in the death of Madame Atomos when the evidence easily supported the supposition. Now he was very suspicious. He refused to give his opinion, but looked meticulously through the humdrum news that the press usually only printed in short items.

So, this evening a few lines attracted his attention. They told briefly about a banal crisis that was running wild among the doctors and all the medical personnel in Rhode Island. Empty hospitals, the pharmacies and laboratories reduced to unemployment, etc.

But it was only a blurb, so Beffort just cut it out and pasted it in his Atomos file, which he faithfully kept up-

[14] See *The Mistake of Madame Atomos*.

to-date. The file contained all the weird news, all the strange events that had happened in the USA since Madame Atomos' disappearance. By experience Beffort knew how the sinister woman acted when she was preparing a new offensive against the Americans. And it always started with a mundane incident, not very likely to arouse any suspicions. When the alarm was sounded, it was usually too late to stop the attack and then they had to fight defensively, hoping to minimize the damage.

Beffort folded the newspaper, stretched his legs and lit a cigarette. Just then the doorbell rang. As Mie opened the door, she cried out in joy and surprise at seeing Dr. Alan Soblen. She invited him in and he walked into the living room where Beffort was relaxing.

"Hello," he sounded like he was in a good mood. "How are you, Smith?"

Beffort smiled, got up and shook his hand. "Well, well! I thought you were called off to Europe, doc? Sit down and let's have a drink to celebrate your return."

Soblen waved it off. "I'll have a drink, but not to celebrate my return because I never left the country. In truth, I was attending a symposium in Providence…"

"Rhode Island?"

"Exactly. We stayed there a month and worked like dogs."

"It looks like it was a success. I've never seen you look so good. Work makes you healthy, eh?"

Soblen nodded and smiled, but a shadow crossed his face. "I got back less than an hour ago and my first stop was to see you."

"That's nice," Mie said as she put down a bottle and some glasses. "I suppose you were in a hurry to see your godson?"

"That's true," Soblen confirmed, "but it wasn't the only reason for my visit. Smith, you have to know that something extraordinary is happening in Rhode Island."

Beffort raised an eyebrow. "If you're alluding to the crisis that's raging in the medical field right now, I'm up-to-date."

Soblen took off his glasses, put them in his pocket and unfolded the newspaper that was lying on the table. Looking at his friends he said, "You know that I'm very nearsighted, right?"

"Many people are," Beffort said politely.

"Yes, but nearsighted is nearsighted and with age it only get worse. Now, I'm sure you won't believe me, but my vision has got much better over the last month. Look, I'll read something from the newspaper."

He did so with no problem and Beffort applauded. "Bravo, doc! You're getting younger!"

Soblen did not have even a trace of a smile. "You don't know how true that is, Smith," he said gloomily. "I'm getting younger."

"That's nothing to be sad about," Mie teased.

Soblen gulped down his drink, jumped over the sofa and started doing amazing gymnastics before the terrified eyes of the Befforts. When he was finished, he sat back down and said, "No more pain, flexible like a kid, perfect reflexes and notice that I'm not even out of breath after that rash of exercise! Almost a month ago it hurt me just to bend over and tie my shoes. What do you think?"

Smith and his wife had nothing to say. Dr. Soblen's demonstration left them speechless. Soblen wagged his finger. "The strangest thing," he hammered out, "is that all the participants in the symposium are just like me! Our eldest member, a fine old gentleman of 83, came to

Providence limping along like a snail. He was using two canes and groaning at every step. He slept through most of the conferences. He looked so run down that many of us thought that he'd be going back in a coffin. But, four days later, he walked to the meeting on his own two feet and spent his nights in the bars!"

Beffort laughed. "It all sounds great," he said enthusiastically. "What are you complaining about?"

Soblen looked gloomier and gloomier. "It may sound marvelous, Smith, but I swear to you that it's not normal."

Beffort whistled. "Oh, I see, doc. You think that Madame Atomos is mixed up in all this. Instead of killing the Americans, she's pampering them like babies, no doubt to make up for her crimes... Very funny, doc." He took the Atomos file and held it out to Soblen, saying in a much colder voice, "I've been putting everything weird into this file for a year. If you look through it, you'll see that nothing can lead us to believe that Madame Atomos is getting ready to launch a new offensive against us. Besides, I'll remind you that our enemy no longer has any means to attack."

"Not in your opinion!" Soblen threw out. "In a year, considering her incredible technology, Madame Atomos could have built up the foundation of a new organization of destruction."

"Impossible!"

"Wrong! Do you remember her secret base in the Pacific?"

"A bluff! Her base was Atomos City and we literally disintegrated it!"

"I don't believe it."

Mie spread her hands out. "Calmly now, please. You're going to scare my son."

Beffort got hold of himself and pointed to the file. "Read it, doc, and we'll talk about it later."

Soblen opened the file nervously. He furrowed his brow and leaned over... farther, farther, farther... "Fantastic!" he murmured. "I'm nearsighted again."

Beffort sat up straight. "You really can't read anything?"

"Really, Smith! And my old pains are suddenly back!"

Mie sat there very cautiously, as if any quick movement could cause a disaster. "I have the feeling," she said, "that it's starting all over again."

Chapter II

Dr. Alan Soblen had just got back all his old pains and his nearsightedness. In short, he became like he was before he had left for Rhode Island. But it remained to be seen whether all the participants of the Providence symposium were in the same situation.

At the Befforts, Soblen made a series of phone calls and, unfortunately, received news to confirm it: the senior member, the 83-year-old man, who was walking without his canes in Providence and going to nightclubs, had died when he got back home. Soblen's other colleagues all complained of various ills, but they were unanimous in their decision to move to Rhode Island.

Soblen hung up after his last call and said thoughtfully, "I have to admit that I, too, would willingly end my days in Rhode Island. It feels so good to be young again!"

It took this statement for Smith Beffort to understand that the whole thing had been set up by Madame Atomos. Of course, he did not know the final results of the operation, but he already suspected that a lot of people would soon want to live in a state where no one was sick and no one died. That was probably the sinister woman's plan. Her goal was obviously to gather together as many people as possible in a relatively small space so that she could exterminate them all at once.

"I wonder," Soblen continued, still musing, "if all the inhabitants of Rhode Island are healthy or if it's only in a few towns?"

"It's happening everywhere," Beffort declared as he recalled the article in the *Herald Tribune*. "The hospitals and pharmacies are empty and the doctors are out of

158

work. Tell me, doc, if Madame Atomos is behind this, as you say, do you have any idea as to how she could keep people in good health?"

Soblen pursed his lips. "How should I know? How could I even imagine it, Smith? Madame Atomos is far in advance of us in every domain and we've never been able to explain… The disintegrator rifle exists, but we do not know the formula. The motor brains in her servants work, but we've never known how. I think that in the present situation Madame Atomos has discovered a way to kill microbes, bacteria and viruses, which are the source of our illnesses, and she has made the Rhode Island air healthier than anywhere else on earth. I know it sounds incredible, unlikely, but everything that Madame Atomos did up till now was the just like this. Remember the preserved corpse of the Boss, dead for two years, lying in a glass coffin in Palm Beach… I saw it recently. He looks exactly the same as when he was alive[15]."

He sat musing for a moment and then added, "In any case, Madame Atomos has not, as yet, committed any heinous crime, right?"

"Right," Beffort agreed, "but do you really believe that this isn't the beginning of something bigger? You and your colleagues are seriously talking about moving to Rhode Island. Who's to say that others won't have the same idea?"

"That's only natural!" Soblen exclaimed. "People want health more than wealth, and the sick want nothing more than to be cured. A short stay would do them a world of good."

Beffort shook his head. "Excuse me for saying this, but you're thinking like a child, doc. If a dying man goes

---

[15] See *Miss Atomos*.

to Rhode Island, he will certainly be cured, but if he leaves, he'll surely die when he gets sick again. Therefore, it won't be a matter of a short stay but a move for good—and probably pretty much forever!"

"Forever! You're exaggerating."

"No, you're the one not thinking it through," Beffort replied calmly. "Rhode Island is a small state where no one has died for six months but where babies are still being born, or at least I imagine so..." He was imagining based on the *Herald Tribune* article and on what Soblen had just told him, but the truth was much worse. He continued, "Until now, the births and deaths have balanced each other out, but what will happen when the old folks don't disappear? Rhode Island will become overpopulated and soon spill over into the neighboring states and..."

"Come on, Smith," Soblen interrupted angrily, "that would take years and Madame Atomos will be dead before her project of overpopulating the United States is accomplished. I don't think the sinister woman has the patience to wait so long. She wants a slow but steady revenge to satisfy her hatred of Americans."

"Revenge is a dish best served cold."

"Cold but not frozen, Smith!"

Mie, who been listening but not taking part in the conversation, suddenly asked, "When are you going to move, doctor?"

"Move? Oh, to Rhode Island? I really don't know. You know, it's kind of up in the air."

"Up in the air?"

Beffort stared at his wife. "What are you thinking, Mie?"

The young woman looked down, filled up the glasses and with a feigned indifference said, "I was

160

thinking that you both could fly out there. After all, it's still the best way to get answers, isn't it?"

Beffort and Soblen landed in Providence the next day.

They instantly thought that the city was unusually busy. When they bought a local newspaper, there was no question about it. Three columns were finally announcing to the inhabitants of the state that they were lucky to live in a special region where sickness had no more hold over human beings. Then a list of names of the miraculously cured. There was a young girl who had suffered from polio for years and who had recovered her health three months ago. Farther down they cited the case of old Douglas and some others who should have been six feet underground a long time ago. In sum, the veil was tearing…

The children were still not growing and the adults remained like they were when the salutary period began. The exact date of this was a matter of controversy. Some said that it had been at least a year; others swore that it was very recent; but nobody was too amazed at this heavenly gift. Men always receive the benefits of nature naturally, as if it was their due, but they howl like demons when the smallest problem arises. So, here, they were happy to report the particularly spectacular cases, but they passed over in silence the little things like the disappearance of colds, toothaches, backaches, etc.

In the end, the ambiance in Providence was one of joy and energy and it was a pleasure to watch.

"Let's hope," Beffort wished, "that it'll last."

"Hm."

"We agree that the wicked mother Atomos is preparing a very special treat for us. She usually kills. Today she's prolonging life. I have the feeling that the bill's going to be steep!"

They made a tour of the city. Chatting with the inhabitants they learned that everything was not as rosy as it appeared. For example, the children were not the only ones not growing; it was the same for the chicks, calves, lambs and eggs that the chickens laid in vain. Meat was already becoming scarce and they had to bring it in from neighboring states. And even though the hospitals were empty, the maternity wards were overflowing with babies born over the last six months. Babies they were and babies they would remain!

"A little while ago," Dr. Soblen said, "You said that we should hope it lasts. If the situation goes on like this, Rhode Island will have a bunch of completely unproductive babies whose number will never stop growing. And then the adults, even though they won't be growing old physically, will end up reaching the age of retirement. So, on one side we'll have babies who are 20 or 30 years old but unable to work and on the other side a lot of retired adults. Who's going to feed everyone, Smith?"

Beffort had a little laugh. "You're looking too far ahead, doc," he reproached. "I have to say that I'm only concerned with the present because Madame Atomos' plan should logically be accomplished quickly. If I'm not mistaken, the population of Providence has probably doubled, right?"

Soblen agreed. "There are, indeed, more people here now than when I left."

"And that was only 24 hours ago," Beffort grumbled. "I wonder how many will be here before the end of the week. For the moment the Americans don't yet know that Rhode Island has become a land of plenty, but it won't take long for the news to spread across the United

States. After that, they'll be talking about it in Europe, Asia and Africa…"

"Everywhere on earth," Soblen finished. "I completely agree with you, Smith, but not about the rush to Rhode Island."

Beffort looked at him wryly. "There will inevitably be a rush, doc," he predicted. "The sick will want to be cured and the healthy will come here not to get sick. It's human. But Rhode Island is small, very small."

Dr. Soblen took off his glasses. "There you go!" he rejoiced, "I can see again! It's wonderful!" All of a sudden he became serious again. "You're right, Smith. Everyone's going to want to live here. A tiny little state that will very soon be bursting at the seams. Do you think that Madame Atomos planned this?"

Beffort did not answer. There was no need.

The first to come to Rhode Island were, naturally, the rich. Elderly, for the most part, they came with their cash, their cramps and their chronic illnesses. They were cured very quickly and immediately decided to stay in the area for life. They bought houses, farms and hotels and made the cost of living skyrocket within 48 hours. By and by, and by the end of the week, the population of the state had grown by a million people. The trouble was that everyone was squeezed into the resort towns like Watch Hill, Block Island and Newport. The sudden immigration raised prices, as always and everywhere the law of supply and demand holds sway. It started a crisis that would, in time, reach unforeseen proportions.

Soon, the less rich arrived. They came from the nearby states of Connecticut and Massachusetts and mostly settled in border towns like Hope Valley and Woonsocket, which were industrialized enough to offer them jobs. Finally, trainfuls of workers came and spread out all over, depending on the availability of work and housing.

Now Rhode Island contained six million extra inhabitants, all sick when they arrived and all healed in less than 24 hours. It was troubling but not yet a catastrophe. On the contrary, business had never been so good in every domain. Those who looked no farther than the end of their nose were rubbing their hands.

In Providence, Beffort and Soblen worriedly watched the huge crowd mulling in the streets. And it was not just at rush hour, but all the time.

"They're all in good health," Soblen remarked sadly, "and they need to move. Wow, even in New York I've never seen anything like it!"

The streets were crammed with pedestrians and cars. The traffic jams became worse and worse. But everyone was still in a good mood about it.

48 hours later a dozen million newcomers filled the cup to overflowing. Rhode Island was now the most populated state in America. Of course, neither jobs nor housing were guaranteed and campsites started popping up around the cities and towns and spreading out into the country where resources and the lines of communication were scarce.

Beffort and Soblen flew over the area in an FBI helicopter. They were amazed to see how bad the situation had got. Everywhere they looked the land was black with people. An extraordinary swarm of healthy beings, hungry, hale and already starting to lack the necessities of life.

"There are still the hills and prairies," Beffort declared. "After that, doc, we're going to witness a phenomenal tragedy if the governor of the state doesn't take preventive measures."

"What do you want him to do?"

"It's urgent that he close the state borders! Otherwise, he won't be able to feed this huge population. Most of them are already without jobs or houses. If it hasn't turned tragic yet, it's because most of them are living off their savings. But imagine what's going to happen next!"

Soblen turned a little pale. "I'm afraid," he said, "that it may be too late to talk about preventative measures, Smith. The governor is overwhelmed by the situation. Everything happened so fast. Soon Rhode Island is going to be the scene of robberies, pillaging and maybe murders." He turned to Beffort and added, "In my opinion, only you and the Green Dragon Force can prevent a tragedy!"

"How?"

"By finding and destroying the means that Madame Atomos is using to prolong the lives of the people of Rhode Island!"

Beffort just nodded. He knew from the start that he and the Green Dragon force would once again be in the eye of the storm.

Chapter III

Beffort made a quick trip to New York and got an immediate appointment with his boss J.E.E. (James Edward Evans). When he entered the office, he collapsed into the armchair that J.E.E. pointed out.

"Cigarette, Smith?"

"Thanks."

"You look exhausted, my boy. Don't tell me that the Rhode Island air isn't doing you good."

"Really, it's doing too much good. It's New York that's choking me. If you think I'm tired, I who am in good health, you can imagine what the sick people who are now in Rhode Island would feel."

J.E.E. pick out a cigar, warmed it with a match and finally lit it with satisfaction. He was very relaxed and Beffort knew that his lack of concentration was a faithful reflection of the government's. Outside of Rhode Island, they did not know the whole story.

"How's Soblen, Smith?"

Beffort got a handle on his irritation. After all, J.E.E.'s behavior was normal, seeing that he did not know that Madame Atomos had just reared her head. Besides, everyone was still thinking that Rhode Island was experiencing some natural phenomenon. Beffort suddenly realized that it would be very hard to convince J.E.E. that Madame Atomos was behind everything—he had no proof.

"Soblen's fine," he answered. Then he asked, "What do you think about what's happening in Rhode Island?"

J.E.E. blew a puff of smoke toward the ceiling. "What should I think? Something extraordinary is happening there, but it's something good. So, why worry yourself sick over it?"

His reasoning was sound. As Head of the FBI, Evans only had to worry about criminals, counterfeiters, drug traffickers… and Madame Atomos, if she made an actual appearance. And this was not the case.

Beffort decided not to mince words. "Madame Atomos is back."

J.E.E. jumped up and put down his cigar, leaning over to Beffort. "How can you be so sure?"

Beffort spread out his hands. "If I told you that the state of Rhode Island was completely razed to the ground, you would easily believe that Madame Atomos was responsible, even if there was no proof of her involvement. Today, Rhode Island is swimming in good health. I just told you that it's thanks to Madame Atomos. Do you believe me?"

"Certainly not!" J.E.E. exploded.

"In that case, goodbye, Evans."

"Hey! Wait a minute, will you… You throw out a rat and then leave me high and dry without any explanation! Is that why you and Soblen are living in Providence at the moment?"

"Every time something bizarre happens in the USA, it's the prelude to an act of destruction by Madame Atomos. The walking dead in New York[16], a giant mushroom in Dallas[17], human robots in San Francisco[18],

---

[16] See *The Sinister Madame Atomos* in *The Terror of Madame Atomos*.
[17] See *Madame Atomos Sows Terror* in *The Terror of Madame Atomos*.
[18] See *Madame Atomos Strikes at the Head* in *Miss Atomos*.

drunks and rattlesnakes in Florida[19], flying saucers against the KKK[20]…"

"You can spare me the rest," J.E.E. cut him off, forgetting about his cigar. "You're talking about Madame Atomos. So be it. I'll remind you that the rocket she escaped in was tracked by our radar to the Hawaiian Islands where she seemed to have disappeared. The search for her produced nothing and…"

"I know, Evans," it was Beffort's turn to cut in, "I know. You think Madame Atomos and her rocket were swallowed up by the Pacific Ocean and the fact that you didn't find any wreckage seems to confirm it. But I still say that I don't agree with you. Madame Atomos disappeared a number of times without leaving a trace and every time they were sure she was dead. They wanted her to be dead so badly, but then after a while our enemy was back. It'll be the same this time, believe me!"

"No!" J.E.E. barked. "It's physically impossible! In one year Madame Atomos could not have rebuilt a City like the one we sank in the shoals of Libegh!"

"Who says she built a new City?"

"Okay. Prove that she's responsible for what's happening in Rhode Island today and it will be easy for me to convince President Johnson that the fight is as important as a world war!"

Beffort turned to leave. "When I came here, I was sure that it would be a waste of time… so, I'm on my own."

J.E.E. furrowed his brow. "The Green Dragon Force, eh?"

---

[19] See *Miss Atomos*.
[20] See *Miss Atomos against the KKK* in *The Return of Madame Atomos*.

168

"Exactly right, Evans."

"What are you going to do?"

Beffort opened the door. "I don't know yet, but I'm sure that our work will clear the way for you by the time you're forced to act yourself! Farewell!" And he went into the hallway, closing the door quietly behind him.

The men of the Green Dragon Force were stationed practically in the middle of the United States, in an underground base located near St. Louis, Missouri. From there, they could respond as fast as possible to any call from Beffort and, in a relatively short time, get anywhere in the country.

Strictly speaking, they were no choirboys. They were all ex-convicts with long records. But to fight against Madame Atomos, they had exactly the kind of skills that were necessary. Plus they had the advantage of being anonymously, in the heart of a crowd, while Madame Atomos had always been informed of the movements of the soldiers and police in uniforms.

Under the command of Owen Bernitz—a tough guy whom Beffort had barely saved from the electric chair—they were training in the use of the paralyzing rifle when the telephone rang and stopped their firing.

Owen swiftly moved his heavy body, slid his eternally unlit, constantly chewed cigar to the other side of his mouth and picked up the phone. "Owen here."

"Hi Owen," Beffort said from New York. "Your playtime's over."

Owen let out a sigh of relief. "None too soon, boss! Where're we going?"

"Rhode Island," Beffort answered simply.

Owen whistled. "No! After pulling us out of the cabin, you're gonna grant us eternal life? Mighty nice!"

"Maybe it won't be all fun and games, Owen."

"Mama what's-her-name?"

"Probably. You have to leave immediately with weapons and baggage."

"How many guys?"

"Everyone! Travel separately. Plan Z. And get in touch with me in Providence. Hotel Columbus. Got it?"

"Got it, boss. How's the kid?"

"Doing great," Beffort said, remembering that without Owen his wife and son would certainly have died in the cottage in Columbus[21]. "See you tomorrow, Owen."

"Okay, boss."

Owen Bernitz hung up and called his men together.

After the telephone call, Beffort went home. It was a rented house in Greenwich Village, under the direct protection of the FBI: a team of six men who did three eight-hour shifts under the command of Eddy Witter. Two G-men kept continual watch over Mie Azusa-Beffort, ex-Miss Atomos, and her one-year-old son. The precaution was necessary because Beffort had not forgotten that Madame Atomos had sworn to kidnap Mie. In the mind of the sinister Japanese woman, this act of revenge was essential, even taking precedence over her vengeance against the United States.

Thus, Beffort had to admit that what was happening in Rhode Island might only be a ploy to catch him in a net where it would be impossible for him to protect his wife and son.

Madame Atomos had more than one trick up her sleeve and could, if need be, play all her cards at once to

---

[21] See *The Mistake of Madame Atomos*.

achieve her evil ends. And since the destruction of the City and the members of the Atomos Organization, Beffort, the FBI and the Green Dragon Force did not know who or what they were fighting against. Would Madame Atomos act alone or had she mustered a new army of crime?

The second solution was more likely. Madame Atomos pulled the strings, but for this she needed puppets. In one year, she could have kidnapped a great many people and submitted them to her will. It remained to see if she had recruited her force in her home country or directly in the United States. In the past, the members of the Atomos Organization were easily recognized because of the kind of automatism that the motor-brain gave to their walk. If Madame Atomos used the same method, everything would be relatively simple. But if her evil genius had discovered another mode of persuasion, it was obvious that anybody could be suspected of belonging to her organization. Under such conditions, identifying them would be impossible.

Beffort entered his house and to his surprise found a G-man in the entry. "Damn! What are you doing here, Hyde?"

"Orders of J.E.E., Mr. Beffort. From now on there will be two men outside and a third inside. Today, I'm the third man."

Beffort smiled. So, Evans had put a little faith in his suspicions after all! Formally denying that Madame Atomos was back, he had, nonetheless, taken measures to strengthen the guard around the Befforts.

Mie and Robert were in the living room. When Smith walked in, Mie got up and went to meet him. Beffort notice right away how pale she was. "What's wrong, Mie?"

"Five telephone calls since yesterday, Smith."

"From whom?"

"No one. They call, I pick up and nothing. I held the phone for ten minutes. I heard the sound of breathing and a low rumble that could be the street, but he or she on the other end of the line doesn't say a word."

"They can trace the calls and…"

"I already asked them," the young woman said nervously. "The calls are coming from a public phone booth in Manhattan." She watched her son playing on his bed and added in a distant voice, "I looked at a map. Each call came from a different location. The first was far away from our house; the second was closer… I'm sure that the next will come from Greenwich Village!"

She whipped around to her husband. Her eyes were a little dilated, her face terribly tense. "It's as if someone wants to make me know that danger is getting closer and closer to us, Smith. Wait, look at this!"

She opened a drawer and took out a map of New York, which she unfolded. In Manhattan, with a red pencil, she had drawn circles that together formed a dotted line that led unquestionably toward Greenwich Village.

"When was the last call?" Smith asked.

"This afternoon. It was at exactly 3 p.m. There was also one this morning and two during last night. The very first was yesterday evening, around 8. They're not regular, like they're waiting for the opportunity to call safely or like they're trying to keep me constantly on edge."

If that was it, Beffort thought, *they succeeded.* Mie was getting more and more nervous, plunged into a feverish state that made her movements jerky and her voice choppy. Someone was trying to panic her, to make her live in agonizing suspense before striking.

It was typical Madame Atomos.

"It's her, isn't it, Smith?"

Beffort took off his hat, sat down and lit a cigarette. He had to keep his cool and calm down his wife, make her admit that she had nothing to fear. The FBI was keeping watch outside and inside the house. Handpicked agents who had fought against the Atomos Organization and who were ready for the unexpected.

"If it's not Madame Atomos," he answered after a delay, "it's someone working for her. Which amounts to the same thing. I would love a drink, Mie…"

His wife stopped staring at him and opened the bar. "Scotch?"

"With a lot of water." He forced himself not to watch her, but he could hear her have a hard time keeping the ice cubes from tinkling in her trembling hand. Mie was panicking. In a few hours she would be on the edge of a nervous breakdown.

"Hyde!" Beffort called. The G-man came into the doorway from the entry. His coat was unbuttoned and Beffort saw the butt of the paralyzing gun sticking out of his special holster. "What are you doing about these telephone calls?"

"Personally, it's not my job, but I know that Witter has all the public booths in the area under surveillance. Every guy is in a car with a radio. When a call comes in here, there will be a red alert and everyone in a booth at the time will be taken in for questioning. In my opinion, there's not much more we can do."

Beffort nodded and took the frosted glass that Mie held out to him. Outside, it was snowing, the temperature dropping. The fact that the young woman had put ice in the scotch proved that she was very worried.

"How have you organized the defense of the house?" Beffort asked again, as if he did not know.

Hyde understood that it was to calm his wife, so he played along. "We put one guy in the house across the street. From there he can see everything that happens in the street and the yard. Plus, this side of the street has got no parking signs on it so that no vehicle can stop without getting a ticket immediately. Another guy is watching the back and sides of your house. The side door is locked and the shutters closed. Sincerely, and given the fact that I'm in the entry, I'd bet my life that a mouse couldn't get in here!"

Mie just barely started to relax. And that was when the telephone rang.

Chapter IV

Beffort stopped Mie from rushing to the phone. "Keep him on the line for as long as possible. No need to talk. He just wants to raise your hackles. He won't hang up first, so Witter's men will have time to nab him. Now, let's go."

Mie picked up the phone and put her pale lips to the mouthpiece while Beffort picked up the other line. "Hello? I'm listening," Mie forced herself to speak.

There was no answer. The minutes started slowly ticking off. Beffort heard shallow breathing, tried to imagine the mysterious caller alone in the glass booth somewhere in Manhattan. It was the end of the workday. The streets were starting to teem with people, cars crawling along bumper to bumper.

In the doorway, Hyde was on edge. He looked like a tiger ready to pounce. Mie gradually turned pale as the time passed. Little Robert had stopped playing and was watching his parents with big, curious eyes. Beffort took this all in automatically. He felt his jaws clench as the minutes went by. What was the G-man doing who was supposed to be watching the booth?

All of a sudden Mie exploded, "Talk! Come on and say something!"

Beffort grabbed her wrist and made a sign to her to calm down. She shook him off, sat down without letting go of the telephone and closed her eyes. Beffort gently put down his phone and walked up to Hyde.

"Mrs. Beffort picked up three minutes ago. It's not long. We have to wait and see. Our colleague is maybe jostling through a crowd."

Beffort nodded, went back to his wife and picked up his phone. The stranger's breathing was still audible, in spite of the low rumble coming from the street. All of a sudden there was a weird crackle and a voice came over the line. "Mrs. Beffort?"

Mie jumped and opened her eyes. The voice was deep, muffled, and it was hard to say if it belonged to a man or a woman. "I'm listening," Mie murmured. "Who are you? What do you want?"

"You should know who I am. You've thought about nothing but me for the past year because I haven't stopped thinking about you..."

"Madame Atomos?"

"You're sitting down," the voice continued undisturbed, "and your husband is listening in. Your son is on the bed. Near the door there's a man with a gun. His name is Charles Hyde. Outside I still see two FBI men. A bugging apparatus set up in the neighbor's house is recording my words. You're all waiting for a federal agent to come and arrest me, but he won't come. He's been dead for two minutes. I will call you one last time at midnight before going into action. Good night, Miss Atomos!" There was a click and the usual buzzing came over the line.

Stupefied, Mie held the receiver in her hand and stared at her husband, who hung up his phone. Beffort grimaced and said coldly, "Hang up, Mie. I think Witter is going to call us very soon."

Mie automatically put down the phone and crossed her trembling hands. "Smith," she whispered, "it's terrifying!"

"Let's say it's troubling," Beffort corrected, trying to hide his worry.

"Troubling! The woman described exactly where we all are. She named Hyde, mentioned the two men guarding the house and she knows that we're bugging the phones! And you say it's *troubling*! My God! I'm sure she's listening to what I'm saying right now."

"In that case," Beffort replied, "be quiet! Hyde?" The G-man came forward. "When did some city workers or employees come in here?" Beffort asked.

Hyde asked for a minute. He went to the entry and returned with a thick, black notebook. Inside were the names of all the visitors who entered the house for the past year. The last dated entry was Dr. Soblen.

Hyde turned the pages and stopped far from the back, on a Tuesday in July, six months before. "On this day," he said, "two city employees from the electric company came to check and repair the electricity. It was at the request of Mrs. Beffort."

"I remember," Mie confirmed.

"One was named Langers," Hyde continued, "and the other Arwood and their job sheet was all in order. From 9 to 11 in the morning. After they left, Witter made sure in person that everything was all right. He marked it here, at the bottom of the page."

"Is the description of the repairs also registered in your book?" Beffort asked.

"The refrigerator and washing machine were having problems," Mie explained.

Beffort turned to her. "Were you here the whole time the men were working?"

"Of course not, Smith. I had no special reason to watch over them."

"Do you remember what they looked like?"

Mie thought for a moment before answering with uncertainty, "I think they were rather young, average height, clean-shaven... but it's been so long, I can't..."

"Good," Beffort stopped her. "Call the office of the electric company right now and ask them whether Langers and Arwood really are working there, then try to get their physical description."

"You don't think Witter will call?"

"He'll call. Hyde, help me take down all the pictures and paintings in this room."

While Mie dialed the number of the electric company, Beffort and Hyde cleared off the walls to no avail.

"What do you have in mind?" the G-man asked.

"A microphone and a camera," Beffort answered. "I don't believe in miracles. In fact, the fridge and the washer are in the kitchen, right? Let's try that."

It took five minutes to find the electronic camera. It was cleverly camouflaged behind a wall clock that had been replaced with a look-alike. The outside of the face was dark, black glass, but on the other side, the transparent side, a camera was hiding, as big as a fist, stuck in a hastily dug out hole in the wall. From the back of the kitchen when the door was open, which was the case, the camera could turn on by remote control and film everything happening in the south part of the living room.

"A real miniature masterpiece," Beffort commented when he tore the camera out of its hole. "*Made in Japan*, as you might expect! For once Madame Atomos was forced to use retail products... How lowly! Now let's see if she's also got a microphone somewhere, Hyde."

Just then Mie rushed into the kitchen. "Langers and Arwood really do work for the repair service of the electric company," she said, "but they've been retired for two years! What's that?"

"Madame Atomos' eye," Beffort joked. "Help us look for her ear, Mie. In other words, an ultrasensitive microphone…"

The telephone interrupted him. He went to answer it in the living room, and caressed his son's cheek as he went by. "Beffort here. Speak."

"It's Witter, boss. We've got a problem. Laumont, who was watching booth 13, was stabbed on the street. He'd barely got out of his car…"

"Is it serious?"

"Fortunately, the blade was deflected by a rib. With a little luck he'll pull through fine, but the guy escaped…"

"The guy?"

"Witnesses saw his attacker jump into a light gray Buick convertible. The area was blocked off, but we arrived a little too late to nab the guy who called Mrs. Beffort."

"The guy or the gal," Beffort corrected.

"Hard to say, in fact," Witter admitted. "I was listening in when he or she was talking and I swear I couldn't tell what sex the voice was." He hesitated before saying cautiously, "How did the person know that Mrs. Beffort was sitting down and that you were listening and Hyde…"

"Camera," Beffort said. "Don't get all hot and bothered. There's nothing miraculous about it."

"Well then," Witter hedged, "it's not like Rhode Island, is it? Something's happening over there that we can't explain."

Beffort smiled over the telephone. Witter had fought directly against the Atomos Organization and had enough terrifying memories for the rest of his life and yet he was always ready to fight again… If you wanted him to. His way of asking to be posted in Rhode Island was discreet and commendable, when you remembered that his father was disintegrated by Madame Atomos and he thought only of personal revenge[22].

"I'm going back to Providence tonight," Beffort offered, "if you want, you can come."

"Okay, boss! With pleasure! What about J.E.E.?"

"One minute, my friend. First you're going to change the security system of my house. I believe Madame Atomos has known since this afternoon that I'm here and she's trying to intimidate me by threatening my family. Only to keep me in New York without really planning to go on the offensive, get it? So, reinforce the guards around Mie and my son. I'll call J.E.E. to tell him that I'm mobilizing you. Get over here when you can, hopefully with the recording of the latest phone call between X and my wife."

Witter assured him that he would be there before midnight. Beffort hung up and went back to Mie and Hyde, who were still searching for a possible microphone in the living room. They went through the room with a fine-toothed comb, but in vain, so they moved on to the kitchen, the bedrooms and the entry, but they could not find the so-called *ear* of Madame Atomos.

"It's 9 p.m.," Beffort said, "so our caller should be in touch in three hours. After that, if they keep their word, they'll go into action. Hyde, you want to see if Witter has changed and reinforced the security outside? In the meantime, my wife will fix us up some sandwiches."

---

[22] See *The Sinister Madame Atomos* in *The Terror of Madame Atomos*.

Charles Hyde went into the yard. The changes had been made discreetly, but the expert eye of the G-man detected very quickly the new security set-up. Two delivery vans were parked across the street. No one was in the front seat, but Hyde knew that his colleagues were spying on the house and the immediate vicinity through tiny peepholes in the body. Hyde walked around the house. The yard was swimming in shadows, but the thick carpet of snow on the ground, which marked the areas free of obstacles, allowed him to proceed without bumping into any of the trees.

"So, Hyde, out for a stroll?"

Hyde looked up. There were four men on the roof of the garage that formed a terrace. From there, they covered the back and one side of the house. The men in the van took care of the other side and the front.

"Where's Witter," Hyde whispered.

"He went to get a walkie-talkie for us. Like that we can give a warning at the slightest sign of trouble. Tell Beffort to turn on the light on the stoop when he leaves. Otherwise he might be taken out. At midnight the property becomes a zone of operations!"

Hyde affirmed and went back to the front door. Witter had pulled out all the stops—no one could approach the Beffort house without being neutralized. And *neutralized* was the right word since the G-men had paralyzing rifles and pistols.

In the living room, Mie was finishing the sandwiches. Robert was sleeping and the house was silent. Beffort and his wife seemed very relaxed, but Hyde felt the tension in the air as soon as he came through the door. He himself could not help feeling a little nervous. Of course, every precaution had been taken, but Madame Atomos never threatened in vain.

"Sit down, Mr. Hyde," Mie invited amiably, "and make yourself at home. Chicken, anchovies or ham?"

Hyde sat down and answered Beffort's unspoken question by detailing the way in which Witter had set up his men. Beffort nodded silently, bit into his sandwich and started talking, strangely enough, about mundane things: sports, politics, the future senatorial elections.

At 10 p.m. Witter arrived with his suitcase.

"Sit down, Eddy," Beffort said. "Do you have the recording?"

Witter took the tape out of his pocket and laid it on the table. "I suppose you have a tape player?"

"Don't worry, I have what we need. By the way, Eddy, I have to tell you that I changed my plans—we're not going to Rhode Island." Mie, Hyde and Witter stared at him, dumbfounded. Beffort pretended not to notice and continued, "The situation is serious here, so I can't leave. I have to think about my family first and I'll pull out the Green Dragon Force."

He took a felt pen and started writing on a napkin while saying, "Besides, I'm convinced that our presence in Rhode Island would do no good. What's happening there is beyond human understanding."

He unfolded the napkin and laid it out so that everyone could read what he had written: *We haven't found the mic, but there certainly is one. So, Madame Atomos is listening to everything we say. She knows that her camera is out of service, but thinks that we've let our guard down. From now on we have to speak for her ears. Of course, we're leaving for Rhode Island. Nothing has changed.*

While Mie and the G-men were reading, Beffort continued his trivial monologue, for appearances sake. Finally Witter played along and with Hyde joined Beffort in a dry discussion so he could write another message: *Witter, you obviously understand that we have to change the security again. Madame Atomos heard Hyde's report and knows exactly where our traps are set. But the change will be purely for form. Madame Atomos won't attack if she really believes we're all staying here.*

The telephone rang, interrupting him. He picked up and a voice said, "Don't wear yourself out, Beffort. You haven't found the microphone or *the second camera!* I'm going to read what you've written. Good night. See you soon… at midnight!"

Beffort swore. The battle was becoming a little too subtle.

Chapter V

During the next hour, Beffort and the G-men found the second camera and the microphone. The latter was stuck with a magnet under the refrigerator whose electricity it fed off of. The camera was ingeniously hidden in the ceiling, in the light fixture precisely, and thus had a view of the table. Its wide-angle lens could film almost the entire living room. It, too, got its energy from the electrical installation.

"Damn!" Beffort swore. "It's crazy what Langers and Arwood were able to do in two hours. And right under the nose of the FBI!"

"We can't be on our guard all the time," Witter defended. "For one year, night and day…"

"Okay," Beffort grumbled. "Don't get all excited, man. We're just going to get out of this house because it wouldn't surprise me to find out that it was booby trapped when it was built."

"Right now?" Witter was scared.

"Why not?" Mie jumped in. "It's not the first time it's happened. We're constantly on the move… Where to, Smith?"

"The furniture…" Witter started.

"Rentals" Beffort interrupted, "just like the TV, the fridge and everything else. In an hour we'll be ready to set off. Mie, can you take care of the suitcases? I have to tell J.E.E. that we're leaving. Hyde, can you help my wife?"

Witter wiped his forehead. Sometimes Beffort and Mie deeply confounded him.

At midnight, there were only two of them at the phone. Mie Azusa-Beffort and her son, accompanied by

Charles Hyde and a squad of G-men armed to the teeth, were flying to a secret hideout in Oregon. Beffort and Witter were listening to the recording of the bugged conversation from earlier in the evening. Even slowed down, it was impossible to tell whether the mysterious caller in booth 13 in Manhattan was a man or a woman.

Between Mie's departure and the first stroke of midnight, the surveillance of the public telephone booths had been reinforced. Witter was expecting positive results this time. At ten after, the two men were still hanging out in front of the silent phone.

Beffort lit a cigarette, blew the smoke toward the ceiling and said, "It's over, Eddy. The contact's been cut off."

"It was a slim chance, but it still might have lead us to Madame Atomos. The move wasn't called for."

Beffort smiled. "Either way, Madame Atomos would stay in the background and we would only have caught her underlings. But her silence proves that she knows my wife and son have left the house. She has a remarkably well organized information network and she will learn that you and I are going to Rhode Island. Therefore, she will try to eliminate us. At the same time she will be forced to get back on Mie's trail again... supposing that she ever lost it."

"You're saying all this so calmly."

"Don't be fooled by appearances, Eddy," Beffort advised. "Right now I feel like I've got two left feet. I know that everything will be all right as long as we can get to Madame Atomos quickly because she can't move faster than a jet plane now. My wife is in a plane. She's untouchable there, but the danger will come when she moves into the house we set up. In Oregon or anywhere else, Madame Atomos will find her."

"Charming. But, since you know that, I wonder what good it does to send your wife and son traveling around."

"It sends Madame Atomos or one of her henchmen traveling around at the same time. We will never spread this terrible woman's forces thin enough, Eddy. While she's chasing my family, we can hope that she'll neglect Rhode Island a little bit."

If Madame Atomos really was neglecting Rhode Island, there was no sign of it. Beffort and Witter noticed this as soon as they got off the FBI helicopter, which had brought them from New York. It was still night, but hundreds or thousands of fires were lighting up the cities and countryside of the tiny state. Rhode Island was packed like a subway train during rush hour. The helicopter was forced to put down on the roof of the local FBI since the airfields were covered with tents, trailers and cars that were being used as temporary housing.

"A temporary situation that might last a long time," Dr. Soblen commented gloomily. "Since you left, Smith, things have got worse. No one now can say for sure how many people are living in the state. Personally I think it's close to 6,000 per square mile!"

"Could be…"

"For sure, Smith! And I'm probably underestimating. As you know, I was thrown out of a $10 hotel room. Now there's a family of six there paying $50. They're sleeping in bathtubs, in hallways, in stairwells… because of the recent snowfall and a sudden drop in temperature."

"Which explains the fires?"

"Naturally. The people are dying of cold. They build fires with whatever they can find that will burn, but it won't last. Supplies aren't coming in anymore because the roads are blocked up and the ones they have are selling on the black market."

"What has the governor done?"

Soblen snickered. "He called a state of emergency. Of course, no one could care less. If an evacuation order were given, no one would be the first to go. If anyone leaves the state, it's considered a gesture of goodwill. They are, for the most part, people who were not really sick before coming here. The others, those who have incurable diseases, are diehards. Right now they're in good health. They'd rather be killed on the spot than leave. And the borders are still open—crowds of people are keep flowing in. We're a hair's breadth from disaster. To avoid it Rhode Island will have to have a first stage…"

"Keep your feet on the ground, doc," Beffort said. "After a first stage, there will have to be others. The solution lies in bringing Rhode Island back to where it was before. Now we know that an earthy paradise is the worst calamity imaginable and we can thank grandma Eve for biting the apple. That said, I think we have to act hard and fast for the government to do something. For J.E.E.'s intervention, of course."

Soblen shrugged, disillusioned. "Outside the state, it's almost impossible to imagine how things have turned out. Today is worse than yesterday, but better than tomorrow. The hours to come might bring tragedy, but it looks like nobody sees this."

"The governor?"

"Graham must not know which way to turn, but he won't show it for fear of laying himself open to his critics. I suspect that he's even put a gag order on the local press while searching for a solution or while hoping that things will just work themselves out."

"You have to admit," Beffort said, "that he's the first one to face this kind of problem. Tell me, doc, how did you meet Graham?"

Soblen got wide-eyed. "What an idea!"

"Talking brings to light, right? This man is in an important position. He's no idiot. If I can convince him that Madame Atomos is behind this thing, I'm sure that he'll take the bull by the horns, put his dignity in his back pocket and make a call to President Johnson."

"And where will that get us?"

"In the first place, we have to close the state borders in order to stop the flood of Americans into Rhode Island. After that, there will be time to clear out some space. It makes no sense for a sick man to come to live here with his whole family. I figure on convincing Graham to decree a partial evacuation."

Soblen shook his head. "It won't work, Smith. People are clinging to this land like ticks on a mangy dog. Besides, they're personally convinced that they deserve what has happened to them and they'll fight like savages to keep their health, which they believe more and more to have been restored to them miraculously be destiny. To understand them, you'd have to have cancer yourself!"

"I understand, doc," Beffort spoke calmly, "but by staying in Rhode Island the sick are putting the lives of their loved ones at stake."

"I know it, Smith!" Soblen exploded. "But they'll never admit it!"

"That's why we have to act without asking for their agreement. Graham can mobilize the army and the national guard without needing to prove that Madame Atomos is threatening his state. I have to meet him."

Soblen pointed his thumb down toward the lower floors of the federal building. "See Sullivan. As the director of the local FBI, he should be able to help you out."

The state's air was good for millions of individuals, but certainly not for Governor Graham. Sitting behind his huge desk at seven in the morning, he looked like an owl caught in blinding headlights. Across from him, Beffort was winding up his presentation while Soblen and Sullivan listened nervously to the monstrous hubbub rising up from the street. Snow had fallen all night long. The temperature was close to freezing and throughout the state, people were off in search of food and firewood.

After his conclusion, Beffort remained silent, waiting for a reaction from the man in front of him. Graham lifted up his eyes and stared without a trace of emotion. Beffort had the feeling that the man had lost all his nerves and muscles and, by some strange evil spell, had been turned into a hunk of lard.

"What you're telling me is unbelievable," Graham murmured, apathetic beyond compare. "Madame Atomos has never spread good around her. Besides, you can't expect me to believe that a human being is capable of abolishing evil on earth... I'm a man of faith, Mr. Beffort, and would willingly go along with you if you were talking about an act of divine intervention."

Beffort gritted his teeth. This guy was drugged or turning back into a child.

"For six months," Graham continued in the same, weird, jerky monotone that made Beffort's hackles rise, "I've been a witness to miracles in Rhode Island...

When heaven is involved, we have to let things go… Can I get you some coffee?"

Beffort and Soblen exchanged glances. Governor Graham was clearly off his rocker. "Certainly," Beffort answered after a short delay.

Graham got up and lumbered out the door, saying, "Please excuse me for a minute. My servants have all gone and I only have a cook left so I have to tell her to do everything… Make yourselves at home." He walked out, closed the door and went down the hallway.

Beffort turned to Sullivan. "Is he always like that?"

The local FBI chief shook his head and whispered, "I warned you that he was weird and you wouldn't get anything out of him. Contrary to what has happened to everyone else, it seems like for the last six months Graham has gotten a lot older."

"It's more than getting older," Soblen reacted. "Your governor seems to have gone soft in the head!"

"Do you know why his servants left him?" Beffort asked.

"No, but I know that Mrs. Graham left at the same time. After that our man has been alone in this huge mansion and was forced to hire the cook he mentioned."

Something went *tilt* in Beffort's brain. The best way to stop a machine was to stop its motor. To take over a state, the best way was to submit its governor to a stronger will. "What nationality is the cook?"

Sullivan made a vague gesture. "Chinese or Japanese. I'm not really sure. Anyway, she's Asian. Why"

Soblen and Beffort exchanged glances again. Sullivan looked at them and pinched his ear. "Tell me," he whispered, "you don't think that would be Madame Atomos down there?"

"You catch on fast, Sullivan," Beffort appreciated.

"If you want my opinion," Soblen warned, "we should get out of here before drinking that cook's coffee—it could very well be poisoned!"

"No rush," Beffort said. "I'll have to admit that I'm very curious to see this woman up close before leaving. What do you think Graham is suffering from, doc?"

Soblen hemmed and hawed and finally said, "I'm going to surprise you, Smith, but I have the feeling that Graham has been hypnotized. He walks like he's floating on air and his eyes seem to be looking inward. His movements are slow, as well as his speech, and he can't keep the thread of an idea for long. Did you see how he offered us coffee?"

"You mean like a third party had whispered to him to offer it to us?"

"Damn," Sullivan groaned, "I don't like this at all! If someone has hypnotized Graham to the point of taking away his personality, we're in serious danger!"

At that moment Graham pushed open the door and entered the room. He looked completely distraught and had difficulty speaking. "Sorry, gentlemen, but my cook has turned in her apron…" All of a sudden he tensed up, like he had an electric shock, then smiled right afterward and said, "But it doesn't matter. We can have something else."

He opened a drawer, made a quick move and turned around, holding a gun in his hand. Beffort dove at him and grabbed his arm, just in time for the first shot to fire into the ceiling.

A second later and Graham was disarmed, staring stupefied at the weapon that Beffort had just wrested away from him. Apparently the governor of Rhode Island was slowly emerging from a long sleep.

Chapter VI

Beffort and Sullivan brought Graham to the infirmary at the FBI headquarters in Providence. Meanwhile, Dr. Soblen was supposed to make contact with one or more members of the Green Dragon Force. For this he went to the Columbus Hotel and sat in front of the entrance. Owen Bernitz would no doubt come in person to get Beffort's orders, as was agreed. If something came up, he would send of his men. A guy whom Soblen might not know could very well show up at the front desk, learn that Beffort was not staying there and then disappear into the crowd again. In that case, there would be a whole mess of complications.

Fortunately, at 10 o'clock sharp, big Owen came up to Soblen without his noticing. "Hey, doc! What's up?"

Soblen smirked and answered, "Health is good but we're starting to lack the necessary space. You should know something…"

Bernitz took the cigar out of his mouth. "A little. I'm starting to wonder how I got so lucky to come here! Where's the boss?"

"I'm going to take you to his HQ. Where are you staying?"

Owen made a sweeping gesture and revealed the suitcase at his feet. "In the street, doc. If you've got a pad for me, I'll take it. As for my boys, they're gonna spread out all over town and it won't be a piece of cake to get them back together."

He put the unlit cigar back between his teeth, looked suspiciously at the crowd rushing through the streets and suddenly declared, "Providence is at boiling point, doc. I've seen this before in the south when the

192

blacks were making their little demonstrations for equality. I'll bet my bottom dollar that it's gonna turn into a riot pretty soon."

Soblen agreed and headed with Bernitz toward the FBI headquarters, which was luckily nearby. As they hurried their way through the crowd, he said, "You and your men are here to minimize the damage, Owen."

"Yeah? Easier said than done. Even with my 300 men, I'm on the losing side."

"Beffort will explain what your job is better than I can. If he brought you here, it's because he thinks you can help. In fact, I believe you'll have to go out looking for the devices that Madame Atomos is using." Soblen pursed his lips. "I don't really know. It's just a guess. It could be that Madame Atomos has found a system of atomic irradiation that can momentarily reverse sickness by stopping it in the cells. But, I repeat, it's only a guess. Nevertheless, even if it's only a rough theory, it's clear that it would have to be implemented by means of something. Atomic science is composed of formulas that can only be materialized by utilizing appropriate materials and even Madame Atomos is dependent on this…"

Soblen interrupted himself when he realized that he was talking to himself. Owen Bernitz was not listening. He did not care about the whys and the hows. He was a man of action, not a theorist. If you asked him to find and destroy the machines, he would destroy them. That's all.

"Is it far, doc?'

"We're here," Soblen answered, a little nippy.

The crowd around the two men continued rushing in both directions down the street. The road was full of cars and the shops full of customers. Everything was still calm, but if the cold continued and if food started getting scarce, things would go downhill fast. However, the situation would not deteriorate completely in the city, at least for the time being. As to be expected, hunger and misery would first arise in the country, far from the sources of supply and that is where a revolt would break out.

Soblen scurried up the stairs up the first landing with Owen hot on his heels. Beffort and Sullivan had got Graham quickly back on his feet with a shock treatment, which luckily came from the healthy air of Rhode Island. The governor was nothing like the larvae he was in the morning. When Soblen and Bernitz entered, he had just ordered the borders to be closed and was on the phone with Washington.

Beffort was looking at a map of the state. He looked up and waved Bernitz over. "Hello, Owen. Sit down. The doctor's brought you up-to-date?"

"Roughly," Soblen offered.

"For the moment," Beffort said, "everything we're doing is rough. We're going to fight in the dark unless a real clue turns up. Owen, this is not going to be a party."

"Doesn't change a thing, boss," Bernitz said calmly. "What do I gotta do, exactly?"

Beffort spread out the Rhode Island map on the desk and traced an invisible square with his finger. "You and your men are going to become investigators. Rhode Island didn't become a spoiled state all at once but little by little, region by region, as if they had first made some trial runs before implementing the system that had not been fully tested yet. According to some reports, the first incident, what some are calling the *miracle*, happened on a farm near Coventry, at the Smiths. So, that's where we have to strike."

"Okay," Bernitz barked. "Let's hit it! But with what?"

"You'll figure that out when you're there," Beffort hesitated. He offered a cigarette and continued, "I'm sorry I can't give you better orders, Owen, but we're really in a sticky spot. Only an exploration in the field can give us any results. Madame Atomos has always stuck her diabolical machines all over the area she wants to destroy. They can be different shapes and sizes, hidden in the ground, in trees or in houses, but they've always been there. Get it?"

Owen nodded.

"No need to tell you that time is of the essence," Beffort said, "and you have to get on it immediately. This building will be our HQ. Give the number to your boys. There will always be a line open. That's it, you can go, Owen."

Bernitz picked up his suitcase, waved and left. He looked like an office worker going to his job, but the job awaiting him was of epic proportions. Bernitz knew it. He was thinking that since he had joined the Green Dragon Force, the problems he faced were infinitely more complicated than when he was knocking off banks with a Tommy gun.

At noon, the army had taken positions along the Rhode Island borders, closed the roads and railroads and waterways. At the same time, the US Navy positioned a swarm of ships two miles off the coast, making an impassable blockade that stretched from Acoaxet to Stonington. All this was the result of the telephone conversation between Graham and Washington and it answered Beffort's desires to the letter.

Likewise, the press, radio and television broad-casted a statement signed by President Johnson declaring the state of Rhode Island off limits. Ten minutes later a second statement was given to the inhabitants of the Rhode Island. It came from Governor Graham and enjoined those who were in good health to leave the state as soon as possible and go to Connecticut or Massachusetts. Graham specified that medical checks would be starting and any violations would be met with immediate expulsion, alone and as is during time of the check, which meant that the members of a family would be separated, scattered and led into a neighboring state without even the chance to pack their bags.

Of course, Graham was bluffing. No medical checks were possible anymore since everyone was in good health! Nevertheless, the threat was not in vain. At two in the afternoon, 100,000 people had crossed the borders with arms and baggage and in the next few hours, thousands more followed. By 5 p.m. the border controls were reporting no new crossings and accounted for a distressingly poor record: 120,000 people had left Rhode Island.

At the FBI headquarters, Graham and Sullivan got the news coming in from all over the state by radio, telephone and teletype. The cold persisted and the snow kept falling. Supplies were very hard to come by because of the traffic on the roads, so only the railroad remained reliable. However, the first alert came around 7 p.m.: a supply train had just been stopped in the country by a group of armed men.

At 7:10 a telex revealed that the train had been literally emptied, the goods were in the hands of the pillagers and entire families were occupying the cars.

"There you go!" Beffort raged. "Madame Atomos has reached her goal!"

"An isolated incident," Soblen commented coldly.

"My foot, doc! It's the beginning of the end. The people are hungry and cold. If supplies and firewood don't come, they'll attack warehouses and stores... You have to understand that they have no more money, no jobs, no housing..."

"Why don't they just leave?!" Graham exploded.

"They'll get sick as soon as they cross the border. In their place, I wonder if I wouldn't do the same. Humanly speaking, they're right."

"So, what do we do?"

Beffort shook his head despondently. "The solution will come from the Green Dragon Force and no one else. If Owen Bernitz and his men find the machines and blow them up, the spell will be broken and the people will lose their health. Then, there will be nothing to keep them in Rhode Island any longer."

"Do you think there's nothing else we can do?"

Beffort patted him on the shoulder. "I know that you're thinking about all these sick people who aren't suffering right now and whom we're voluntarily going to plunge back into pain and despair, but it's the law of nature, Sullivan! Maybe Madame Atomos is using Rhode Island as an experiment before prolonging the lives of all Americans. If she succeeds, it would be a disaster!"

"Still," Sullivan protested, "this time we can't accuse her of killing people!"

Soblen jumped in with unusual vigor. "I know the problem here, gentlemen, and I can assure you that Madame Atomos will kill more people by prolonging their lives than by just killing them outright. My friend, the sociologist Philip Hauser, at the University of Chicago, has just finished a very serious study of the issue. In the present state of things, he says that if nothing limits births, the global population, which is 3.3 billion people this year, will reach the incredible number of 7.4 billion by the end of the century! Hauser pointed out that seven nations—China, India, the USSR, the USA, Indonesia, Pakistan and Japan—in 1960 had a total of 1.75 billion inhabitants, or 60% of the world population and that nothing short of a miracle will be able to keep these seven nations from reaching 3 or 4 billion by the year 2000, that is as many as the entire world today![23]"

Soblen caught his breath and continued, "That's what we're seeing in Rhode Island today, I mean famine, lack of housing, lack of jobs... This will spread all over the world if nothing is done to stop this terrifying demographic explosion! Now, Madame Atomos is speeding up the process. Thus, she is the greatest criminal of the century, far worse in cruelty than the effects of the atomic bombs in Hiroshima and Nagasaki, which are the cause of her hatred against the United States. So, don't worry your conscience, Sullivan. For the world to survive, people have to die."

A profound silence followed Soblen's speech, but a ringing telephone and rattling teletype quickly brought the four men back to the present.

---

[23] True. This warning was pronounced on July 28, 1966 by the sociologist Philip Hauser in New York at a national conference on the subject of Population and Expansion (Author's Note). To be sure, at the end of 2006 the world population had, in fact, reached 6.5 billion people according to the UN (Editor's Note).

Near the northern border, between Wallum and Slatersville, armed commando teams were attacking the army that was forbidding them entrance into Rhode Island. They were commandos of sick people who had lost all hope and who sometimes charged with bayonets, which the soldiers had to ward off with violence.

In the south, in Rhode Island Sound, the navy was also busy intercepting all kinds of boats that were trying to run the blockade. Admiral Greens stated that he was forced to act with violence in order to make them respect the ban.

Over Usquepaugh, they spotted three civil aircraft dropping parachutes. The clandestine immigrants were all people suffering from incurable diseases.

In the interior of the state, attacks, pillaging and fights broke out one after another at a frightening rate as the sun began to set. They broke grocery store windows, forced their way into apartments and kicked the people out, most of the time after a battle in which someone lost their life.

Organized gangs roamed the countryside, invading and pillaging farms, killing cattle and immediately butchering and sharing the meat. They stole wood, coal, vegetables and money when there was some. Barricades were built on the roads and railways, which stopped trucks and trains carrying precious supplies to the city. They let them leave, empty. Elsewhere, the fields were ravaged and storerooms robbed before the eyes of the helpless police.

At midnight, a telex arrived at the FBI headquarters: *Big mob of rioters (around 6,000 men) heading for Providence. Right now spotted at Esmond. We have no way to stop them. Awaiting orders.*

Graham went pale. "If this mob reaches here, it'll be a civil war."

Beffort stared at him and said coldly, "To stop them you'll have to kill them. What do you want to do?"

Chapter VII

Graham remained silent, frozen, and neither Soblen nor Sullivan had the courage to intervene. The decision was beyond question that of the State Governor, but blood would flow no matter what the choice.

"There are only two solutions," Beffort said in a strained voice. "You can let these 6,000 men come all the way to Providence and they'll attack the city, rob the stores of food, clothes and fuel, and then go back to the country after getting hold of vehicles to transport their booty, leaving behind them the corpses of whoever tries to stand in their way. Doing that, you'll prove that you are powerless and the looting will set a dangerous precedent. The other solution is to pit the army against the revolt."

"You know very well that I don't have enough forces for that!" Graham defended.

"A simple call to Washington and troops will be flown in and dropped at a strategic point in less than an hour."

"The army will open fire!"

Now it was Beffort's turn to remain silent. For the second time since the affair in San Francisco[24], Madame Atomos had succeeded in pitting Americans against one another. Today, things were more serious. Everything was happening in an overpopulated area, already on the edge of severe unrest, and the smallest spark could light the fuse.

"I believe," Soblen suddenly spoke up, "that there's a third solution."

---

[24] See *Madame Atomos Strikes at the Head* in *Miss Atomos*.

"Tell us, doc," Beffort said.

"Just now you said that with a simple phone call, Washington could drop troops at a strategic point. Instead of that, why not drop two or three tons of food, clothes and fuel on the demonstrators? Basically, that's what they're asking for, isn't it?"

Beffort, Graham and Sullivan stood agape. Then the governor snapped out of it and ran to the phone. By the time he had hung up, he knew that 50 cargo planes with full loads were taking off from various airports in the neighboring states. If all went well, tons of food, clothes and fuel would be dropped over the demonstrators within the next hours.

"Esmond is only a few miles from Providence. Let's hope that the planes will arrive in time... Sullivan, can you check to see where the mob is right now?"

Sullivan left the room, got on the radio and returned quickly, with a long face. "Esmond is being sacked," he said, breathless. "I got through to police headquarters, but they're under siege by thousands of rioters who are looking for weapons. They've already cleaned out the local gun stores and seized cars and trucks. Their final goal is Providence, more particularly the governor's mansion."

Graham jumped up. His face was pale, but he made no comment.

"Their number is only increasing," Sullivan continued. "I'm afraid the parachutes of supplies won't be enough to stop them. After this latest update, it might even be too late to negotiate with them. The rioters are aware of their strength. They know that the army won't be too pleased to stand against them and the government in Washington won't be too quick to treat them as enemies. In short, a civil war looks inevitable!"

Beffort gritted his teeth as he went to open a window. The cold immediately penetrated the room and snow flurries splattered on the floor. Outside, cars were having trouble getting around. The pedestrians were still wandering in the streets in spite of the late hour; they slipped and sunk up to their knees in the thick layer of snow that covered everything. "What we can't do," he said, "nature will. If this bad weather persists, no one will be able to move anywhere in Rhode Island except by crawling on their bellies. Let's wait."

As for the rioters, it was not as easy as the Esmond police report claimed. In fact, everyone was dying of hunger, cold and fatigue and really fighting to save their life. There were women and young children among them—those lovely infants whom they had to feed as best they could, protect from the cold and take everywhere in their arms or in strollers.

It was crazy how many births there had been in Rhode Island over the last six months. Of course, the babies had been conceived before Madame Atomos' intervention, but because of their small size (that is, the size they had the day they were born), it looked like there was an entire generation spontaneously born in the last few minutes.

In the snow and bitter cold, all these little ones wailed and fidgeted and added more worry to the anguish of the parents, who were already overwhelmed by the circumstances. Then the men turned into wolves; they had to protect their families. Forgetting that they had put themselves in the desperate situation, they accused the governor of not taking the necessary steps in time. As always, the mob paid no attention to the general interest, saw only individual issues, their own personal problems, and was obviously looking for a scapegoat. Now, Graham was all set up to take on the role and that is why the mob was marching on Providence.

Marching is maybe putting it nicely. *Crawling* is more like it because, just as Beffort had foreseen, raging nature started hitting them hard.

In Esmond, among the rioters as well as the inhabitants, there was panic. The attacked became attackers, matching blow for blow and coming out the better for it. During the night the battle turned to havoc, mostly one on one. An incredible free-for-all in which it was hard to know who was the enemy. Members on the same side were frequently pitted against each other.

In the north of the city, a gang had started a fire with the wreckage from barns and hangars and the flames had got out of control, quickly spreading to the closest buildings that were devoured recklessly while the fire fighters were stuck downtown.

Some buildings fell into the hands of the rioters after bloody brawls. They took over the apartments, emptied them of food and lit fires to fight against the cold. Now they had to defend their positions against those who were kept fighting in the streets with women and children. Small groups formed spontaneously and tried to survive by setting upon other groups, who were just as panicked and likewise trying to save their own lives.

Outside of Esmond, on the road leading to Providence, the mob formed again. They recognized one another there because they were going in the same direction with the same goal, but no one was sure that the individuals were actually the same ones who had come from the country a few hours earlier. In Esmond, everything was mixed up. A crazy brew of crowds whose hatred and desperation were the only point in common. An immigrant coming from Texas walked side by side with a native of Rhode Island, maybe after fighting with him, and needed to know nothing more because their suffering was shared.

This mob marched painfully slowly. It had cars, trucks and a bunch of other vehicles of all kinds, stolen in the first hours of battle, but the snow and cold were making them useless. At their head three big, fully loaded trucks were trying to open a passage. Their wheels dug through the fresh snow until they hit a layer of cold-hardened ground and slid to the sound of revving, wailing engines. Then the men got down onto the land swept by icy winds, pushed their heavy trucks for a few yards and climbed back in when their energy was spent. The trucks went on for a short while, got stuck again and everything started over.

Gas was getting lower in the tanks. The men's strength declined with their courage. But the storm kept on and even seemed to be getting stronger. At two in the morning, the three lead trucks were stuck on the open road and it was impossible to get them going again. One of them had run out of gas, another had fallen into a ditch and the last, which they tried to drive across the fields, was sunk up to its hubcaps in another ditch.

In the meantime, the cargo planes had accomplished the mission ordered by Washington. Unfortunately, because of the bad weather conditions, the parachutes were dropped rather far from the planned target, near Georgiaville, on a camp of calm, resigned immigrants. The miraculous manna stirred up their appetites, spurred on the hesitant and, as there was not enough food for everyone, they now fought over a crust of bread.

In the end, throughout the land, Madame Atomos was racking up points.

Owen Bernitz lowered the barrel of his paralyzing rifle and said, "Okay, Lucky, you can stop this old heap."

Lucky Simms turned into the courtyard of the Smith farm, cut the engine of the Jeep and pulled the handbrake. In the back of the car, Ralph Sutton and Art Baxter also lowered their arms. To get there, the four men of the Green Dragon Force had to clear a path through the hate-filled crowd that cluttered the roads and fields. The former killers were luckily cool-headed and did not use the submachine guns that were hidden under the waterproof seat covers at their feet.

In spite of everything, on their long trip from Providence to the Smith house, not far from Coventry, there were a few corpses and many bodies left prostrate in their wake. The paralyzing rifles had floored the men for 60 minutes, but the wheels of the Jeep always managed to avoid them. Still, Lucky had to force himself to limit the damage, knowing that you cannot make an omelet without cracking eggs.

Now, in the snow and bitter cold, Owen Bernitz was examining the apparently deserted farm. Here, too, there had been a fight. Even though the main buildings were intact, the minor structures had been reduced to ashes. The rioters must have attacked the Smiths while they were barricaded behind the thick walls of the farm, no doubt shooting back with a hunting rifle and managing to protect the house but not the livestock or other buildings.

A dozen frozen corpses were lying in the snow and the walls of the farm were riddled with bullets. The attack must have been heated and the defense very violent because no one had dared to inhabit the farm afterward.

Owen Bernitz went up to the solid front door. Art Baxter said to his back, "Watch out, Owen! The guy who's in there could snipe you right quick."

Owen nodded, but kept on, clutching his weapon between his frost-numbed hands. He banged on the door with the butt of his rifle and it opened, revealing an unexpected sight: the house had been pillaged, the Smiths murdered and the entire back of the house had collapsed along with a good part of the roof. Even though the front seemed intact, the living room and others looked directly out on the fields, blowing in the snow and cold all the way up to the front door where Owen Bernitz was standing.

In the middle of the ruins Bob Smith, his wife Jeanne and young John were taking their final rest. Owen chewed his cigar, mechanically closed the door and lumbered slowly back to the Jeep.

"Well?" Ralph Stutton asked.

Owen sat in the front seat, closed the canvas door and looked pensively at the two beams where snow flurries were spinning in the headlights. "Nobody's gonna give us a tip at the Smiths. Gonna have to deal with it on our own, boys."

"Okay," Baxter grumbled. "Where do we start?"

"Start by turning off the headlights," Owen said as he peered suspiciously into the night. "I figure they could try to pinch our wheels."

Lucky turned off the lights and grabbed his submachine gun. "This time we won't be giving it away, right?"

"Not enough time," Owen agreed. "You stay in your heap and fire at anything that moves. We'll go explore the area. If you have any trouble, just honk once or twice, got it?"

"Got it."

Owen Bernitz, Baxter and Stutton got out after grabbing their weapons and fanned out silently around the farm. Lucky watched them disappear into the darkness and turned to keep an eye on the immediate surroundings. The Jeep was an army vehicle borrowed from the base in Providence on Sullivan's orders. It was fitted with a two-way radio, so that Lucky only had to make one move to be touch with Beffort's HQ. The other members of the Green Dragon Force were crisscrossing the state in similar vehicles, so they, too, could get in contact with Beffort in case of an emergency. 300 men in teams of four had taken off, which meant 75 cars to comb a vast, incredibly overpopulated area. The men of the Green Dragon Force were handpicked tough guys, but the job they had to accomplish was overwhelming.

In any case, Owen Bernitz was not thinking of this as he stomped slowly through the snow. He simply told himself that it was a damned complicated business, whispering to himself in that colorful, though not very proper language of his. "Man, you're up shit creek. Digging up Mama-what's-her-name's batteries when it's nice out is no walk in the park, but in this mush, it's bullshit. I could walk on this snow without seeing anything, going round in circles for hours like an idiot. The boss said we gotta search in the trees... I think his head's in the clouds. They're too bare for Mama-what's-her-name to be sticking her dirty machines up there. No, I figure she was digging..."

He stopped to think about it. If he was right, it was obvious that Madame Atomos had not buried her devices in farmable land. Bernitz got off the field he was inspecting and went into the bushes, making a wide circle. He walked around for 30 minutes before running into Art

Baxter who was standing in front of a patch of soil where, strangely enough, the snow was melting before it touched the ground.

Chapter VIII

Eddy Witter had requested and received authorization to conduct a personal investigation alongside the research undertaken by the Green Dragon Force and the local FBI. Witter hated groping in the dark. For him, an investigation kicked off with the start of a trail and the trail here was in the Graham residence, in the person of the Japanese cook who had fled when Beffort first showed up.

Witter was finishing his search of the ground floor and was starting to give up hope when he found a door leading to the cellar. From the beginning, a fact that no one seemed to have paid any attention to had struck him: how did the Japanese cook get off the property without being noticed by the police who were watching the premises? It was surrounded by a fence that could not be climbed without a ladder. So, Witter had made sure that nothing like this was lying around the perimeter. Since the policemen on watch had not seen anyone, the cook's disappearance was a mystery.

Witter did not believe in miracles.

He turned on the light and went carefully down the stairs into the basement, unholstering his paralyzing pistol. The cellar was huge but uncluttered. Witter walked quietly, keeping on his guard, sidestepping a cabinet with dusty files, until he finally came to a window that looked out onto the big yard. It was pretty much in the middle of the cellar and through it he could hear the low rumble of the city that was still in turmoil in spite of the late hour. Except for this noise, Witter heard nothing and felt a little like he was in a vault in the middle of a cemetery.

Witter was not a particularly emotional person, so he wondered why this macabre idea came to him and then almost right away noticed the smell. A sickly smell, barely perceptible, but very real, floating around him though he could not determine the source.

Moving silently, the G-man walked around the cellar, but he did not see anything out of the ordinary. He returned to the bottom of the stairs and sniffed the air. He could not smell the nauseating stench there, so he reasoned that it had to be coming from the other end of the basement.

He trampled over the hardened earth again until he came to the back wall and realized the odor was a lot stronger. Nevertheless, the place was completely empty; there was not even a door or a window. He went through the motions of feeling along the wall, to put his mind at ease and also because the odor had to be coming from somewhere. His fingers ran along the coarse concrete and felt a small protrusion. He followed it and found that it formed a circle around two and a half feet in diameter, perfectly invisible in the darkness at the back of the cellar. The G-man sparked his lighter to see the line better. The clean circle was too perfect to be a natural formation in the concrete.

He hit the center of the circle with the butt of his gun and heard a solid sound. He repeated the action all over the strange target but in vain. It did not sound hollow. Anyone else but Witter would certainly have given up. But the G-man was stubborn, incredibly persistent. In fighting Madame Atomos he had learned how much the diabolical woman loved basements and tunnels and how ingeniously she knew how to hide the entrances.

And the Japanese cook had disappeared to quickly, without a trace, as if swallowed up by the earth…

Patiently Witter started looking for some anomaly on the ground, walls and ceiling of the cellar. If the circle was an entrance to a tunnel, there had to be a way to open it from both sides. In 30 minutes, the G-man had shaken everything that could be shaken, pushed a countless number of bumps and tried turning things sticking out of the wall but without any effect. Finally, he sat down and had the sudden realization that a cook is usually in the kitchen and this room was located exactly above the cellar and...

He dashed up the stairs to the ground floor and searched the kitchen feverishly. He found what he was looking for in the broom closet: a switch, half-hidden by a shelf with a wire running into the wall. Witter flipped it and ran back downstairs. He got into the cellar at the exact moment when the concrete circle was quietly swinging open into a narrow tunnel.

Witter entered without a second thought and was suffocated by the hideous odor that came from the remains of a decomposed dog whose skull had been crushed. It had been dead for at least six months. Witter stepped over it. When the round door automatically closed, he was startled to find himself in total darkness. He sparked his lighter and walked as quickly as the flickering flame allowed. The tunnel was solidly propped up, but the earth was still crumbling in spots, forming small mounds on the ground where footprints had been left, which were obviously those of the Japanese cook taking flight. The prints were of a small shoe, light and faint, as if the woman were running.

He continued down the tunnel clutching the butt of his paralyzing pistol. After 50 yards he found a ladder leaning against the end of the tunnel. Still cautious, he extinguished the flame and climbed the rungs in the dark until his head hit a big, heavy piece of wood. It felt like it could have been a trapdoor. Metal bands, hinges, etc. Witter listened hard, but heard no sound. He pushed the trap open with his shoulders. A second later he was in a small room that looked like an old storage closet, feebly lit by a small window.

The G-man slowly closed the trapdoor and climbed onto a rickety stool to look through the grimy pane. The first thing he saw was the source of light: an old oil lamp sitting on the floor. Then his gaze drifted over to a bed on which a woman was calmly sleeping, a brunette, rather young and clearly Asian.

Witter cracked a smile. By extraordinary luck, if he was not mistaken, he had just found Governor Graham's cook!

Miles away from Providence, in the snowstorm, Owen Bernitz and Art Baxter stood dumbfounded before the small patch of earth on which the snow was not falling. A 6 X 9 foot triangle, dry and warm, still covered with green grass, like it was the middle of July!

"In this weather it kind of makes you want to lie down and take a nap, eh?" Baxter whispered.

"Better not," Owen grumbled, chewing his stub of cigar, "you might turn to ashes."

Baxter stepped back and squatted down. "You think we've hit the jackpot?"

Owen avoided the question. "Go to the car and tell the others to get back here with the explosives. When we've blown this thing to bits, I'll give you my answer."

Baxter stood up and hustled away into the night. Five minutes later the Jeep engine came purring nearby and stopped. There was a moment of silence, then Art Baxter, Ralph Stutton and Lucky Simms appeared carrying crowbars, a shovel, a pickaxe, sticks of dynamite and a big electric lamp.

"Hey," Stutton shouted, "have we got it this time?"

"Shut up!" Owen raged. "When you're gonna pull a trick like this on Mama Atomos, better just keep quiet. Gimme a crowbar instead of opening your trap."

Stutton understood that he was serious and gave him a crowbar. Owen took it and slowly swung it at the green grass. A few clods flew up revealing the oily soil that a strange radiation made phosphorescent. Owen yanked away the iron bar and jumped backward, his face turned pale. "Get back!" he ordered. "We gotta tell the boss before touching this thing. Lucky, get on the horn."

Lucky slipped between the bare branches, jumped into the Jeep and warmed up the radio before Owen and the two others joined him.

"Well?" Owen asked impatiently. "We're waiting."

Lucky gave his signal and received an immediate response from Providence. All of a sudden he was in direct contact with Smith Beffort, to whom he explained the discovery that his team had just made.

"There's certainly no danger," Beffort assured him. "The most important thing is to destroy whatever's buried under that grass. Have you probed it at all?"

"No, we wanted your advice first."

"You have it! Blow the thing up and call me back!"

"Okay. Out."

Lucky sign off and got out of the Jeep. Art Baxter was smiling. "Maybe there's no danger, okay?"

Owen shrugged his shoulders, went back to the grass patch and started digging without saying a word. Lucky and Stutton joined in and then Baxter got to work, too. The phosphorescent dirt crunched under the shovel, crumbled under the pickaxe and crowbar and lost its luminous glow as soon as it was removed from the ground. After ten minutes of toil, the pickaxe that Stutton was swinging hit a metal surface. It sounded like a gong and it petrified the four men.

"We're there," Owen whispered, his brow sweating in spite of the cold. "Now we have to go slowly." He took the shovel and went at the dirt around the metal plate, which shined menacingly. The big lamp cast a pale, sideways light on the ditch and suddenly revealed six thin rods sticking up like antennas, which were apparently at ground level before the men began digging. It was clearly these rods that were emitting the mysterious, health-giving waves that the inhabitants of the state were feeling. The device that Bernitz saw could not have covered a very large territory. There were others somewhere that they would have to find and destroy one by one without taking the time to understand how they worked.

Owen redoubled his efforts until the plate was completely uncovered. It looked like the hood of a car, but there was no sound underneath it. He straightened up and said, "All yours, boys. Dig around the sides and I'll prepare the fireworks."

Lucky, Stutton and Baxter took their places. Owen took four sticks of dynamite and tied each fuse to a longer one. He was knotting everything off when he felt an imperceptible change in the air. It was as fleeting as the shadow of the sun, but Owen felt something real and disturbing. He looked around, but could see no change. Lucky, Stutton and Baxter were still digging in the dim halo of the electric lamp. The cold was just as bitter. Maybe the snow was falling a little more lightly…

All of a sudden Owen noticed that the six antennas were slowly sinking into the metal hood. At the same time, its luminosity was growing weaker and weaker. All this was happening very slowly, without any sudden change, so that Owen's partners, who were right on top of it, were still unaware.

"Let it go!"

Stutton, Baxter and Lucky turned to Owen. "What's up with you" Baxter groaned. "We're almost done."

Stutton and Lucky did not say a word. They dropped their tools and hopped out of the hole fast, which told volumes about how nervous they were. Baxter laughed. "Hey, don't panic now , boys!"

Owen snatched up a submachine gun and aimed it at Baxter. "Come over here, Art," he roared. "Right now!"

Baxter saw that Owen was not joking. He jumped out of the hole leaving his crowbar behind and followed Owen and the two others who were backtracking to the Jeep.

"Good God, are you going to tell us what's going on?"

A whistling shot out in the night, screeching like an alarm, and a thin tongue of fire danced over the hole.

"Get down!" Owen shouted.

The reflexes acquired during their training came instantly into play and the four men dove for cover behind the nearest embankment. A few seconds passed in utter silence and Baxter lifted his head, looked at Owen. "What were you expecting?"

"Shut up and get down!"

Baxter hunched back down and felt the ground vibrate beneath him. The very same second a huge explosion shook the air and a burning wind blasted over their heads, sweeping away the snow and frying the trees and bushes. A mighty tornado, full of red-hot shrapnel, destroyed everything in its path.

Then silence fell again, the air quieted down and the snow stopped swirling. Owen stood up, his ears humming, and looked around. For over 200 yards in all directions, everything had been blown away. The Jeep was lying in a ditch, wheels in the air and its canvas top was sailing off, waddling ridiculously over the ravaged ground.

"Well, I'll be!" Baxter spit out.

Owen walked up the hole where Madame Atomos' device had been buried and saw a huge crater, totally empty. The big lamp, miraculously spared, cast its pale light toward the sky. Owen picked it up and searched for the crowbars. He found only a thin fragment, half-melted and twisted like hairpin.

"Scary," Lucky stated calmly.

Owen nodded and continued his inspection. He was searching for some debris from the device, a trace of some kind that could prove to Beffort, materially, that he and his men were not dreaming. But his efforts were useless. The machine obviously had the power to automatically self-destruct when it was unearthed. Madame Atomos' final precaution.

Since Beffort and Soblen had stolen the makings of the paralyzing ray, the sinister woman was becoming more careful, preferring to disintegrate her inventions rather than have them fall into the hands of the Green Dragon Force.

But it was a two-edged sword. In fact, there was no need to carry around explosives anymore. They only had to spot the places where there was no snow, dig until the telescopic antennas started going back into their housing... and then clear off—a substantial improvement for which Madame Atomos was directly, though unintentionally, responsible.

Chapter IX

In order to avoid any resistance, Eddy Witter had plunged the Japanese woman into an even deeper sleep by hitting her with a quick shot from his paralyzing gun. Afterward he got in touch with Beffort's HQ and Sullivan sent an ambulance to transport the woman.

Now she was slowly waking up on a bed in the infirmary. They already knew that her name was Yukiko Kimura and that she was born in Tokyo 30 years ago and had been living in the United States for eight months. Her passport was in order, her visa good for four years and she had her smallpox vaccination certificate.

"Nothing to complain about at first sight," Beffort commented.

"Except that she left Graham's house through the basement where there were the decomposed remains of a dog," Sullivan said. "In fact, this dog?"

Witter lit a cigarette and watched Yukiko Kimura blinking her eyes. "It belonged to Graham."

"When did it disappear?"

"Graham claims that he can't remember exactly, but he thinks it was a little before his wife and servants left. We can't forget that at that time Graham was pretty much under the influence of Madame Atomos."

"That remains to be seen," Sullivan said. "In theory, this Yukiko Kimura worked for Madame Atomos and probably has a strong hypnotic power that she used to keep Graham muzzled. We can even suppose she was responsible for the departure of Mrs. Graham and the rest of them, but if she doesn't talk, nobody will be able to prove a thing."

Beffort motioned to the G-man to be quiet because the Japanese woman was sitting up groggily. She looked at the nurse with a dilated eye and then stared at the three men who were sitting at her bedside. In perfect English, she asked, "Where am I?"

It was so typically commonplace that Beffort almost smiled. He was betting with himself that the banalities would continue. He won his bet when she said, "What happened to me?"

"You fell off your bed," Beffort answered with a straight face.

"I'm sorry…"

"You fell off your bed," Beffort repeated, deadpan, "and unfortunately knocked over the oil lamp on the floor. The fire spread quickly. You owe your safety to the lucky passing of a patrol car. You're not even injured."

"In that case," the woman muttered suspiciously, "why was I taken to this hospital?"

"You were sleeping so deeply," Beffort assured her, "that it worried us. Well, we're wondering if someone didn't slip you a narcotic before knocking over the lamp to make it look like an accident. Hmm… That's a little wild, but it wasn't a natural sleep, was it?"

The woman's gaze fixed on the clock hanging on the wall and became very thoughtful. She obviously did not know that Witter was the cause of her deep sleep, so she must have been asking herself all kinds of questions about it.

"Moreover," Beffort added wickedly, "considering that your door was locked from the inside, our men were wondering how your attacker got in and out of your room. Then they discovered an underground tunnel that connected your closet to a nearby cellar."

The Japanese remained as silent as stone, but her eyes looked disturbed. "An underground tunnel?"

Beffort's smile spread as he said, amiably, "The most extraordinary thing is that the tunnel led to the house of your ex-employer, Governor Graham. Funny, isn't it?"

Curiously and very unexpectedly, Yukiko Kimura also smiled, which made her very seductive and exuded a magnetic attraction that none of the three men were expecting. In her persuasive voice she said, "I can explain it to you. In truth, I work for Madame Atomos, who ordered me to control the actions of Governor Graham. The tunnel was supposed to allow me to escape in case of danger, which I did when you showed up, Mr. Beffort."

"You're confessing very quickly," Beffort kept his voice friendly. "That's surprising."

"Why deny it? You're all very intelligent and it's obvious that you already know what to make of my role in the affair. I hope that you'll admit, however, that I'm not so responsible when you learn that Madame Atomos threatened me with death to get me to help her. All things considered, I'm a victim, too."

Beffort, Witter and Sullivan figured, personally, that she was right.

"You know, Yukiko Kimura continued, "I was living peacefully in Tokyo when Madame Atomos got hold of me. I came to the United States against my will, only in order to escape the threat that loomed over me. I'm not the first. Before me, there'd been Miss Atomos, Catherine Lomakine[25] and others whose names I don't

---

[25] See *Madame Atomos Sows Terror* and *Miss Atomos* and *Miss Atomos vs. the KKK*.

know. No one works for the Atomos Organization of their own free will."

She interrupted herself, but kept smiling, keeping a close eye on the three men. Right away she saw that were beginning to suffer the effects of her hypnotic power. If all went well, she knew that they would not hesitate to throw themselves out of the window if she told them to.

"I'm just a poor woman," she went on in her monotone. "You shouldn't use your justice system against me. It's Madame Atomos that should be judged, provided that she really is the criminal you think she is... After all, she's just taking revenge... Her family was killed by the American atomic bombs dropped on Hiroshima and Nagasaki during the last world war..."

Smith Beffort perceived that Yukiko Kimura was about to put him and his partners to sleep, but he was already powerless to fight against the kind of cerebral numbness that was growing in him. It was a little like his brain was detached from his body and was becoming unable to control the situation soundly. A kind of local breakdown, spreading in certain brain cells whose sudden cessation was paralyzing his whole nervous system. In fact, Beffort felt like he was splitting in two. On one side was the man who liked what the Japanese woman was saying and on the other remained the Usual Beffort, but his resistance was weakening every second.

"Those thousands and thousands of dead," Yukiko Kimura was saying, "and hundreds of houses destroyed in a few seconds is the greatest crime of humanity. Japan was already defeated. That demonstration of power was useless, don't you think?"

Sullivan nodded and spoke in a faint voice, "It was useless and cruel."

"Not worthy of us," Witter mumbled.

As Beffort remained silent, the Japanese addressed him in particular because she was feeling an unusual resistance in him. "And you, Mr. Beffort?"

Beffort's muscles tightened up and he answered, despite himself, "It was, indeed, a great crime..." And then he added, "But there was a war."

Yukiko Kimura's eyes blazed. Madame Atomos was right to be wary of this man. He had a powerful will. No one had ever resisted Yukiko's power of persuasion. "Mr. Beffort, you're tired and you can't hold a coherent thought. Your friends will take you home. Get up, please."

The three men stood up.

Yukiko pointed to the fourth floor window and said, "Leave by that door."

At that precise moment, Dr. Soblen entered. He aimed his paralyzing rifle at the Japanese and pressed the trigger. There was no explosion or flame, but Yukiko Kimura was jolted and fell back on her pillow. Soblen put down his weapon and jumped in front of the three men who were walking slowly toward the window. He started hollering and shaking them mercilessly.

"Wake up! It's not a door but a window! Come on, wake up!"

Just like Governor Graham a few hours earlier, Beffort looked like he was coming out of a coma. He shuddered, stared at the little doctor and said, "Doc, if it wasn't for you, I think we'd be goners."

Soblen smiled. "I was monitoring from the start, just like we agreed, Smith, remember... Anyway, right now we have proof of this woman's guilt. That's what you wanted, right?"

While these events were unfolding and the morning was approaching, the situation in Rhode Island and at its borders got worse. The hundreds of thousands of sick people being retained in Connecticut and Massachusetts by the army were close to considering their ban as a direct attack on their lives. Unaware that Rhode Island had been transformed into a witch's cauldron, they tried, in spite of all opposition, to break through the barricades that were cutting them off from the land where all suffering ceased.

In the snow and biting cold of the early hours, the army had to confront the attacks of veritable commando teams. The border was turning into a front where they were killing each other at close range. The troops, stuck between the immigrants and the rioters from neighboring states, had to be supplied with ammunition and food by parachutes. Washington had tried to bring in armored vehicles, but General Hiver stopped them in the middle of the countryside, bogged down in traffic jams that held them up surprisingly fast. And the officers and soldiers hated fighting against their fellow countrymen; they were in no hurry to get to the theater of operations.

On the sea in Rhode Island Sound, Admiral Greens' fleet had, unfortunately, no other alternative but to open fire. Every minute saw a racing speedboat or simple dinghy trying to break the blockade, not stopping despite the warnings. In the ghostly gleam of the onboard spotlights, they had to sink them, pick up the survivors and care for the wounded. A rather unsavory job that disgusted the crew, who were already exhausted by the endless vigil.

As to the state itself, it was chaos. In spite of the intense cold and hunger, no one was dying. In this, Madame Atomos' devices performed their roles admirably, protecting the population against all natural attacks. Nevertheless, if a natural death was no longer possible, nothing could stop a bullet from penetrating bodies or fire from burning flesh.

They were battling here, too. For a little heat, a little food, a tattered blanket...

In only one place in the territory had things gone back to normal. Order had just been restored in Coventry, in a rather large square of land that surrounded the Smith farm where everything had begun.

After the stupendous explosion that had literally disintegrated the device discovered by Owen Bernitz and his team, the four men had flipped the Jeep back onto its wheels. Following Beffort's orders, Lucky got in touch with Providence right away. He informed them that the devices were rigged with a self-destruction program, so all they had to do was dig them up, after which the six antennas would go back into the hood and trigger the explosion. Owen Bernitz on the headphones was sure that the radio operator was passing on the information to the other teams of the Green Dragon Force and giving orders to depart.

Now, the Jeep had reached the suburbs of Coventry. On the road, the silence and stillness of the crowds huddled together in the fields and on the roadsides had struck Owen and his men. Once in town, they finally understood that this passiveness was due to the breakdown of the machine.

They themselves felt the cold bite harder and the effects of fatigue. But they were in good health and so reacting normally to the sudden lack of health-giving waves, which was not the case for the immigrants. Deprived of the kind of permanent painkiller they had enjoyed since their arrival in Rhode Island, the sick were immediately plunged back into their former condition. They recognized with horror that they were not cured—their sickness had simply been sleeping.

The awakening of ills happened in a flash and it seemed that the accumulated delay in the development of the sickness since passing over the border came back all at once by the return to normal—the normal that had always governed human existence.

Therefore, everywhere within the perimeter surrounding the Smith farm hundreds of sick people dropped dead, giving up the ghost with unheard-of suddenness, as if they were mowed down by invisible gunfire.

Owen Bernitz and his team saw very quickly that this corner of Rhode Island had more dead than living inhabitants and the survivors would be too troubled to think about fighting or even just to survive. Passiveness succeeded aggressiveness and the one was no better than the other.

"If they don't start moving a little," Owen grumbled through his unlit cigar stub, "the cold and hunger are gonna get the better of them before sunrise."

"You wanna help them, Owen?"

"No time. Our job is to find the other contraptions of Mama Atomos. We have to get them dug up as soon as possible. That's what the boss said… except now we're searching blind."

Ralph Stutton leaned over the back of the seat and said, "Not as much as you think, Owen. As long as we see the dead, we're inside a circle that was controlled by the device we just destroyed. After, when we meet up with the rioters again, that'll mean we entered a zone with waves from another device. If we calculate the distance between the site of the last explosion and the edge of the other zone, we'll get a line from which we can draw a circumference. The center of the circumference will give us the position of the other device and then the whole installation network. If it's consistent, Rhode Island can be freed before noon."

Owen whistled. Stutton was a guy with a right good melon.

Chapter X

This time Yukiko Kimura had no chance of escaping by using her extraordinary hypnotic power. Just when the effect of the paralyzing ray was wearing off, Dr. Alan Soblen injected her with a needle full of a strong dose of scopochloralose. This tried and true mix of scopolamine and chloralose was one of the best weapons of the FBI and CIA. Thanks to this product, the most stubborn will would automatically reveal what torture could not have got out of them. Yukiko Kimura could not resist.

Beffort pulled a chair up to the bed in which the Japanese woman was lying and asked the first question: "How long have you been working for Madame Atomos?"

The woman did not hesitate for a second; she answered in a weak voice, "Since the beginning."

"Were you in Atomos City?"

"No. I belong to a team of specialists who performed research on the island in the Pacific."

"What's the name of this island?"

"We call it Atomia."

"Where is it located?"

"Off the coast of Hawaii."

"More precisely?" Beffort insisted.

"Off the coast of Hawaii," Yukiko Kimura repeated.

Dr. Soblen interjected, "Drop that question, Smith. She doesn't know anything else about it."

Beffort nodded and moved on to the second part of the interrogation. "What happened to Mrs. Graham and the governor's servants?"

"I was in charge of persuading them to leave, which I did easily. After that they were probably taken by Madame Atomos. Since the destruction of the City, we've been short on staff. But I don't really know what fate Madame Atomos had planned for them."

Graham clenched his jaws and squeezed the bedposts, but he did not say a word. Beffort gave him a sympathetic look and then continued his questioning, forcing himself to keep his voice calm.

"You live in a house next door to the governor's. This house belongs to a Mrs. Bernheim whom no one has heard from for around one year. Do you know what became of her?"

"I don't know who she is. When I arrived in Rhode Island, I had orders to live in the house and await the start of Operation Sweet Death."

"Did Madame Atomos give you the signal?"

"No. I've never seen Madame Atomos."

Beffort looked at Dr. Soblen, who was waving him to continue. It was useless to question the woman any further about Madame Atomos, who was very careful to preserve her safety so that no one could say that they had ever met her face to face. Women who more or less looked like her played her part on several occasions. One of them had, perhaps, really been the real Madame Atomos, but this was not certain—it was merely a guess.

"What is Operation Slow Death?"

Yukiko Kimura balked and everyone understood that the effect of the drug was wearing off. The woman was fighting against the fog in her brain, trying desperately to take control of her will. The doctor reacted immediately. He filled a syringe, leaned over the woman and gave her a new injection of scopochloralose. Yukiko Kimura winced but gave in quickly.

"What is Operation Sweet Death?" Beffort repeated. "And when did it start?"

"It hasn't started," the Japanese said, to the great astonishment of her audience. "At the moment, the devices installed throughout the state are emitting health-giving waves to make Rhode Island an earthly paradise. This is only the debut of Operation Slow Death, which is supposed to unfold in two, totally opposite phases. The first should attract a maximum population to Rhode Island. According to our forecast, the state should hold half the population of the USA by the end of the month. And that's when the devices will inverse their emissions and send off a series of deadly, supersonic waves that will eliminate every trace of life in Rhode Island. The government of the United States will not be able to dispose of the millions of corpses in time and epidemics will inevitably break out and spread like wildfire across America. Madame Atomos and her computers figure that the USA will be turned into a desert before the end of March."

Beffort ran his tongue over his dry lips. So, that was how Madame Atomos had decided to pass into action. For years she was literally playing cat and mouse with the United States, delaying her vengeance in order to savor it better, plunging the Americans into the most revolting panic with utmost cruelty and then stepping back by taking away their last hope, which her operation embodied. Right now and probably since the destruction of Atomos City, the terrible woman wanted to finish things off.

Yukiko Kimura was telling the truth. If providence did not get in the way of Madame Atomos' plans, the United States would become, in a short time, a huge cemetery!

Dr. Soblen took off his glasses, automatically dried the lens and with a worried look said, "So, Yukiko Kimura's confession has taught us nothing that we didn't already know. Madame Atomos remains unknown and keeps her Pacific hideout secret…"

"An island off the coast of Hawaii," Witter cut in. "It shouldn't be impossible to find."

Beffort shrugged. "For now that's secondary. Before anything, we have to keep these deadly devices planted all over Rhode Island from doing their duty. Where are we with this, Sullivan?"

"Owen Bernitz, as you know, found one of the machines around the Smith farm. The discovery was made easier by the snowfall because the place where the thing was buried was dry and green and melted all the snow. With their information my men have determined that each device should cover an area with a diameter of approximately 16 miles. This means that only a dozen machines are controlling the conditions of life in all of Rhode Island. Moreover, by a simple calculation, we know their approximate positions. In all probability, we'll be rid of these devices today. But this depends solely on the men of the Green Dragon Force."

Sullivan's tone alarmed Beffort.

"Why do you sound so reluctant?"

"Frankly, Beffort, I doubt your boys can get there without a lot of problems. The latest news is that the roads are impassable. And Rhode Island is in a revolution. Armed gangs are pouring through the countryside and infesting the towns. Whenever they can take a car, they don't hesitate to kill its occupants."

"Don't worry about that," Beffort responded. "My boys weren't born yesterday and they have a pretty powerful arsenal to fight off any assaults. What time is it?"

Soblen looked at his watch. "Almost 7 o'clock."

Beffort pointed at Yukiko Kimura who was still under the influence of the drug. "Tie this woman up tight and don't let her put the guards to sleep. We're going to launch a counter-attack."

Soblen's eyes widened. "What do you mean by that, Smith?"

Beffort shook his finger. "Never to my knowledge has Madame Atomos put all her trust in her machines. In previous affairs there was always a servant of the Atomos Organization nearby. Now, we have to keep our enemy from learning too quickly that we're trying to destroy her machines, otherwise she'll figure out a new method of death to reach her goal."

"Right," Soblen agreed, "but will you tell me how you can recognize a member of the Organization?"

Beffort leaned over Yukiko Kimura, parted her hair and showed the famous half-moon scar. "Motor-brain, doc! Nothing new as far as the main form of persuasion that Madame Atomos uses."

Soblen did not hide his surprise. "How long have you known?"

"It was more of a feeling than a certainty," Beffort confessed, "but this woman's behavior wasn't completely normal. And her hypnotic power is far beyond human capabilities. Yukiko Kimura is being remote-controlled. We have to find and destroy the local Great Brain that is guiding her."

Soblen sat down. "Wow!" he exclaimed. "You come to the damnedest conclusions!"

"I've had a year to think about it, doc," Beffort replied.

"Me, too…"

"Yes, but you don't have at hand a subject as remarkable as my wife! Don't forget that Mie was Miss Atomos, that she was under orders of the Great Brain and that her subconscious is full of memories that she doesn't even know about. During the night, these memories escape her. I take due note of them, that's all."

"Well," Soblen said, "the scopochloralose?"

"Ineffective, doc. Yukiko Kimura was drugged physically, but her motor-brain was in perfect working order. She told us what the Great Brain dictated to her. Nevertheless, our trial will have been useful in the sense that this woman's eyes and ears couldn't transmit our conversation. So, Madame Atomos still doesn't know that we've spotted her devices."

"The one in Coventry blew up," Soblen recalled.

"It could have been an isolated incident," Beffort retorted, "and Madame Atomos won't necessarily deduce that her whole system has been found out. But we have to act fast. Between 9 and 10 a.m. we'll take advantage of the usual hour of neutralization of the Organization members. We'll have to interrogate Yukiko Kimura again. Depending on the answers we get, we'll either keep her prisoner or free her in the hope that she can lead us to one of Madame Atomos' hideouts."

"Okay!" Witter said. "Until 9 o'clock, what can we do to further things along?"

"Not much, unfortunately," Beffort moaned, "except keep up to date on the results of my men. Let's start by calling Owen Bernitz."

The Jeep that Bernitz was in charge of was driving deeper and deeper into the danger zone. To fulfill its second mission, it had to get to Clayville and search for the device that was filling the region with health-giving waves. The problem was that the rioters there were particularly lethal. The Jeep had already braved a lot of gunfire and it was miraculous that none of the four men were injured.

Of course, Bernitz, Baxter and Stutton had used their paralyzing rifles freely, thus creating a certain panic among their assailants, but the weapons' reserves were running low before their eyes.

Lucky, who was driving, summed up the situation in a few words, "If this continues, we'll have to use the submachine guns."

There was no need to say more for each of them understand that it would be adding fuel to the fire. As long as the paralyzing rays were working, with no sound and no flame but with fantastic efficiency, as was their way, the rioters would fall back in disorder. But when it came to conventional weapons, they would understand that the passengers in the Jeep had no supernatural powers and they would attack in force.

Bernitz and his team were at risk of being flooded by the mobs without even the possibility of a quick retreat because of the terrain over which they were driving. Also, the storm had not let up. The snow was piling up everywhere, leveling the countryside, wiping out roads and blurring signposts so that the ride was turning slowly into an exploration.

"If only we knew exactly where we were going," Bernitz grumbled.

Baxter looked up. "According to the compass, Clayville is straight ahead. Our destination is a little farther north."

"How far?"

"Two or three miles is all. But we'd do better to side-skirt the town to avoid getting hit hard."

Bernitz spit out his cigar, which had been reduced to a plug of tobacco and observed, "To avoid any obstacle, gotta know where it is and we can't see anything in this mess. Good thing Lucky has cat's eyes!"

Lucky said nothing. The wipers were barely sweeping off the packs of snow forming on the windshield. Most of the time he had to drive with his head sticking out of the window. From time to time he spied a telegraph pole, saw the spectral form of a post surge up in the dull glare of the headlights and he figured that he was still on the right road, probably the 102...

Fortunately the night was over. A grey strip was already appearing in the east. Only a few minutes before the darkness would disappear completely.

Lucky pushed the Jeep for 100 yards or so and the radio started crackling. Owen put on the headphones and heard a distant voice signing in: "Car 7 calling G.D.F. Clayville sector... Car 7 calling G.D.F."

G.D.F. was the code for the Green Dragon Force; car 7 was Brady Castleman's. "G.D.F. here," Owen barked into the microphone, "car 1."

"Owen?"

"What are you doing over there, Brady?"

"I just came across a patch of dry land still covered with grass, but there's something I don't like. Right next to it..."

"What?"

"I don't know, Owen. It's like a little tank. A kind of barrel with treads... in your report to the boss, did you talk about this kind of thing?"

"What, you're afraid of a barrel?"

"Uh..."

"Brady? Hey, Brady?"

Lucky leaned over, listened and said, "Let it go. There's nobody on the line."

They did not know it yet, but a mile to the north Brady Castleman's Jeep had just been disintegrated.

Chapter XI

All this happened just when Beffort decided to get in touch with Bernitz' Jeep and the radio post in Providence picked up the short conversation between the leaders of cars 1 and 7.

Beffort, Soblen and Witter entered the radio room. The operator slowly took off his headphones and said, "You're just in the nick of time, Mr. Beffort. Something very strange is happening around Clayville..."

He repeated what Brady Castleman had said. Beffort furrowed his brow. "A barrel with treads?" He was flabbergasted.

"That's the description Castleman gave. After that he didn't answer Owen Bernitz. Right now Bernitz is trying to reestablish contact, but Jeep 7 is silent."

The operator gave his signal and got an immediate response, then he left the radio to Smith Beffort. "Hey, Owen, any problems?"

"Not for me, boss," the tinny voice of Bernitz came back, "but I think Brady hit a snag. You know anything about this barrel on treads?"

"No... Needless to say, you don't know where Castleman was?"

"Roundabout, he can't be too far from us. Baxter thinks he's where we told him to wait for us, which is where we figure the second device is in the northwest sector. That's logical. Brady based his search on the coordinates given by the office in Providence. What I can't figure out is why there wasn't another team in the area."

"Another team? Owen, hold on..."

The operator knew what Beffort wanted. He held out a folder with the most recent positions of the Green Dragon Force Jeeps. Out of 75 cars, 50 were still active. In the northwest sector, which Bernitz thought was abandoned, four vehicles were heading toward Clayville. Elsewhere they were looking for other devices.

Beffort got back on the radio and advised Bernitz to get in contact with the four teams in his sector. Brady Castleman's sudden silence could have been due to a breakdown. There was no need to go overboard. But there was no need to take pointless risks either. One organized action was called for. In case of strong opposition, Bernitz had orders to inform Providence, which would alert the air force.

A barrel, even armored, stood no chance against two or three tons of well aimed bombs.

At 8 a.m., in the snow and gloomy light of the eerie day, Bernitz' Jeep met up with the other four teams in the northwest sector. They formed a small but well-armed convoy that the rioters were content to watch from a distance. With no worries about this, the men of the Green Dragon Force could crisscross the area extending north out of Clayville. At 8:30, car 45 rounded up its team members.

Owen got out of the Jeep and look through his binoculars at the barren piece of land squeezed in between two ditches. The highway passed by at a distance. Farther on there was a pine forest. Between the tract of land and Bernitz the falling snow was filling up the double grooves left by the tires of Brady Castleman's Jeep. But as far as the eye could see, there was no vehicle.

Bernitz panned his binoculars all around until he finally spotted a strange object sitting near the ditch. It was half-covered with snow but was unquestionably in the form of a barrel. The tire tracks that Bernitz had noticed stopped right in front of the barren land where Madame Atomos' second device was obviously buried... but there were none coming back.

"'Bout says it all, huh?" Lucky said.

Owen Bernitz lowered his binoculars. "Disintegrator gun. Bet your bottom dollar."

Stutton was nervous as he stepped up. "Do you think this spot is unsafe, Owen?"

"We're 600 yards away," Bernitz replied coldly, "and its range is only 500."

The men got out of the Jeeps that were lined up on the edge of the field. Their faces betrayed their anxiety. They had been driving all night without a minute of rest and fatigue was starting to act on their nerves. And it was obvious that Brady Castleman and his three men had got themselves killed. See, little Brady was a tough guy with a long-standing, solid reputation. He would not be easy to trick. He was careful, crafty and extremely clever.

Moreover, the situation was creating a tension that was hard for the men to bear. They were not fighting against Madame Atomos but against her diabolical inventions. They did not have an enemy before them but a whole array of arms with unpredictable effects. Now Owen Bernitz was talking about a disintegrator gun and was sure that its range was 500 yards. Figuring there was a margin of safety of around 100 yards... but that was only his opinion. Others did not see things that way. On the field, which was totally white because of the snow, distances were hard to estimate. And the disintegrator gun could have been improved!

Owen felt the men of his commando team were dreading the next step of action and he fully agreed with them. It was impossible to fight against the disintegrator ray when it was shot by an entirely mechanized apparatus because in this case the paralyzing rifles were taken out of play.

"Lucky," he ordered, "tell the boss that we're at a standstill. No way to go and dig up the device. Madame Atomos has mobilized a robot-guard that can disintegrate anything within a range of 500 yards. Give him the exact location of that damn machine and get us some bombers. We can direct their fire from here."

Lucky let out an involuntary sigh of relief and headed for the Jeep.

Very far from there, in Oregon, Mie Azusa and her son were just waking up. Around the bungalow, located in a big suburb of Burns, FBI agents were keeping watch. It was cold, gray and a little icy rain had been drizzling over the area for 24 hours. The countryside was silent and the nearby road not very busy. The G-men did not talk much; they were constantly watching the surroundings through their binoculars. Charles Hyde, who was in charge, kept in touch with Washington, giving hourly updates about the situation to J.E.E. He had a two-way, self-powered radio for this, which a power outage in the area would not put out of service.

Everything had been prepared to answer a surprise attack by Madame Atomos, but the federal agents knew that there were never enough precautions when it came to fighting the terrible Japanese woman. Their behavior revealed their worry. Everyone kept his finger on the trigger and showed a hardened face that no smile ever softened. Periodically, they called for a listening period.

Total silence in the house. If little Bob was crying, Mie had to shut herself up with him in the small closet that was entirely soundproofed. Then the federal agents would proceed with the inspections imposed by the security: listen to the ground for the digging of a tunnel, identification of the so-called neighborhood sounds: humming machines coming from a factory located a mile to the north, squawking poultry from a nearby farm, passage of a train every 30 minutes on the Burns-Newport line; a permanent tracking of the few vehicles driving on the side road from Izee to Burns; constant spotting of airliners flying over the area, etc.

At 3 in the morning, an unidentified vehicle stopped on the secondary road. An alert was given right away and two G-men were immediately dispatched to the place in one of the five Chevrolets at the service of the group. Stuck in the middle of nowhere, the suspicious Buick only held a couple of lovers. Charles Hyde still took the young couple's identifications, their addresses and the car's registration number before ordering them to move on.

At 8 a.m. the detector captured a series of faint sounds among the so-called neighborhood noises. They came from the ground or underground; in any case they were quite disturbing. Another general alert; again a lightning fast move—a man in his yard was cutting down a dead tree with an axe before going to work.

All of this made for an insupportable environment and Mie was constantly on edge. Even though she was used to this kind of life, the young woman had become more timid since the birth of her son. The ex-Miss Atomos was just a mother jealously watching over her child whom Madame Atomos had sworn to kidnap. The circumstances—for the first time in a year—were particularly favorable to this kind of attempt: Smith Beffort, Alan Soblen, Owen Bernitz and the Green Dragon Force were busy in an endless battle at the other end of the country.

Obviously, Mie had confidence in the FBI protection, but she would have far preferred to have her husband next to her. Privately she was sorry that Yosho Akamatsu, the ace of the Japanese *Tokkoka*, had not yet shown up in this new affair because, except for Beffort, he was the most capable man to combat Madame Atomos and her formidable Organization.

At that very moment, the man whom Mie Azusa-Beffort was thinking about was stepping incognito off a plane at the airport in Burns. Bearded, wearing glasses and cheap old clothes, Akamatsu was unrecognizable.

He was not in Oregon by chance but at the request of the old fox J.E.E. who was more afraid than he liked to admit of a lightning quick attack by Madame Atomos against Mie Azusa-Beffort and her son. Coming directly from Tokyo, Akamatsu had already been informed about the events in Rhode Island and he supposed that Madame Atomos in this case could have wanted to engage in a tactic that fit with her one-year-old plans. For her, getting Mie back would be the finest prize for her vengeance, but capturing little Bob obviously bordered on the sublime.

So, Yosho was absolutely convinced that the affair in Rhode Island would not end without a violent attack against the bungalow that was the temporary residence of Smith Beffort's little family. A residence which he knew about thanks to J.E.E.'s care and of which he knew the defenses. Even before sizing them up, he thought they would be insufficient if Madame Atomos pounced.

After renting a car in Burns, worry stayed etched in Akamatsu's face. He had to work in the shadows to better guarantee the safety of Mie and little Bob and this posed certain problems.

Once in the car and outside the city, he opened up the suitcase he had been lugging around from Tokyo and took out a black box that looked in every way like a big camera from the Golden Age. It could be carried by a strap and fit in perfectly with the moth-eaten clothes, shaggy beard and clouded glasses of the Japanese special agent. But the camera could not take any pictures. It was a laser developed by the *Tokkoka* laboratories, who were experts in miniaturization, and it could burn through diamonds, pierce the hardest metals and, above all, kill a man without fail at 2,000 yards.

This weapon, which did not belong to the arsenal of Madame Atomos, could be particularly effective against her diabolical machines and would remain so as long as the Atomos Organization did not know what it was. Because to fight against this death ray called the laser, all that was needed, unfortunately, was a layer of reflective paint to bounce the ray back to its sender[26].

In the meantime, Akamatsu knew that he possessed a formidable weapon of average size which—the greatest advantage—looked nothing like a weapon. Who, indeed, would be suspicious of a photographer carrying such an old, out-dated camera?

Akamatsu closed his suitcase and set off again for the bungalow.

---

[26] True. Otherwise the laser would have long ago been considered the ultimate weapon dreamt of by soldiers… and novelists.

There were a dozen of them. Men who looked and acted like workers going to a construction site on bicycles. Only the bicycles seemed outmoded, but there were few people to watch the group pass by on the quiet road from Izee to Burns. A well-informed observer would immediately understand that this kind of vehicle was actually the best adapted to moving silently: no engine rumbling, no gears grinding, practically no tires rolling. The men were not talking to one another and they avoided, as much as possible, the strips of gravel on the side of the road. In fact, they were trying to travel as noiselessly as possible and they succeeded almost perfectly.

It was as if they had trained for a long time for this cold, rainy day in order to reach a difficult goal, demanding much skill and finesse. But these men did not really look human with those strange instruments slung over their shoulders: a slender object, like a glass cane, whose bulging handle was stuck inside a waterproof casing with a square sack from which an antenna stuck out—its purpose was a mystery.

After what must have been a long trip, they arrived at the intersection of the road with a dirt track leading to the bungalow of Mie Azusa-Beffort, her son and the federal agents. Once there, they got off their bikes, hid them in the ditch and continued on foot, being even more careful.

Apparently, Madame Atomos was going on the offensive by means of her mechanized servants.

Chapter XII

In Rhode Island the weather was still awful. But for once, the elements were helping the good-hearted men and fighting indirectly against the Machiavellian projects of Madame Atomos.

The rioters had to slow down everywhere. Washington, following through on Dr. Alan Soblen's original idea, took this time to set up an impressive airlift. Hundreds of planes parachuted supplies throughout the state; giant *Sea Knight* helicopters dropped tons of winter clothes on the ground, as well as fuel and combustibles, tents and thousands of leaflets telling the population to stay calm. At the same time, the teams of the Green Dragon Force were uncovering, one by one, Madame Atomos' devices.

On the wall map in Sullivan's office, Beffort was sticking in colored pins. There were a dozen of them now, showing the exact position of each device. The national guard was helping the Green Dragon Force to evacuate the danger zones because, according to the latest information, small disintegrator tanks were defending the devices everywhere.

At 9 o'clock Sullivan entered the office, collapsed in a chair and, after lighting a cigarette, said, "There's no way to get any information out of Yukiko Kimura. I think it'd be easier to get a brick wall to talk."

Beffort looked at the clock on the wall. "A few more seconds and it'll be the neutralization hour. If nothing has changed in the Atomos system, everyone who works for it will come back to themselves until 10 o'clock. We'll have to take advantage of it."

Soblen raised an eyebrow. He looked exhausted. "Take advantage of it," he repeated cynically. "It seems logical to me, but I wonder how we're going to go about it. In an instant, the planes are going to bombard Madame Atomos' devices and Rhode Island will go back to normal. On that score, the danger will be over, but it won't bring us Madame Atomos."

Beffort crushed his butt in the ashtray. "We're going to let Yukiko Kimura go, doc."

"Okay, Smith," Soblen mumbled. "She'll wander around for an hour like a lost soul..."

"Agreed. Except, when the Great Brain takes control of her again, she'll be no more use in Rhode Island. Her mission was to hypnotize Graham so that he wouldn't interfere in the operation. Now, Graham escaped her... Mission terminated for Yukiko! In all probability she'll join back up with a group from the Atomos Organization, thereby leading us to some gathering place. Before their base was Atomos City, so they must have found a new one, right?"

Witter nodded. "In my opinion, Yukiko Kimura will act just like you say. I volunteer to trail her."

"No," Beffort refused. "She knows you too well, Eddy. Sullivan will have to get a new man. Can you?"

Sullivan nodded and answered simply, "Richard Speck."

"Perfect. Free the Japanese and have Speck stick to her tail. He'll have to keep in contact with this office or, if it's not possible, with any FBI office in the US. Tell him that his mission is of the utmost importance."

Sullivan gestured that he understood and left the room.

Beffort picked up the telephone. "And now it's the bombers turn!"

Above Bernitz and his team, the sky looked like it had drawn a thick curtain. The ceiling was low and the visibility poor, so the bombers offensive was going to be undertaken in miserable conditions.

Nothing had moved in the field. The army, police and national guard had forced the rioters, who were quieter after getting some supplies, to evacuate a large tract of land in order to minimize the risk of accidents. Bernitz and his men had also withdrawn to the highway, a mile away from the target. Elsewhere in Rhode Island, at strategic points, the same scene was unfolding. The United States was getting ready to strike a decisive blow at Madame Atomos and her Organization.

At 9:10 a rumbling broke the silence and then Lucky's walkie-talkie started blinking. Straightaway the surprisingly close voice of the squadron chief was heard. "Kilo Bravo here, do you read me Green Dragon?"

"Loud and clear, Kilo Bravo."

"Watch for the flare." A few seconds passed and then a green light streaked across the sky before slowly falling on the field.

"You're right on top of it, Kilo Bravo," Lucky said. "Stay at 2,600 feet. There's a disintegrator ray down here!"

"Got it, Green Dragon, let the operation begin! Keep talking…"

Lucky started counting slowly into the mic. He knew that up above Kilo Bravo was using his voice to locate his position and from there the target located a mile to the north.

All of a sudden the barrel-like tank started shaking. Owen, who was watching through his binoculars, grunted and said, "Right, now the birds are in firing range of the disintegrators. Tell them to climb, damnit!"

On the ground the tank spun around with remarkable smoothness, got rid of its jacket of snow and pointed a group of antennas on top of its turret toward the sky. At the same time, a long rod emerged from the turret, straitened up and let out a short, blinding flash. A huge explosion instantly rattled the atmosphere and then silence fell again, heavier than the minute before.

A bomber had just been disintegrated in mid-air to the deafening din of its load of bombs, but no debris fell to earth. It was exactly as if it had never existed.

With his throat in knots, Lucky kept counting.

"What are they doing?" Owen yelled. Before he had time to finish, hell broke loose on the deserted ground. The first stream of bombs fell too far to the west of the target, but the next hit the tank directly and its wreckage whistled through the air in every direction. Two seconds later the bombers hit the device emitting radiation.

Kilo Bravo had taken its time but it knew the exact position of its target. The squadron dropped ten tons of bombs on the device and when the roar of the explosions finally died down, there was nothing left in front of Bernitz but a huge crater.

At the same time, hundreds of sick people died within the liberated perimeter.

Richard Speck had been following Yukiko Kimura for ten minutes when he knew that her behavior was not what Beffort had predicted. Sullivan had told Speck that Yukiko Kimura would wander around the city for 60 minutes showing all kinds of signs of confusion. But it was nothing like that. On the contrary, the Japanese woman looked like she knew exactly where she was going and what she had to do.

At the corner of the street, she almost got away from the young G-man who was held up in a crowd. Speck sprinted ahead while making sure that the Chevrolet on duty was still following. He got to Kennedy Road just in time to see Yukiko Kimura climb into a cream-colored Cadillac sedan. At the wheel was a man whose face Speck could not see. In the backseat was an older, white woman whose face seemed somewhat familiar to the G-man. The Japanese sat next to the driver and the Cadillac pulled away from the sidewalk.

Speck jumped into the Chevrolet that pulled up and started a difficult chase through the traffic jams. But the Chevrolet's driver, David Mansur, was what you would call an experienced driver. That was exactly why Speck had picked him for his team.

In a few miles, Mansur had caught up with the cream Cadillac, overtaken it and started skillfully following it from the front. It was an acrobatic stunt in which Mansur was supposed to predict the reactions of the Cadillac driver. Strangely, it felt like the Cadillac was following the Chevrolet now.

Coming out of the city on Highway 95, as the traffic was flowing better, Mansur let the Cadillac pass. Now the chase was really on and Speck took the opportunity to send Beffort his first message over the radio. The operator took it down and sent a man to take the message to Beffort, who was flooded with reports coming from all over Rhode Island, so he did not pay much attention to it. Speck was following Yukiko Kimura—that was the main thing.

If his mind were less preoccupied, Beffort would have had the time to analyze Speck's message and realize right away that Yukiko Kimura was not acting as predicted. He would have logically concluded that Madame Atomos had abolished the 60 minutes of neutralization or, even more logically, that she had changed the hour... as she had also changed other things, like the number of team members working together.

In Oregon, the dozen men of the Atomos Organization were still making their way to the bungalow. Around two miles from the cabin they separated into two groups to make a wide circle across the country.

The day was still dark. A storm was threatening and would probably break out before noon. Meanwhile, the rain did not let up, blanketing the landscape with a thin curtain that greatly reduced visibility.

Silently the men of the Atomos Organization closed their circle around the bungalow. Even though very far from each other and without precise landmarks, they managed to locate themselves perfectly, within an inch of the imaginary circumference with the house at its center. To do this it was obvious that they were being directed by a higher force that left nothing to chance and removed all personal initiative from its servants.

As for the federal agents, except for the two false alarms during the night, the situation could not have been calmer. Each of them was at his post. They kept monitoring the detector that was recording the so-called neighborhood sounds and because of this the atmosphere was a lot more relaxed.

Little Bob was playing in his playpen. Mie Azusa-Beffort was listening to the news coming from Rhode Island. On the terrace, Charles Hyde was lazily inspecting the surroundings. The rain bothered him, pattering on his raincoat and finally creating a background noise that drown out all other sounds.

At 9:20 the Atomos men pulled up the telescopic antenna sticking out of the square sack that they carried over their shoulder, thus answering a signal from the Great Brain, which activated the electronic mechanism in their motor-brain. All together the men plugged the kind of glass cane into a socket in the sack and pressed a button.

No change could be seen, but the surface of the circumference was penetrated by paralyzing rays that quickly froze every living thing within the circle. Birds plummeted out of the sky and crashed to the ground. A hare, hit as it was hopping, rolled on the grass and stopped moving. On the terrace, Charles Hyde collapsed in a heap at the same time as his colleagues and little Bob looked like he was sleeping on the floor of his play-pen. Mie Azusa-Beffort was not worried because she, too, was curled up in the armchair and lost to all reality.

Then, the Atomos men retracted the antenna and started walking. Ten minutes later, they entered the bun-galow and carried Mie and her son into one of the agents' cars. Four of Madame Atomos' servants climbed into the car and took off immediately toward the west.

At 9:40, the bungalow was left empty except for the federal agents who were sleeping soundly, but still alive...

Yosho Akamatsu had stopped his car at the inter-section of the road and the private drive leading to the bungalow. Chronologically speaking, he got there a few minutes after the arrival of the pack of bicycles ridden by the men of the Atomos Organization.

Akamatsu had chosen this place because it was unquestionably the most strategic. Of course, two other roads ran near the bungalow and off into the country, one to the north and one to the west, but Akamatsu thought that the federal agents would be watching them more carefully and that there was nothing to worry about on that account.

He hid his car as best he could and sat behind an embankment. He was not at all comfortable in the light rain, but the Japanese special agent was prepared to stay there for hours if he had to.

In the next few minutes, he saw two trucks pass by heading toward Burns and then an ambulance rushing off to Izee. None of the three vehicles slowed down near the road and Akamatsu, one minute on alert, crouched back against the embankment.

Much later, considering how slowly time goes by in certain conditions, Akamatsu heard the rumble of an engine. He rose up and saw a black Chevrolet coming from the bungalow. The car took the turn at full speed and sped off toward Burns. The vision was only fleeting, but between the two men in the backseat, he recognized the face of Mie Azusa-Beffort. Her head leaning back against the headrest, eyes closed, the young woman looked like she was sleeping.

It was not the time nor the place and the men on either side of her did not look like G-men. Akamatsu jumped into his rental car and tore off. He was sure that destiny had put him there to stop a dreadful tragedy.

Chapter XIII

When he was forced to put his glasses back on, Dr. Soblen knew that Rhode Island was completely freed. However, this freedom looked like a catastrophe, in the sense that hundreds of thousands of sick people had died. No one wanted to remember that these sick had postponed their date of death by coming to live in the state and that they would have been dead a long time before if they hadn't.

But the piles of corpses that they found everywhere in the state obviously made quite an impression. All these fatalities could not have been removed in 24 hours. Of course, Washington took emergency measures, but it was an enormous task.

"To think," Witter said, "that Madame Atomos' curse is going to be fulfilled after all."

"What's the temperature?" Soblen asked calmly.

"Around 33 degrees."

"So, don't worry. Rhode Island is a cold room right now and the corpses will stay in good shape. Nature is really with us!"

It was true. If the weather had been mild, a frightening epidemic would have been able to grow and as Yukiko Kimura had said, it would have spread through the US like wildfire. So once again, nature opposed the sinister plans of Madame Atomos and they had to see a sign of destiny here.

Toward noon, the snow stopped falling and the cold became worse, but Smith Beffort did not care about these things anymore because in the meantime he had learned of the kidnapping of Mie and his son. The news came to him by telephone through the mouth of J.E.E., who was literally devastated. The FBI chief had not imagined that Madame Atomos could strike so fast and so hard. He was clutching to the hope that his federal agents would quickly get on the trail of the missing...

Beffort knew exactly where things stood. The one and only chance of saving his wife and son lay in Richard Speck. As for Yosho Akamatsu, (J.E.E. had told Beffort that the Japanese special agent was in the United States), there had been no news from him and they had to conclude that he was, unfortunately, no longer in the game.

On the other hand, Richard Speck was still following the Cadillac. After four hours of traveling west, through all kinds of traffic jams, the Cadillac finally stopped on the edge of a private airfield located in the suburb of Hartford, Connecticut. There, Yukiko Kimura and her partner stepped out of the car and onto the airstrip while the Cadillac left for an unknown destination.

Richard Speck knew what was going to happen. He asked his partner to follow the Cadillac before he in turn entered the airfield.

At the end of the runway, Yukiko Kimura and the other woman were already sitting in an air taxi. Richard Speck snuck along the buildings and entered the office. He presented his FBI identification and was told that the plane had been held for three days and was going directly to Wilmington, North Carolina.

While the air taxi was taking off, Richard Speck went to the phone and called Providence. He was put in touch with Smith Beffort right away and repeated what he had just learned. To his great surprise, Beffort screamed and said in a raspy voice, "Watch out, Speck! You're sure that it's really going to Wilmington, North Carolina?"

"Absolutely, *sir*."

"Will you check that, please?"

Speck went to the desk to confirm the destination of the air taxi and came back to the phone.

"Unbelievable!" Beffort yelled.

Very intrigued now, Speck became bolder. "Excuse me, but I don't see what's so amazing here."

"You didn't follow the last affair, otherwise you'd know that Yukiko Kimura came to that city when Madame Atomos had a hideout there before her City was destroyed. A little to the east of this city and almost on the water, there's a very remote house. It belonged to a certain Arthur Flower. The man disappeared during a visit to Europe and I'm sure that Madame Atomos pulled him into her Organization only to use his house."

"Amazing!" Speck said. "It doesn't seem likely to me that Madame Atomos would reuse a hideout that you already know about. It's a huge mistake!"

"Or a stroke of genius," Beffort added. "If you weren't following Yukiko Kimura, not me or anyone at the FBI would ever for a second think that she would hide out in that city. Listen, Speck, you go and rent a plane and get to Wilmington as soon as you can. I'll do the same from over here. The first one there will wait for the other in the airport lounge."

As for Akamatsu, he had just crossed the western US in a little over three hours. Still following Mie, her son and their kidnappers, he had done exactly what Richard Speck was about to do. In Burns the four men had transported Mie and little Bob, still unconscious, onto an air taxi and the Japanese special agent had followed them on board another plane, an emergency rental.

254

Now, a little after 12:30, the necessary layover to fill up with fuel was made in Des Moines, Iowa. Knowing that he could do nothing useful without putting Mie and her son at risk, Akamatsu dashed into the office, showed (like Speck) his FBI card and two minutes later was on the phone with J.E.E.

"Holy smokes," J.E.E. shouted, "I thought you were dead."

"Not so fast," Akamatsu protested calmly. "After Madame Atomos missed me a dozen times, I'm beginning to think I'm indestructible… Anyway, I have news, Evans."

"Shoot. My tape recorder's on."

"I'm in Des Moines and…" Keeping an eye on the runway, Yosho ran through what had happened since the morning. In spite of his emotions, J.E.E. kept his cool. He saw right away the connection between the direction of the plane transporting Mie and the one that Yukiko Kimura had taken. There was a time difference, but it was only due to the distance separating Burns from Wilmington. Wilmington seemed definitely to be the meeting point of the Atomos Organization. It was certainly not the least surprising news in the affair, but no one could have any idea about what was going through Madame Atomos' twisted mind in bringing all her pieces together in the area that saw her bloodiest defeat.

"Call me when you get to your destination," J.E.E. advised. "If you lose them in North Carolina, I'll do what I can to hook you up with Smith."

Akamatsu agreed, hung up and ran back to his plane.

Beffort and Speck were watching the house from the attic of an abandoned building, which had been used for the same purpose during the last affair. Beffort felt like he had turned the clock back one year.

At first sight, the house looked deserted, but Speck knew that Yukiko Kimura and her partner were hiding inside.

"I don't understand," Beffort said worriedly, "the property has only one way in or out and is therefore a trap."

Speck took a bite out of his sandwich and with his mouth full said, "In my opinion, Madame Atomos was thinking that Yukiko Kimura would give us the slip and we would never search for her here."

His reasoning was good, but Beffort did not see things that way. "I have the feeling that Madame Atomos has done all this just to bring us here. You know, Speck, we can never underestimate…"

He stopped himself when he heard the stairs creak, but it was only Witter coming from Providence.

"What's new, Eddy?" Beffort said automatically.

"I snagged a message from J.E.E. when I passed by the FBI office in Wilmington," the G-man said. "There's news from Yosho…"

Beffort turned a stony face to him. "My wife and son?"

"Exactly. Akamatsu's been tracking them from Burns. Right now the two planes are flying over Kentucky."

Beffort had a little jolt. "Good God," he roared, "you mean they're heading for Wilmington, too?"

"That's what J.E.E. believes. Personally, I think it's too good to be true."

Beffort nodded. Witter knew the unscrupulous cunning of Madame Atomos and could not accept the idea that the evil woman was making such a monumental mistake.

Witter continued, "I've got a car outside with a radio. If you want, you can get in touch with Evans."

Beffort went downstairs. He was hiding his anxiety, but he had stopped living since Mie and Bob were kidnapped. It was like an inevitable fatality. Madame Atomos spared nothing and nobody, struck with blind fury at what was dearest to her enemies. If she succeeded in getting Mie and Bob out of the United States, Beffort was absolutely sure that he would never see them again.

He sat in the car, warmed up the radio and signed on. He was relayed through Norfolk and Atlantic City, waited a second and was on line with Evans.

"Hello!" J.E.E. forced himself to sound cheerful. "Did Witter give you the good news?"

"He gave me the news," Beffort corrected. "Do you know where the airplane is right now?"

"Of course," J.E.E. grumbled. "Since Yosho called me, the plane's been on our radar. Plus, we've got two squadrons ready to intercept it in case it decides to head for Cuba or the Bermudas…"

"Intercept, huh?" Beffort sounded gloomy.

"What of it?"

"With my wife and son on board, don't tell me you trust that! The plane could fly to hell before you give the order to open fire!"

"It won't go that far," Evans replied. "It had to stop in Des Moines to get fuel, so it can't, physically, go farther than Wilmington."

"No, but nothing can stop it from landing somewhere else."

"Let it land, let it land," the FBI chief muttered. "That's all we're asking. Wherever it goes, it can't escape us."

"Just now you said that it could head for Cuba or the Bermudas…"

"Listen, Smith, don't nitpick! We've taken all precautions and I assure you that this plane can't slip through the net I've thrown out for it. And remember that your friend Akamatsu has been on its tail since Burns. Well, no one has ever shaken Yosho, right? So let's have a short but useful talk: What are you planning to do when the plane lands in Wilmington?"

"When will it arrive?"

"30 minutes, if we predicted accurately."

"First of all, we have to let it taxi off the runway to avoid any accidents."

"Careful," J.E.E. warned, "your family is surrounded by four guys from the Atomos Organization. At the first sign of trouble, they could execute them."

Beffort grinned. "There won't be any trouble, Evans. I'm simply going to surround the airfield with G-men and then I'll sit there alone on the terrace…"

"Discreet but completely ineffective."

"Then I'll open fire from above with a paralyzing rifle," Beffort finished.

"On Mie and Bob?"

"I'd rather put them to sleep for an hour than see them fall into the claws of Madame Atomos! Besides, it's the best way to neutralize the guards."

J.E.E. was silent for a few seconds, but finally said, "You have carte blanche, Smith. You take care of it. I'll take care of the rest."

"What does that mean?"

"The bungalow was attacked by a dozen men who came on bicycles. Four of them are with Mie and Bob, but the other eight took off in the service cars. It's strange, since all the members of the Organization seem to be heading toward Wilmington—but they left for the north and west."

Beffort felt a weird void. "Who did you stick on their tail?"

J.E.E. snickered. "Charles Hyde and his team. They were guarding the bungalow and got had like little boys. I don't need to tell you that they're literally raging. Last heard two of the cars were found in Newport and the others in Astoria. All four were empty, but Hyde is following a lead that's taking him to Coos Bay."

"What kind of lead?"

"A witness says he saw four guys and an Asian woman getting out of the Chevrolets parked in Newport. All of them were carrying big packages. They crossed the street and climbed into a Dodge truck covered with a tarp that got on the road for Coos Bay."

"This woman," Beffort inquired, "what did she look like?"

"I know what you're thinking," J.E.E. replied, "and I already asked the question. The witness didn't see her face and couldn't give her age, even approximately. She was wearing a salmon-colored raincoat, a rain hat and white rubber boots. Almost a disguise! Anyway, we need to understand that it wasn't easy to identify her under such conditions. Still, it really could be Madame Atomos!"

Beffort white-knuckled the microphone. "Don't screw it up, Evans!" he urged with hate in his voice.

"I'll do my best, Smith. In the meantime, try to get Mie and Bob back without too much damage."

Chapter XIV

The airfield in Wilmington looked no different than usual, but the upper terrace was closed for repairs and a lot of civilians were bustling around the runways. These civilians were federal agents armed to the teeth and Smith Beffort was in the corner of the terrace that over-looked the landing strip. He was crouched like a hit man waiting for his victim. His hands welded onto his para-lyzing rifle. His prey was still flying somewhere over Bladen county and would be forced to come to a stop less than 50 yards from him. A target practically imposs-ible to miss, even for an inexperienced shooter, which was not the case. Still, Beffort's forehead was beaded with sweat.

He pressed the button on his walkie-talkie and asked, "How long?"

"Ten minutes, sir. The plane has just been picked up by the Emerson radio and has already given its posi-tion to the control tower."

"How is the pilot acting?"

"Normal. He's probably not in on it, seems totally self-controlled. His name is Robinson and the investiga-tion by our colleagues in Burns concluded that he's above suspicion. For him it's just a routine flight."

"The ambulance?"

"It's ready, sir. When you shoot, we'll do our best to act quickly and quietly."

"Thanks," Beffort said.

He signed off and got into a more comfortable posi-tion behind the railing on the terrace. From his post he could see the whole airfield, the runways where a plane took off every seven minutes, the crowd of passengers walking around the departure lounge, but his attention remained fixed on the horizon.

Very soon the plane carrying his wife and son would come out of the northwest to throw itself in the trap that the Wilmington airfield had turned into. Just like Witter rightly said, *it was too good to be true*. Unbelievable that Madame Atomos had not taken more precautions.

The walkie-talkie hummed. Beffort clicked it. "I'm listening."

"Yosho Akamatsu has just asked permission to land."

Beffort gritted his teeth. He would have preferred that his friend stayed behind the plane that he had been following from Burns. "Okay. Tell him to join me on the terrace when he can."

The control tower cut off communication. Almost immediately a small yellow biplane appeared in the north, soared twice around the field and made an acrobatic landing at the end of the runway. It taxied quickly toward the buildings and stopped in front of Beffort, who saw a bearded man wearing glasses get off. He did not know that it was Akamatsu until one of the federal agents went up to him and pointed at the terrace.

Akamatsu waved discreetly and then disappeared from sight. An instant later he stepped onto the terrace and walked over to Beffort smiling. "Hello! I won't ask you how you're doing, Smith."

"We'll talk about it later, if you want. Where's that damn plane, Yosho?"

Akamatsu sat next to Beffort and calmly lit a cigarette. "Don't worry, Smith. The hard part is over. Now the plane can't land anywhere else but here. It's running low on fuel and Wilmington was registered as its destination on the flight log."

Beffort looked hard at the Japanese. "Doesn't this all seem weird to you, Yosho? Madame Atomos is acting as if we didn't exist."

Akamatsu shrugged his shoulders. "I'll never understand the underlying motives that make Madame Atomos tick, but it doesn't matter. All that counts is that it's almost over: in a few minutes Mie and Bob will be safe and sound."

"Did you clearly identify them?"

Akamatsu jumped. "Unfortunately I didn't have the opportunity to see them up close, but I guarantee you that no one left that plane during the layover in Des Moines."

"What happened in Burns?"

"Your wife and Bob were sleeping. The four men of the Atomos Organization took them in the plane and it took off. That's all."

Beffort nodded silently while looking again at the end of the runway. Airplanes were lined up to take off and land but no taxi plane appeared.

"*Hurricane 800*," Akamatsu said softly, "twin engines, eight seats, bright red. You can't miss it. Relax a little, Smith."

Beffort did not answer. He looked at his watch. "It was over Bladen county ten minutes ago and the control tower had its position. Logically it should be landing."

"30 seconds late. That's nothing to worry about."

Beffort did not listen. He got on the walkie-talkie and spoke nervously into the microphone, "Well, where are we?"

"Everything's okay, sir. The plane is going to land any minute now."

Beffort was about to say something, changed his mind and gently put the walkie-talkie down while staring at the horizon over the hills. He admitted that his anxiety might seem childish, so he tried to control it, but it took a great effort. Something told him that it was not going to go as smoothly as the FBI plan anticipated.

All of a sudden, a red, twin engine popped up.

"There it is," Akamatsu said. His relief contradicted his earlier confidence.

Beffort breathed more easily and nestled the butt of his rifle in the hollow of his shoulder. He carefully inspected the airfield, the runway and especially the buildings. Nothing had changed. Except an ambulance had just backed into the exit drive while the federal agents were closing in the circle. There was no turning back now for the forces of order.

The red plane landed faultlessly on runway 2 and rolled slowly toward the buildings, veering off onto the clearance strip. Just as a Boeing was crawling up off the runway with a roar of its jets, the small plane stopped below the terrace. Its door opened and a man stood in the doorway, leaning out, waiting impatiently for the runway worker to bring the stairs.

"That's one of the four men," Akamatsu whispered. "He was driving the car in Burns."

Beffort did not hear. His eye was riveted on the plane. He was ready to open fire.

The stairs were hooked up to the *Hurricane* and the worker ran off to another plane that just started its engines. Two men got off the red plane and then a woman carrying a child appeared. She was dressed in black; a veil covered her face. She hesitated for a second and then finally started down the stairs with a kind of mechanical step that made Beffort's heart skip.

"Shoot, Smith!" Akamatsu ordered. "What are you waiting for?"

Beffort still waited. The ambulance was backing up to screen the *Hurricane* from the main hall. At the same time, the G-men were circling around. When the ambulance was in place, the woman had stepped off the stairs, but the two other men were still coming down. At that instant, Witter raised his hand and dashed forward. Beffort pressed the trigger of his weapon.

The *Hurricane* pilot collapsed in his seat and the four men of the Atomos Organization keeled over, but Witter got there in time to catch Mie and her son in his arms. After that everything happened in a flash: the federal agents rushed in and transported the seven victims of the paralyzing ray in the ambulance. Someone slammed the ambulance doors shut and sped away around the buildings where it was immediately escorted by a team of motorcycles to the hospital in Wilmington.

Beffort followed the action as much as he could, turned to a smiling Akamatsu and said, "Unbelievable, Yosho."

"Come on, don't tell me that you're still on pins and needles."

"No, but I can't really believe it. Something happened that I don't understand and I hate not understanding."

Akamatsu pinched his mouth. "Madame Atomos lost this round, Smith. Whatever you think, she took all her normal precautions. She even went so far as to dress your wife in mourning clothes. The veil was a good idea. I admit that I would never have recognized Mie under that veil."

Beffort grabbed his arm and dragged him toward the stairs. "Come on, a car is waiting to take me to the hospital in Wilmington. Mie will be happy to see us at her bedside when she wakes up."

General Hospital, seen from the inside, looked like a fortress. Because of the continuing threat that surrounded Mie Azusa-Beffort and her son, dozens of G-men, armed with paralyzing rifles, were stationed at every entrance to the huge building. Outside, radio-equipped cars were parked between the trucks with flamethrowers mounted on them and policemen had cordoned off the area.

Beffort and Akamatsu found Witter in front of the main entrance to the hospital.

"Everything's fine," Witter said, wiping his forehead. He stared at Beffort and grimaced. "Now I can admit that I was scared stiff. If a bookie was taking bets, I would have taken Madame Atomos at ten to one."

Beffort patted him on the shoulder and asked, "What room?"

"908."

The three men took the elevator and were shot up to the ninth floor. There was no need to ask where Mie's room was. A crowd of G-men were blocking the corridor and milling about the door. A doctor popped up and Beffort grabbed his arm. "How are they?"

"The mother and child are doing just fine," the doctor answered, somewhat ironically. "I don't think they really wanted you to put them to sleep."

Beffort pushed open the door and walked in. He stopped, petrified. The woman who was sleeping between the white sheets was not Mie and the child in the crib was not his son…

Chapter XV

After waking up, the woman first said that she remembered nothing and especially not the child she was carrying. Her name was Soo Fergusson; she was Korean. In Korea she had married an American soldier and naturally followed him when he moved to Oregon and that is how she came to live in Burns. That morning she had driven away from home to go to the supermarket downtown. That was the last thing she remembered. And she was absolutely certain that she had no mourning clothes in her closet.

With two telephone calls Witter identified the child. His name was Frank Davis and he had been kidnapped around 9:40 in front of a store in Burns where his mother was making some purchases. Without a doubt Soo Fergusson and little Davis looked a little like Mie Azusa-Beffort and Bob.

"The resemblance would certainly not have fooled any of us," Witter concluded, "but the Atomos men were careful not to give us a good look at Mrs. Fergusson and little Davis, always keeping them at a distance..."

Akamatsu looked very sad. He mumbled, "I'm sure that Mie was in the car at the crossroads. I recognized her instantly and got on their tail right away."

Beffort looked wearily at him. "Give it up, Yosho. There was a substitution between Burns and the airport or between the bungalow and Burns, but it's not important. Madame Atomos prepared her feat down to the last detail. She had us all the way, even anticipating that we would let Yukiko Kimura go, who was supposed to lead us to Wilmington. While we were acting just like she wanted, my wife and son were led into..."

He stopped suddenly and jumped on the telephone. "What's got into you, Smith?" Akamatsu asked.

"One second, Yosho." When he had J.E.E. on the line, he told him how Madame Atomos had tricked the FBI and asked, "Do you have any news from Charles Hyde?"

"He's making progress. At the moment his men are examining that Dodge truck that was found empty on the docks in Coos Bay."

"Empty?"

"Except for some boxes, it was."

"Were the boxes big enough to hold a one-year-old baby, Evans?"

J.E.E. whistled. "I'll be damned! Do you think?"

"If you've got a better idea…"

"I don't know what to think!"

"Listen, Evans, it's highly likely. The cars started almost at the same time from the bungalow. They went in pairs but ended up going in different directions. At Newport, the witness you were talking about saw four men and an Asian woman get into a Dodge truck. Mie is Japanese and the boxes were there only to fool anybody watching. One of them could very well have been holding Bob! So, you've found the truck. Great! What is Charles Hyde doing?"

"He's inspecting the boats."

"Blockade the bay. Coos Bay is on the Pacific. If we don't act quickly, Madame Atomos is going to be able to get Mie and Bob out of the United States!"

"Calm down, Smith. I know how you feel, but Hyde is doing everything he can. There are hundreds of vessels moored between Coos bay, Empire and North Bend. I guarantee you that it's not trivial affair."

"Good God, if I could…"

"You can't be everywhere, Smith. It'll take you six hours to get to the west coast. You have to trust Hyde. Don't move and I'll call you when I get some news."

He hung up and Beffort flopped into a chair. All he could do for the moment was to recapture Yukiko Kimura and worm some information out of her.

J.E.E.'s message reached Charles Hyde five minutes after the conversation between the FBI chief and Beffort. Knowing now that he was looking for Mie and Bob, Hyde suddenly felt the weight of responsibility fall on his shoulders. He asked for reinforcements and managed to get, in record time, 2,000 policemen and 5,000 troops. At the same time, an aircraft carrier and two destroyers sailed for Coos bay while three groups of supersonic fighter jets stood ready to take off at the first signal.

Now the attack force was ready. They just had to flush out the prey.

Charles Hyde played his part like a game of chess, with skill and a sense of strategy that was absolutely remarkable under such conditions. Two hours after initiating the operation, a suspicious yacht was spotted south of Cape Arago. They tried to contact it by radio but got no response. Hyde and 20 G-men boarded a heavily armed coast guard ship and went after the yacht, which was sailing lazily along the coast.

The coast guard caught up to it quickly. Since the radio remained silent, they ordered it to stop its engines before firing a warning shot. The yacht was shut down and Charles Hyde climbed on board with his men. The bridge was deserted, as well as the pilot-house. Hyde and his team moved cautiously, entered the cabins, the kitchen and the lounge without meeting a soul.

It was not until they were in the ship's hold that they discovered the still warm corpses of a young Chinese woman and four men. Their descriptions matched those of the Newport witness. They obviously belonged to the Atomos Organization, as the half-moon scar on the skull proved, and had acted as a diversion very similar to the role played unwittingly by Soo Fergusson and young Frank Davis.

When their duties were done, Madame Atomos' Great Brain eliminated them, pure and simple.

Downhearted, Charles Hyde got in touch with J.E.E.

Smith Beffort, Akamatsu, Witter and a team of federal agents had encountered no trouble entering the house by the sea. Yukiko Kimura had put up no fight; she just smiled when Akamatsu found the body of the woman who had accompanied her. She had been shot in the neck by Yukiko. Searching her purse told them that her name was Julietta Graham, the wife of the governor of Rhode Island, who had disappeared six months ago.

Yukiko Kimura was clearly under the influence of the Great Brain. Her eyes were empty, her movements mechanical and she was totally unconscious of the present. Beffort made her sit down and asked, "I presume that I'm talking to a robot?"

"You're right, Mr. Beffort," the voice of Madame Atomos said. "Yukiko was supposed to stay there so I could talk to you through her."

Beffort was expecting this. Madame Atomos was probably hundreds of miles away from Wilmington, but she could still speak, hear and see whoever was before her through the senses of Yukiko Kimura.

"Mr. Beffort," Madame Atomos continued, "you are a brave adversary. Rhode Island did not fulfill the mission I gave it, thanks to you, and I will have to strike again later. But, from now on, I am going to be in a position to dictate my conditions because Mie and your son are in my power!"

Beffort turned pale. He had not yet contacted J.E.E., so he was totally ignorant of the failure of Charles Hyde in Coos Bay. Madame Atomos laughed. It was bizarre to see Yukiko Kimura express emotions that were not her own.

"What do you plan to do?" Beffort asked in a distant voice.

"That all depends on what you and your government do. To save the lives of Mie and your son, the United States will have to give me California, Nevada and Arizona! Moreover, the American armed forces have to leave South Vietnam and give up any idea of using the atomic bomb! All this will have to take place within six months…"

"Madness!" Beffort screamed. "You're completely mad!"

"During these next six months," Madame Atomos continued undisturbed, "your wife and son will suffer no abuse. They will be treated well. But at the end of six months, if I don't get what I want, they will be operated on by my surgeons and become servants in my Organization! No, don't say a word! Take some time to think about it and try to convince your country. See you soon, Mr. Beffort. You will find my signature on the back of the woman who is about to die."

Silence fell over the room and Yukiko Kimura collapsed in a heap on the floor. Akamatsu ran to her and felt for a pulse. "She's dead," he whispered. He turned her over, unzipped her dress and revealed the Madame Atomos' signature, which was tattooed between her shoulder blades: *Hiroshima, Nagasaki, compliments of Madame Atomos...*

Shattered, Beffort staggered over to the window. Akamatsu joined him, put his hand on his shoulder and said, "Don't lose hope, Smith. We have six months to save Mie and Bob."

Beffort did not answer. It was a hope in which he could not believe, but he knew that he would do everything in his power to make it come true.

Matthew Baugh:
The Way of the Crane

Hiroshima, 1966

Kato stepped into the sunlight, a small urn in his hand. He paused to watch the people pass. The park had been built to commemorate the darkest day of Hiroshima's history, but it was still a park. There were mourners, young couples, even children playing in the beautiful weather.

He moved to the statue of a young girl holding a stylized crane. Hundreds of origami birds sat sheltered beneath it. He took a square of paper from his pocket and folded his own crane. He held it as he pressed his palms together in a reverent gesture.

"Prayers for peace will not comfort the dead."

Kato turned. The speaker was a woman in her 50s, stern and regal.

"Excuse me, Ma'am," he said. "I don't understand."

"Only the weak beg for peace," the woman answered. "The strong find a way to take revenge."

Kato felt his cheeks flush.

"I'm afraid we disagree, Ma'am," he said. "Please excuse me."

He picked up the urn to go.

"Do I upset you, Hayashi-san?"

Kato turned back.

"How do you know my name?"

"When the ashes of your grandfather were identified, I knew that you would come to take them from this place."

"Do I know you, Ma'am?"

"You were not yet born the last time I saw your grandparents," she replied, "but the Kato and Yoshimuta families have been friends for many generations."

"Yoshimuta?" Kato's eyes widened at the name. He glanced around warily.

"There is no need to be alarmed," she said. "I have not come to harm you. My wrath is for the Americans."

"How can you be here?" he demanded. "You're wanted by the *Tokkoka*!"

"Madame Atomos goes where she pleases."

"Why have you come?"

"To pay my respects to your grandfather. Also, I hoped to recruit you for my organization. I understand that you are a resourceful man, and there is the connection of our families."

Kato was speechless.

"Don't act so shocked, Hayashi-san," she continued. "I have investigated you. I know that you work for the criminal organization of the Green Hornet. I offer you the chance to use your skills in a nobler cause."

"I am not a murderer!" Kato protested.

"Nor am I," she replied. "I am an avenger. I mete out justice for the angry spirits of all who died here and in Nagasaki."

"This is no place to talk of revenge." Kato gestured to the paper cranes. "Each of those is a prayer for peace. The statue of the little girl is..."

"I know the story of Sadako-san," she interrupted. "She believed that if she made a thousand paper cranes, the gods would cure her. But childish superstitions are useless in the face of evil. That little girl died of leukemia from the radiation of the American bomb."

"Her prayer wasn't just for herself," Kato replied. "She prayed for peace so that no other child would suffer so."

"My aims are the same," Madame Atomos replied. "When I am done, no child will ever again suffer at the hands of the Americans."

"What of the American children you have killed?"

"An unfortunate necessity."

"That sounds like what the Americans must have said when they dropped their bombs."

"Do you think to compare me with them?" Madame Atomos snapped. "How many innocents died? Was it 100,000, 200,000? How many more need to die before people like you understand that such an act must be punished?"

"I don't defend the actions of the Americans, but is punishing atrocities with more atrocities the answer?" Kato shook his head. "The cycle of vengeance will never end."

"It will—when I have crushed them," she retorted. "I will not leave the survivors the strength to rise against me."

"There have been many who have tried to do that," he countered. "Have any of them ever succeeded?"

"I will succeed!"

"Please reconsider," Kato said. "Revenge is like sugar. The first taste is sweet, but it gives no nourishment and leaves you craving more. If that is what you live on, it will rot you from within."

"You sound more like a monk than a gangster!" There was contempt in her voice. "Do you honestly believe they deserve my forgiveness?"

"Forgiveness is not for those who deserve it," he replied. "If we were all virtuous, there would be no need for it."

"To forgive is to excuse the guilty!" Madame Atomos shot back. "It is a denial of reality."

"I do not excuse them," Kato said. "It was a terrible thing that we cannot forget. But in remembering, we must let go of hate. That is the only way that healing is possible."

They had been moving through the park; now, they paused near a statue of a young girl with a fawn.

"I am disappointed, Hayashi-san," Madame Atomos said. "Your grandfather deserves better. For his sake, I ask you one more time: join me."

"For his sake, I ask you to seek another way." Kato held out the crane he carried.

She snatched the folded paper from his hand, and tossed it away. It landed at the base of the statue.

"For the sake of the friendship our families once shared, I will not have you killed," she hissed. "Do not try to stop me. I have snipers around the park. You might evade them, but they would kill others."

Kato's eyes widened. There were dozens of people around them, unaware of the danger. He was silent as Madame Atomos crossed to a limousine that bore her away.

When she had gone, Kato moved to the statue. There was a poem inscribed on the base.

"O god of evil, do not come this way again.

This place is reserved for those who pray for peace."

Kato picked up the crumpled paper and smoothed it until it was a crane once more, then he placed it at the foot of the statue.

SF & FANTASY

Henri Allorge. *The Great Cataclysm*
Guy d'Armen. *Doc Ardan: The City of Gold and Lepers*
G.-J. Arnaud. *The Ice Company*
Cyprien Bérard. *The Vampire Lord Ruthwen*
Aloysius Bertrand. *Gaspard de la Nuit*
Richard Bessière. *The Gardens of the Apocalypse*
Albert Bleunard. *Ever Smaller*
Félix Bodin. *The Novel of the Future*
Alphonse Brown. *City of Glass*
André Caroff. *The Terror of Madame Atomos; Miss Atomos;
The Return of Madame Atomos; The Mistake of Madame Ato-
mos*
Félicien Champsaur. *The Human Arrow*
Didier de Chousy. *Ignis*
Captain Danrit. *Undersea Odyssey*
C. I. Defontenay. *Star (Psi Cassiopeia)*
Charles Derennes. *The People of the Pole*
Georges Dodds (anthologist). *The Missing Link*
Harry Dickson. *The Heir of Dracula*
Jules Dornay. *Lord Ruthven Begins*
Alfred Driou. *The Adventures of a Parisian Aeronaut*
Sâr Dubnotal *vs. Jack the Ripper*
Alexandre Dumas. *The Return of Lord Ruthven*
Renée Dunan. *Baal*
J.-C. Dunyach. *The Night Orchid; The Thieves of Silence*
Henri Duvernois. *The Man Who Found Himself*
Achille Eyraud. *Voyage to Venus*
Henri Falk. *The Age of Lead*
Paul Féval. *Anne of the Isles; Knightshade; Revenants; Vam-
pire City; The Vampire Countess; The Wandering Jew's
Daughter*
Paul Féval, *fils. Felifax, the Tiger-Man*
Charles de Fieux. *Lamékis*

Arnould Galopin. *Doctor Omega; Doctor Omega & The Shadowmen*

G.L. Gick. *Harry Dickson and the Werewolf of Rutherford Grange*

Nathalie Henneberg. *The Green Gods*

V. Hugo, P. Foucher & P. Meurice. *The Hunchback of Notre-Dame*

Michel Jeury. *Chronolysis*

Octave Joncquel & Théo Varlet. *The Martian Epic*

Gustave Kahn. *The Tale of Gold and Silence*

Gérard Klein. *The Mote in Time's Eye*

Jean de La Hire. *Enter the Nyctalope; The Nyctalope on Mars; The Nyctalope vs. Lucifer; The Nyctalope Steps In*

Etienne-Léon de Lamothe-Langon. *The Virgin Vampire*

André Laurie. *Spiridon*

Gabriel de Lautrec. *The Vengeance of the Oval Portrait*

Georges Le Faure & Henri de Graffigny. *The Extraordinary Adventures of a Russian Scientist Across the Solar System* (2 vols.)

Gustave Le Rouge. *The Vampires of Mars*

Jules Lermina. *Mysteryville; Panic in Paris; To-Ho and the Gold Destroyers; The Secret of Zippelius*

Jean-Marc & Randy Lofficier. *Edgar Allan Poe on Mars; The Katrina Protocol; Pacifica; Robonocchio; Tales of the Shadowmen 1-8*

Xavier Mauméjean. *The League of Heroes*

José Moselli. *Illa's End*

John-Antoine Nau. *Enemy Force*

Marie Nizet. *Captain Vampire*

C. Nodier, A. Beraud & Toussaint-Merle. *Frankenstein*

Henri de Parville. *An Inhabitant of the Planet Mars*

Georges Pellerin. *The World in 2000 Years*

J. Polidori, C. Nodier, E. Scribe. *Lord Ruthven the Vampire*

P.-A. Ponson du Terrail. *The Vampire and the Devil's Son*

Maurice Renard. *The Blue Peril; Doctor Lerne; The Doctored Man; A Man Among the Microbes; The Master of Light*

Jean Richepin. *The Wing*

Albert Robida. *The Adventures of Saturnin Farandoul; The Clock of the Centuries; Chalet in the Sky*
J.-H. Rosny Aîné. *Helgvor of the Blue River; The Givreuse Enigma; The Mysterious Force; The Navigators of Space; Vamireh; The World of the Variants; The Young Vampire*
Marcel Rouff. *Journey to the Inverted World*
Han Ryner. *The Superhumans*
Brian Stableford. *The New Faust at the Tragicomique; The Empire of the Necromancers (The Shadow of Frankenstein; Frankenstein and the Vampire Countess; Frankenstein in London); Sherlock Holmes & The Vampires of Eternity; The Stones of Camelot; The Wayward Muse.* (anthologist) *The Germans on Venus; News from the Moon; The Supreme Progress; The World Above the World; Nemoville*
Jacques Spitz. *The Eye of Purgatory*
Kurt Steiner. *Ortog*
Eugène Thébault. *Radio-Terror*
C.-F. Tiphaigne de La Roche. *Amilec*
Théo Varlet. *The Xenobiotic Invasion*
Paul Vibert. *The Mysterious Fluid*
Villiers de l'Isle-Adam. *The Scaffold; The Vampire Soul*
Philippe Ward. *Artahe*
Philippe Ward & Sylvie Miller. *The Song of Montségur*

MYSTERIES & THRILLERS

M. Allain & P. Souvestre. *The Daughter of Fantômas*
A. Anicet-Bourgeois, Lucien Dabril. *Rocambole*
A. Bisson & G. Livet. *Nick Carter vs. Fantômas*
V. Darlay & H. de Gorsse. *Lupin vs. Holmes: The Stage Play*
Paul Féval. *Gentlemen of the Night; John Devil; The Black Coats ('Salem Street; The Invisible Weapon; The Parisian Jungle; The Companions of the Treasure; Heart of Steel; The Cadet Gang; The Sword-Swallower)*
Emile Gaboriau. *Monsieur Lecoq*
Steve Leadley. *Sherlock Holmes: The Circle of Blood*

Maurice Leblanc. *Arsène Lupin vs. Countess Cagliostro; Lupin vs. Holmes (The Blonde Phantom; The Hollow Needle)*
Gaston Leroux. *Chéri-Bibi; The Phantom of the Opera; Rouletabille & the Mystery of the Yellow Room*
William Patrick Maynard. *The Terror of Fu Manchu*
Frank J. Morlock. *Sherlock Holmes: The Grand Horizontals; Sherlock Holmes vs Jack the Ripper*
P. de Wattyne & Y. Walter. *Sherlock Holmes vs. Fantômas*
David White. *Fantômas in America*

SCREENPLAYS

Mike Baron. *The Iron Triangle*
Emma Bull & Will Shetterly. *Nightspeeder; War for the Oaks*
Gerry Conway & Roy Thomas. *Doc Dynamo*
Steve Englehart. *Majorca*
James Hudnall. *The Devastator*
Jean-Marc & Randy Lofficier. *Royal Flush*
J.-M. & R. Lofficier & Marc Agapit. *Despair*
Andrew Paquette. *Peripheral Vision*
R. Thomas, J. Hendler & L. Sprague de Camp. *Rivers of Time*

NON-FICTION

Stephen R. Bissette. *Blur 1-5; Green Mountain Cinema 1; Teen Angels & New Mutants*
Win Scott Eckert. *Crossovers* (2 vols.)
Jean-Marc & Randy Lofficier. *Shadowmen* (2 vols.)
Randy Lofficier. *Over Here*

HEXAGON COMICS

Franco Frescura & Luciano Bernasconi. *Wampus*
Franco Frescura & Giorgio Trevisan. *CLASH*
L. Bernasconi, J.-M. Lofficier & Juan Roncagliolo Berger. *Phenix*
Claude Legrand, J.-M. Lofficier & L. Bernasconi. *Kabur*

Franco Oneta. *Zembla*
L. Buffolente, Lofficier & J.-J. Dzialowski. *Strangers: Homicron*
Danilo Grossi. *Strangers: Jaydee*
Claude Legrand & Luciano Bernasconi. *Strangers: Starlock*

ART BOOKS

Jean-Pierre Normand. *Science Fiction Illustrations*
Raven Okeefe. *Raven's L'il Critters*
Randy Lofficier & Raven OKeefe. *If Your Possum Go Daylight...*
Daniele Serra. *Illusions*